**Just a kiss. Nothing they couldn't walk back from.
Nothing too significant.**

Nick's world narrowed down until the only thing filling it was the heat of Sabrina pressed tight against him. The way the ocean breeze wrapped around them and blended with the smell of her shampoo, driving him closer to crazy. The soft lights under the tent warming her skin. The music languidly mixing with the waves in the background. And the deliciously plump temptation of her mouth.

His hands fisted against her lower back, gripping the silk of her dress before he could stop himself. Would the silk rip? He could replace the dress if it did.

He couldn't drag his gaze away from her mouth. When she licked her lips again, he leaned down. She pressed up, her breath brushing his cheek, and that almost broke him.

Why wasn't he supposed to kiss her? He was sure there had been a reason. Otherwise, he wouldn't have resisted this long. Something important, right?

Tabitha. Her best friend. His neighbor. The woman who would kill him if he got involved with Sabrina.

Nick watched Sabrina's eyes drift half closed as her arms tightened around his neck. Death didn't seem so bad just then. Not with Sabrina so close, her lips just right there, her little sigh humming in the air between them.

A kiss wouldn't be too bad, right?

Just one kiss.

DESIGNED FOR YOU

KAT SIMONS

T&D PUBLISHING

DESIGNED FOR YOU
Copyright © 2022 by Katrina Tipton
All rights reserved.

Published 2022 by T&D Publishing
Cover design: © 2022 T&D Publishing
Cover art: © Nyul, © Iofoto | Dreamstime.com
Interior book design © 2022 T&D Publishing
ISBN-13: 978-1-944600-52-5 (Trade Paperback Edition)
ISBN-13: 978-1-944600-53-2 (Large Print Edition)

This is a work of fiction. All of the characters, places, organizations, and events portrayed are either products of the author's imagination or are used fictitiously. Any resemblance to actual persons, living or dead, business establishments, events, or locales is entirely coincidental.

First printing T&D Publishing edition: July 2022
For information, contact T&D Publishing: https://www.tanddpublishing.com

DESIGNED FOR YOU

For my beloved family. Because. Always...

Chapter One

The house was perfect. The setting was perfect. Everything about this entire thing was perfect.

And Sabrina Mitchell couldn't have been happier. For the first time in a year, she took a deep breath and felt all the worries and cares that had plagued her fall away.

Everything would be all right here. She could feel it. Sea air always had a healing effect. That's what she needed. Tabby had assured her the months here would clear out all the cotton clogging her mind, and as she stood on the back deck, looking out over the rolling Atlantic waves, the midday sunshine sparkling on the white sand, the screeching seagulls flying over the rough grass-covered dunes, the air brushing her hair in a salty fresh breeze, she thought her college roommate and best friend might just be right.

How could she not breathe easier here?

All she had to do was babysit Tabby's two dogs and do a little work on the second floor of the cottage. A whole summer stretching out before her with nothing but beach, walking dogs, reading novels, and redoing the second floor of a glorious beach cottage with good bones. All her favorite things.

She turned away from the tempting whoosh of waves and headed back inside. She still had to unpack and assess the work she needed to do on the second floor. And find the dogs who were likely upstairs playing hard to get.

She hadn't been out to the beach cottage for months. Six months at least. The changes Tabby had managed in that time, while still finishing her book, were pretty amazing. She'd opened up the entire back half of the house, leaving a fancy sitting room and a library at the front of the house, but the entire back was just one big open space. A living room area to the right, with a giant sectional couch in front of a large, flatscreen TV mounted above a small stone fireplace. An open kitchen to the left with rustic wooden finishes and shiny chrome appliances. Fit for a chef. Which, technically, Tabby wasn't, but she was an extraordinary cook, so the fully decked out kitchen suited her.

Sabrina admired the polished and darkened hardwood floors—Tabby had debated and debated keeping them this more natural color or painting them a sage green. Now that she saw it in person, Sabrina had to agree with Tabby's final choice. Natural wood against the white walls and blue and green accents were perfect. The furniture was white, which Sabrina had balked at since Tabby had dogs. But Tabby assured her the color was fine because her standard poodle, Justin, didn't shed and was white anyway, and her brown Pekingese shed up a storm, but the hair was easier to see on the white and so easier to clean.

Since this was Tabby's home, Sabrina didn't argue, but she'd have gone a different way for a client's house if they had shedding pets.

Speaking of pets… She called for the dogs, wondering why they hadn't come down to greet her. She'd probably have to take them for a walk since Tabby had left on a predawn flight. That alone should have motivated them to greet her at the door.

"Princess! Justin! Where's my hello?"

No pitter patter of little dog feet. Huh. Definitely playing hard to get.

She returned to the front door, a straight line from the back of the house, and hefted up her suitcases, which she'd unceremoniously left there. The dogs knew her well and had always come to the door to greet her on previous visits. But the Pekingese, Princess, was a true to her name, so Sabrina supposed she could be holding out, waiting upstairs for Sabrina to come to her, establishing who the real boss in the house was. That was a very Princess move. And since Justin didn't leave Princess's side for many reasons, he'd stay upstairs if she did.

While Sabrina had visited Tabby here often, she'd never been in charge of looking after the dogs before. Normally, Tabby hired a professional dog sitter for them if she had to travel for work. Finding one out here in the Hamptons wasn't hard either. But this time, with Tabby being away on a book tour in Europe for three whole months and Sabrina being in such a bad place with work, Tabby had thrown her a bone. So to speak. Giving her the time here she needed to get her head on straight.

In exchange, Sabrina had not only agreed to dog sit, she'd volunteered to help work on Tabby's second floor, which was still mid-update and modernizing. Sabrina wouldn't try doing the plumbing or electrical work. But she could paint, and install fixtures, and buff and refinish floors, and finish the bathroom tiling. Tabby had been so delighted she wouldn't have to wait on finishing the upstairs until the fall, she had even offered to pay Sabrina.

Sabrina had been very tempted. She was going to need a real, proper job soon. Again. But the free summer house and money enough to eat and feed the dogs would do for now. She'd managed to sublet her Brooklyn apartment to a friend's little sister for the summer, so she didn't have to worry about that. And the money she had saved while she'd been working gave her a little cushion. She'd worry about the rest later. The work on Tabby's house felt like *her* paying Tabby back for her kindness anyway. A no-brainer.

The stairs up to the second floor had been sanded and polished since her last visit, but Tabby was still debating putting down a carpet runner or leaving them exposed. The polish made them a little slippery, Sabrina noticed as she hefted her largest suitcase up the stairs. A carpet runner would probably be best for Princess.

Maybe that's why the Pekingese hadn't come downstairs. Maybe she slipped on the stairs? If so, Sabrina would have to watch her carefully, make sure she didn't get hurt when she did attempted them.

On the landing, she called out to the dogs again. "Hey guys. I know it's been a few months. I'm here to keep you in food and treats and walks while your mom is in Europe."

Still no doggy noises. No one came out to greet her. Weird.

Where were they?

Maybe hiding in Tabby's bedroom? She'd left for the airport really early, and Sabrina hadn't been able to leave the city in time to get out here before dawn. She'd had to meet with and hand over the spare keys to her apartment to her friend's sister, pick up her other friend's car she was borrowing for the summer, and finish clearing out some of her stuff to a storage locker. Then there'd been traffic on the drive out—because of course there had. It was after noon now. Maybe the dogs had just camped down in Tabby's bedroom and gone to sleep since they didn't have any human company?

She wasn't a dog expert, having never had one of her own, and she wasn't sure how the dogs reacted to Tabby's sometimes long work trips. It was possible they got sad the first day and would have to be coaxed out with some treats. Poor babies.

She pushed into the guest bedroom, a large space, with a giant king-sized bed pushed against one wall and lovely large windows that looked out at the ocean. There was even a small balcony off this room, which would be a nice place for her morning coffee.

The room itself was still pre-update, so the white walls needed a new coat of paint and there wasn't any real interior decoration. Just a basic, cheap side table beside the huge bed and an overhead fan-light that would be nice on the hottest days of the summer. The wooden floor was scuffed and covered by a couple of colorful rugs. Tabby had made up the bed with cool pale yellow sheets and a bright orange comforter. Even without all the freshening that Tabby intended, the room was cozy and comfortable and Sabrina would be very happy ensconced here for the summer.

She dropped her big suitcase next to the bed. There was a small closet but no dresser in here yet, so she'd be living out of her suitcase. She didn't mind that either, though. Felt like being on a real vacation, which she hadn't had in so long she barely remembered what they felt like. Living out of the suitcase would remind her regularly she was on vacation here. Mostly. Which seemed like a great thing.

Once she assured herself the dogs weren't hiding in here for some reason, she went to Tabby's room, hoping to find them there.

The master bedroom was mid-update, but still pretty rough. In fact, the room was in rougher shape than the guest bedroom, probably because Tabby had ensured the guest bedroom would be livable for Sabrina in a way she hadn't bothered with for her own room.

There was another giant bed, covered in white sheets and a blue and green comforter and pillows. And the rugs covering the unfinished floor were fluffy and soft. The windows were covered by sheer white drapery that let in plenty of sunshine and a view through the thin material to the ocean. But the walls had splotches of paint samples on them. The new dresser and side tables were pushed haphazardly to one side of the room where they still had to be sanded and repainted and some of the drawers repaired. And the bookshelf braced against the wall was empty and in need of sanding and painting too.

The dog beds were under the windows, near the gauzy curtains. But despite her expectations, neither Princess nor Justin were laying in their beds. Frowning, Sabrina checked the master bathroom.

Another room still in need of updates. The new sink and tub had been installed, but the tiling, the paint, and the finishes still had to be done. She was looking forward to getting this room perfect for Tabby before she got back.

Once she found the dogs, of course.

Where the hell were they?

Worry started to claw at her now, tightening in her gut. They hadn't been downstairs, she was sure. She'd poked her head into the formal sitting room and library. The back door had been firmly locked when she'd arrived. The sunroom off the kitchen had been empty. Although, she hadn't checked under the furniture so Princess *could* have been there. But Justin was way too big to wedge himself under the couch or coffee table.

She was certain if they'd been downstairs, they would have already shown themselves. So they had to be up here somewhere. Right?

She checked Tabby's office, which faced the front of the house. No dogs there.

The small room next to the office contained boxes and paint canisters and various tools. This was the room Tabby used for staging the renovations because she hadn't decided what she wanted to do with it yet. Sabrina checked carefully around the stacks of supplies. Still no dogs.

Her worry turned into a full blown panic.

She hurried downstairs to hunt, searching the sunroom more closely, including under the big sectional couch, the two rocking chairs, and under the wicker coffee table that didn't have much of an under. She searched the kitchen. She searched the library. She searched the formal living room. She even checked inside the fireplace because panic had her imagining the worst-case scenarios.

Nothing.

She glanced toward the back door, the large window in the top half of the door giving her a great view of the ocean.

That door had definitely been locked when she'd arrived. There was no way Princess and Justin could have gotten out there. Right?

They hadn't been inside the small, fenced off backyard. The patch of beach grass and bushes wasn't that big. Well, okay, Princess could hide under one of the bushes, but Justin couldn't.

Justin could, however, jump the short wooden back fence. It was just a row of rough, unpainted, worn wooden slats that only came up to Sabrina's thigh. Easy leap for the standard poodle. But he wouldn't jump out of the yard without Princess. And even if he had, Sabrina would have seen Princess at the fence. The two dogs were inseparable. Where one went, so did the other. So Justin didn't jump the back fence because he'd have to leave Princess to do that.

Still, the worry, the possibility that he'd gotten out onto the beach had her hurrying to the back door again. What if they were lost on the beach? What if someone took them? Or worse, they'd gotten swept out to sea? Her gut churned at that idea.

She reached for the door, only to stop in her tracks as she heard a key in the front door.

She spun, her heart hammering. Was Tabby home? Had something gone wrong?

The door pushed open and Justin in all his giant poodle glory bounded into the house, spotted her, and made a beeline for her, all long legs and tightly shaved white curly fur. She barely had time to brace before he jumped up on her, front legs on her shoulders as he greeted her with a big smacking lick on the face. She chuckled and gave him a hug.

"Hey boy, where have you been?" A little imperious yipping sound, brought her attention down to the Pekingese next to her ankle. "Princess!" She let Justin drop back to his feet and then dropped to her knees to give Princess as thorough scratch, sinking her fingers into the little dog's long, soft coat. "Where have you guys been? I was so worried."

She looked up toward the doorway, expecting to see Tabby standing there.

But it wasn't Tabitha Reynolds filling the door frame.

Sabrina froze. Just…froze, for a full thirty seconds, as she met the newcomer's gaze.

Shocked at coming face-to-face with the one massive kink in her summer plans to rethink and regroup.

Tabby's next door neighbor.

Nick West.

Chapter Two

Sabrina scrambled to her feet, brushing dog hair off her jeans as she faced Nick. She'd met him before, of course. He and Tabby were friends. Tabby introduced them to each other the very first time Sabrina had come out to see Tabby's new beachfront house—and been stunned and tongue-tied then, too.

When she'd taken Tabby up on this offer to housesit for the summer, she'd been so desperate to get out of the city, she'd managed to forget about the complication of the criminally handsome next door neighbor.

Now, here he was, filling up the doorway with his over six-foot frame, all glorious shoulders and hard jaw. Dark hair cut short but loose, dark eyes, a build that could make Greek gods weep, and a face that should be painted and hung in museums. It wasn't just that Nick was handsome. He was one of those handsome men that made you stop on the street, do a double take, and blink a few times. Like, he shouldn't be walking around in real life because that kind of absolute stunning attractiveness shouldn't exist in the world. Just in movies and on TV. Where there was good lighting and makeup artists on hand.

The fact that he just casually lived next door to her best friend, looking that gorgeous without any effort or backlighting, always struck

Sabrina as a little unfair. He shouldn't live in an ordinary house next to people. He should be living on some estate on Mount Olympus or something.

The one good thing about Nick, though, was that he was so far out of her league, he didn't seem to notice she went slack-jawed whenever he walked into a room. Which meant she could crush on him in peace without him realizing. He'd only ever barely given her the time of day, so she knew she wasn't someone *he'd* stop on the street and blink at like he'd been hit by a bus. And there was freedom in knowing he didn't notice her—*especially* because he didn't notice her bus-hit blinking at him.

"Nick," she greeted. Then had to clear her throat, which had probably dried out while she was gawking. She smiled because he was Tabby's neighbor, and she had manners. "What are you doing here?" Then she frowned down at the dogs. "Why were the dogs with you? Was something wrong? Did something happen?"

New worries for the dogs replaced her awkwardness, and she dropped down to inspect the them both, running her hands over their sides and heads, reassuring herself they weren't hurt or wrapped up in bandages or anything.

"Sabrina," Nick said, she supposed by way of greeting.

His voice was very deep and rumbly and she had to make an effort not to shiver. She'd always loved his voice.

"Tabby left really early," he said, "and didn't know when you'd arrive. The dogs needed a walk."

"They could have waited for me," she said. "I'm not that late." She'd got caught in traffic getting out of Queens. And then again on the freeway outside Syosset. But it was only a little after noon.

"But I didn't know when you'd be here, did I?" Nick said.

"I was worried when I couldn't find them."

"I was worried when you weren't here by eleven." He stuffed his hands into his pockets, which called her attention to the lovely way he filled out his jeans.

She dropped her gaze to Princess. No ogling the neighbor, Sabrina. That would be rude. Even if he didn't seem to notice.

She couldn't resist a little eye roll at his comment, though. "You didn't need to panic," she told him. "I just got caught in traffic."

"Didn't want them pissing all over the house before you arrived," he grumbled.

She had to suppress a smile. He sounded very annoyed when he admitted that.

To the dogs, she said, "How was your walk? Did you have fun with Nick?" She glanced up at him. "Where did you take them?"

"The beach. Princess will need some of the sand combed out of her fur."

"No problem at all." She gave Princess a little face squish and a scratch behind the ears. "We'll have a whole session of grooming and catching up, won't we?"

She kept most of her focus on the dogs. It was always easier to be around Nick if she didn't have to look directly at him too much. In fact, now that she'd gotten over her initial, and usual, stunned response to seeing him for the first time in months, she decided she could get through the summer just fine living next door to him. Not like he'd be over a lot to visit or anything. She'd probably barely see him. She could keep her crush in check, focus on the dogs, the beach, the renovations for Tabby, and her future. No problem.

She glanced at him from the corner of her eye. Hmm. Maybe problem.

No boys allowed, she scolded her lusty brain, checking her spiraling fantasies. She didn't have time for boys. Except for Justin, of course. But standard poodles didn't count.

When Nick continued to stand silently in the doorway, she finally looked directly at him, though it took an effort to pull enough brain cells together to say words that sounded like human speech. "Thanks for walking them. Even though it wasn't strictly necessary."

"You're welcome." The words were little more than a grunt.

She pressed her lips together. He sounded so annoyed. She was very tempted to ask what had him so irritated. Except that would lead to more conversation. More of him standing in the doorway looking all hot and gorgeous. She wasn't sure she was up for that. Her heartbeat was already pounding too hard—between the adrenaline rush of thinking the dogs were missing and her first view of Nick in months, she needed some time to calm down.

After another silent moment, she raised her brows at him. He was hovering there in the doorway, not leaving, but he didn't look like he intended to come inside either. "Is there something else?"

Another grunt, which wasn't really an answer.

"Did the dogs eat yet?" she asked, because he still didn't move.

"Yes."

She waited. Nothing more. Okay. "Well, thanks again." She rose after giving Justin another head scratch.

Nick continued to stand in the doorway, not moving, glowering at the floor, which was starting to weird her out a little.

"You okay?" she asked. "Something wrong?"

"No."

She waited some more. But that seemed to be the extent of his answer. Well then. "Okay, well, I guess, thanks again. We're good now, the dogs and I. Although, maybe warn me in the future before taking them for a walk. I'd rather not have another heart attack."

She said that last with a grin, attempting to joke and lighten the silence, but instead of amusement, or even an eye roll for her over dramatic statement, his brows snapped down with his frown.

"I didn't even know you were here yet," he said, sounding defensive. "I wasn't trying to worry you."

"I…know."

Wow. Guess she shouldn't try to joke with him. Either she was very bad at it—entirely likely—or he didn't have much of a sense of humor. Although, in this case, she was probably the one who'd flubbed the joke. She blamed him for that, though. How was she supposed to act like a normal human in a normal human conversation when he stood there looking like he'd just come down from the seat of the gods?

"I have to go," he said suddenly.

"Okay," she said, because he still wasn't moving. "Well. Uh. Have a nice day?" She wasn't entirely sure what was happening but got the feeling he had more to say.

He opened his mouth. Closed it. Shook his head. Then pointed to the dogs and said, "Be good for Sabrina while she's taking care of you."

Justin plopped down into a sit and wagged his tail. Princess let out a little yippy bark.

Nick grunted, nodded once, then spun back out the door, stalking away like he was mad at the ground. Without any parting word to her.

"Uh," she said again to the empty doorway. "Bye."

She shook her head and went to close the door. "Well that was an interesting way to start this summer visit, wasn't it? Guess I won't have to worry about seeing him. Not sure he likes me very much."

To be fair, in the years Tabby had lived here, Sabrina hadn't talked to Nick all that often. He'd say hello—or rather grunt hello—but then she wouldn't see much of him during her stay. Despite the fact that she secretly watched for him, hoping to see him. She had no idea if he liked her or not. Or had any opinion on her one way or the other. Tabby swore he was a good neighbor and they got along great. But he'd always been…distant with her.

Probably for the best, she assured herself. He couldn't notice her crush if he wasn't around. And that couldn't complicate her already complicated life. He'd go about his life. She'd go about reevaluating her life. Nothing to worry about. Gorgeous neighbor wouldn't be a problem.

She glanced down at the dogs, who'd followed her to the door. "I am glad you're okay and there was nothing wrong, though."

Justin pushed his head into her hand for another scratch.

"Want to help me unpack now that you're all refreshed from your walk? And maybe you can tell me what crawled up Nick's butt and put him into such a bad mood."

Princess barked and then started bouncing up the stairs in the little leaps required of her short legs. Justin nudged Sabrina's thigh once before following Princess, taking the steps slowly as he waited for her much slower progress.

Sabrina grinned and followed them both, relaxing now that the encounter with Nick was over.

No reason to let the fact that he was right next door bother her or interfere with her plans. She had a whole summer stretching out in front of her, to relax and reassess her future, and she didn't intend on letting anything get in the way of that.

Not even the gorgeous neighbor.

CHAPTER THREE

Nick slammed into his house, the door rattling behind him as he swung it shut. Of all the times, and all the people, Tabby just had to pick Sabrina Mitchell to dog sit.

Sabrina.

No professional dog sitter. No innocuous person Nick didn't have to think about. No.

Sabrina fucking Mitchell.

How the hell was he going to get through a summer with her living right next door?

He did not have time for this. He had a big job on the line, and the potential to lose a shit ton of work—as well as his most influential clients—if he didn't play the next few weeks just right. His career was *important* to him. He had to concentrate. He had to focus.

That got significantly harder with Sabrina Mitchell living next door.

Not that he even entirely understood why Sabrina got under his skin. She just…did. She stood there smiling at him, looking all adorable and shit, and he got restless and uncomfortable and couldn't seem to carry on a normal conversation.

And to top it off, he'd worried her. So now he was kicking himself for worrying her. Except he hadn't *meant* to worry her. Was it his fault he didn't know when she'd arrive? Was it his fault she was late and the dogs would have left her a house full of shit and piss if he hadn't taken them for a walk?

The fact that he'd been hovering around all morning waiting for her to arrive and dreading her arrival at the same time was beside the point. He'd done her a favor, taking the dogs out. He wasn't trying to worry her. So he shouldn't feel like such an ass right now.

He supposed he could have left a note.

Running his hands through his hair, he tugged hard, then shook himself in a vain effort to refocus. Enough. He had work to do. He couldn't spend what was left of the day mulling over all the ways he'd been an ass that morning. But an entire summer of Sabrina as his neighbor stretched out before him, and he couldn't stop thinking some higher power was trying to torture him. For what, he had no idea. Some sin he'd committed in a previous life, probably.

Instead of heading into his office, where he should have been all morning, he wandered into the kitchen and stood staring at the coffee machine on his counter. There was still a bit left in the carafe but the machine had shut off an hour ago. The coffee was probably cold. He deserved cold coffee.

No. He did. Scowling, he snapped the carafe out and dumped out the old stuff. A new pot of coffee was exactly what he needed. It wasn't too warm today. There was a nice breeze blowing in off the ocean. He should open the back door. Maybe bring his laptop out to the deck to work.

He glanced past the kitchen door, to the full wall of windows at the back of his house. The bright sunshine and rolling Atlantic were absolutely beautiful today. He'd bought this house specifically for that view, for the wall of windows that gave him unfettered access to that view. The fact that he didn't take advantage of it, and of his own deck, more often was a travesty. He had comfortable chairs, a table, even a couch out there. On purpose. When he moved out here, away from Manhattan and all that craziness, he'd promised himself he'd live slower, work on the deck when he wanted, enjoy the breeze and sea air.

He hadn't done that nearly enough over the last five years. He liked his office in the house—he'd set it up specifically so he would enjoy spending time in it. His large drafting table was even positioned so he could still easily glance out the window and take in the ocean view. But he should take advantage of his luck and this location. Most of what he had to get done today he could do on his laptop. He could easily work outside. Sit on the deck. Breathe in the salty sea air.

And that desire had absolutely nothing to do with the fact that he could see Tabby's deck and sunroom easily from his deck and so might just happen to see Sabrina.

He dumped water into his fancy coffee machine, which was, ironically, a gift from Tabby last Christmas. He'd been happy enough with his basic Coffee Mate, but she knew how much he loved his coffee and had gotten him one that had a timer and the ability to brew single cups as well as carafes, and had a few other bells and whistles he'd never bothered to learn. She'd stopped short of getting him one of those big ass espresso things, fortunately, because then he'd feel the need to use it. But he just wanted easy coffee in the morning. Thinking about how to manipulate one of those giant machines would just complicate things and piss him off.

Fortunately, Tabby knew him well enough not to do that to him.

He glared at the machine as he scooped fresh grounds into the filter. Tabby did know him pretty well. They talked a lot. He was closer to her than he'd been to any of his neighbors in the city. Not as close as he was to his best friend Diego. He and Diego had grown up together. Diego knew all his life secrets, mistakes, and triumphs. Tabby didn't know that many details. But they were close enough they talked about personal shit and not just the weather. She knew him as well as anyone out here.

She knew him well enough that right after she'd introduced him to Sabrina, she'd warned him away from her, and promise to kill him if he hit on her best friend.

Had she purposefully gotten Sabrina to house sit just to torture him? Had he done something to offend her, and now she was punishing him?

He rolled his eyes and slammed down the top on the coffee machine, hitting the on button hard enough to push the machine back into place against the kitchen wall. Of course Tabby wasn't trying to torture him. She was too nice for that. Too genuine. She'd bought him the perfect coffee machine, for christsake.

If she wanted to torture him, she'd have just come right out and said so before doing it.

The kitchen filled with the scent of fresh brewing dark roast. He pulled in a deep breath, hoping the smell would settle some of the restless energy making his skin itch. He supposed he could clean the kitchen. Except he'd already done that this morning when he couldn't sit still long enough at his computer to work on the proposal he was supposed to be doing. The chrome appliances gleamed. The dark blue granite countertop sparkled in the sunshine. The Spanish tiled floor was clean enough to eat off.

All the dishes were out of the dishwasher. The random boxes of food left on the countertops had been returned to the small pantry. He'd even straightened the few cooking gadgets he had on the counter and dusted the cookbooks—two of which were signed Tabitha Reynolds cookbooks—on the tall, narrow shelf near the fridge. Nothing left to clean in here.

Still, restlessness had him pacing the galley kitchen as he waited on the coffee.

Stalking out into the open living room, which took up almost the entire back half of the house, he looked out the story and a half wall of windows at the white sand beach and blue ocean beyond. Sunshine warmed his light, hardwood floors. The ceiling fan, high overhead in the peak part of the roof, worked hard to keep the living room air circulating. But the ocean breeze would cool the room off even better.

He opened the accordion doors, folding them back fully, and stepped out onto his wide wooden deck. Without thought, his gaze went to his neighbor's deck, covered and shaded against the bright sunshine. No one there. The pang of disappointment that settled in his gut had him cursing again.

What the actual fuck was wrong with him?

With an irritated grunt, he stalked back inside. He couldn't work on the deck. He'd spend the whole time tense, waiting for Sabrina to show. Like he'd been doing all morning. This was ridiculous.

He stomped into the kitchen, got his coffee, and returned to his office, determined to put his temporary neighbor and nemesis out of his head. He had a report to finish. A proposal to write. A job to do. He didn't have time for this, or for her.

An admonishment he kept repeating to himself.

Every ten minutes.

For the rest of the day.

Chapter Four

Once unpacked, reacquainted with the dogs, and everyone was properly fed lunch, Sabrina spent the afternoon going through the supplies Tabby had left her for the upstairs work.

Enough paint to get the two main rooms finished, maybe even tackle the hallway, which was lower on the list of to-dos but still on the list. Tiles for the two bathrooms—a pretty white tile with some smaller, decorative sheets of multi-shaded blue tiles for the guest bathroom; a soft sandy color intermixed with a gold flecked maroon for the master bath. Enough drop sheets, paint brushes and trays, detail tape, grout, towels, a small step ladder, and assorted tools to get the basics done. There were even a few carpet samples, which Sabrina thought might be for a stairs runner.

Everything she needed to get started.

Tabby, organized as she was, had left a long list for Sabrina of all the equipment, what she wanted done in each room, and what she was thinking about doing in the spare room once they no longer needed it for a staging area. She knew Tabby would call, probably once a week, so they could discuss some of this during those conversations. But she had to appreciate Tabby's attention to detail. It was what made her so good with pastry and desserts.

The afternoon crept by as Sabrina worked out where she'd start, and even got some of the set up for painting in Tabby's bedroom ready. At least, she got the stuff she needed moved into Tabby's room.

By the time dinner rolled around, she was tired and hot and needed to relax for a bit. The dogs followed her all through the afternoon, watching her every move and keeping her company, but otherwise not getting very involved in the process. She appreciated their dedication to watching her, though. And it was nice having someone to talk to, even if they didn't talk back.

If she ever got her life back on track, maybe she'd get a dog of her own.

She really needed to figure out what to do with herself. Where she wanted to go next. How to fix the mess she'd made of her life.

But not all at once. And not immediately. She wasn't going to recover and start fresh on the very first day here. Certainly not expecting a miracle just because she was near the sea and breathing clean, salty air. Of course she wasn't.

She sighed and wandered into the kitchen to figure out dinner. That was at least something she could do today.

The dogs were easy. Tabby had a specific, small fridge set aside for their fresh food—which was delivered twice a week apparently—and there was another instruction sheet detailing everything tacked to that little fridge.

"Half a tube for Princess," she said aloud as she cut open one of the patty sausage-like rolls of dog food. "A full tube for Justin. Twice a day. Dog biscuits for treats no more than twice a day." Sabrina looked down at Justin, who tapped his fluff-tipped tail against the floor at the mention of dog biscuits. "Only twice a day, huh?" She wondered if Tabby stuck to that rule herself or just wanted to make sure Sabrina didn't overcompensate by overfeeding.

Princess ate like food might vanish if she didn't suck it all down in half a second. Justin went through his at a more measured pace, but they still both gobbled up their dinners in record time. Sabrina barely had a chance to clean up after setting their bowls on the floor before they were both back to watching her. She got a feeling the admonishment about dog biscuits wasn't so much to keep Sabrina from spoiling them, but to keep her from panicking that they hadn't eaten enough and compensating with dog biscuits. If Tabby hadn't left her the note, she'd be looking into those doggy eyes right now thinking she hadn't given them nearly enough food.

"Good thing your mommy is organized," she told the dogs.

Justin's tail thumped the floor again. Princess sat and started to lick her paws clean, a bit like a cat.

Sabrina went to the double-wide fridge and hunted in the freezer. True to her word, Tabby had left some frozen meals for Sabrina, to get her through the first few days here before she'd have to go shopping. Given how tired she was this evening, she sent up a silent thank you to her friend's thoughtfulness and pulled out a plastic container labeled chicken and roast veg.

The chicken was glazed in some sort of sauce Sabrina couldn't name, something both sweet and a little spicy, and the roasted potatoes and carrots were sprinkled with lemon zest which added a nice citric touch. Tabby, of course, left detailed instructions on how to re-heat everything without losing the flavor and integrity of the food.

Once her dinner was ready, Sabrina took herself out to the back deck to eat. No point in spending her first night inside when the evening was so glorious. This was the wrong coast to watch the sun set, but the darkening evening, the soothing swoosh of the waves, the occasional seagull squall, all seemed too perfect to waste.

And it would have been perfect.

If she hadn't made the mistake of glancing next door. Where Nick was sitting. On his deck. Looking scrumptious and off limits.

She supposed she should have expected that. She couldn't avoid him the entire time she was here. They were neighbors, at least for the summer. She'd sort of hoped the fact that they were in houses and not an apartment building would make avoiding him a little easier, though.

So much for that hope.

She settled at the large round table on the far side of the deck, trying to pretend she hadn't noticed him. Hoping they could sit out here and ignore each other so she could eat in peace. And maybe think big thoughts about her future.

But when she glanced back in his direction, she found him looking her way, frowning slightly. She forced out a grin and gave him a little wave. That was friendly enough, right? He lifted his bottle of beer in a return greeting, then faced the ocean again.

Okay, then. He didn't want to talk either. That made things easier.

She settled in with her glorious dinner and made an attempt to keep her attention on the ocean and her food and *not* on her neighbor.

She managed to at least not look at him every forty-three seconds. More like every two minutes. She counted that as a win. And she did only sneak those peeks from the corner of her eye, which also seemed like a win because he wasn't likely to notice.

Not that Nick noticed her crush anyway. The relief of that had always left her a little giddy. This whole thing could be so much more awkward if he actually realized she secretly had a thing for him. Especially since he obviously didn't return that interest. They'd both be super uncomfortable if he actually *knew* she lusted after him.

The dogs followed her out to the deck, and while Justin sat under the glass-top table, Princess plopped down right next to Sabrina's chair and stared up at her during the entire meal as if waiting for her portion to be served.

Tabby had said nothing about feeding the dogs from the table. And Sabrina couldn't remember if she'd ever seen Tabby feed them off her own plate. So she was hesitant to give in to Princess's stare. But eventually, when she was down to one last bite of chicken and a few carrots, she gave in and dropped a carrot. The Pekingese swallowed the bite whole before it hit the ground.

"Well that was impressive," Sabrina murmured.

Because she wanted to be fair, she dropped another carrot chunk under the table. The glass top was see-through, so she was able to clearly see Justin snatch the carrot off the wooden deck lightning quick. She wasn't even sure he chewed it before he thumped his tail and glanced up at her, through the clear tabletop, as if expecting more.

"Wouldn't do that if I were you," Nick said, his deep voice traveling across the space between them easily.

She started at the sudden break in their silence. "What?" she asked, mostly to give herself some time to recover from the sound of his voice.

"You feed them your own food, they'll never leave you in peace for another meal again."

She looked down at the dogs. "That true?"

Justin thumped his tail again, his tongue hanging out in what looked suspiciously like a grin. Princess gave a little yip, spun in a circle, and attempted to sit up. She wobbled a little and dropped back into a normal sit as she shot glances between Sabrina and her nearly empty plate.

"Told you," Nick said, as if the dogs had confirmed his comment out loud.

She grinned. "Fair enough. Although I have a feeling they're going to find multiple ways to take advantage of my ignorance of the rules."

"Didn't Tabby leave you a list?"

Now she laughed. He obviously new Tabitha Reynolds well. "She did. Lots of them actually. But so far, I haven't seen one mentioning table scraps."

"Look again. I'm sure there's something there."

Sabrina gave both dogs a look. "Yeah, you might be right." She glanced at him, but he was staring out at the ocean again, beer bottle held loose in his grip. "Thanks for the warning."

He grunted and lifted his bottle in a little solute.

Why did that make her want to laugh again? He was so... Well. Nick. She wasn't sure how else to put it. Helpful while being irritated about being helpful. Hard not to crush on that.

She made an attempt to relax in her seat, enjoy the view, ignore the dogs still looking up at her pathetically like they hadn't been fed since last week. Ignore the man sitting out on his deck just next door.

She failed at that last thing pretty spectacularly.

He was impossible to ignore. And she kept stealing glances in his direction from the corner of her eye. More interested in studying him than studying the rolling waves. The sun was low behind them, casting long shadows through the yard and across the beach. It would be dark soon. Would that be better? She wouldn't be able to see him in the dark. But she wasn't sure she could take the sound of his sexy voice floating across the darkness to her. Too intimate.

Not that he was doing any speaking. He was as much ignoring her as she was *attempting* to ignore him. She couldn't blame him. There was no rule you had to carry on conversations with your neighbor just because you were both out on your deck. In fact, there might be a rule that you were supposed to ignore each other to give a sense of privacy? She didn't live in the Hamptons. What did she know?

In her apartment building, she spoke with her neighbors in the hallways and elevators, in the laundry room, but there were very clear privacy lines with the neighbors. Not a lot of interaction once she was inside. Not unless she invited someone in. Which she rarely did because, until three weeks ago, she'd always been too busy and hadn't been *in* her apartment enough for that.

Here, though, she didn't have anywhere to be and the decks weren't blocked by trees or convenient bushes. She'd have to ask Tabby why she hadn't built a barrier between hers and Nick's deck, for the privacy. Tabby had her backyard enclosed, though she said that was for the dogs. But still. Tabby liked her privacy. She lived out here *because* she liked her privacy and didn't want to be nagged by a lot of people looking for autographs and food advice. She could manage in the city without too much trouble. It wasn't like she was on TV—yet. Still, Tabby was just famous enough with the foody crowd, she did occasionally get stopped on the streets in Manhattan and Brooklyn. So she'd moved out here the minute she could afford it to preserve some privacy.

The fact that she'd left her deck open to full view of one of her neighbors suddenly struck Sabrina as strange. She knew Nick and Tabby were only friends because Tabby would have told her if anything romantic had ever happened between them. Tabby talked about Nick like he was a close cousin or sibling or dear friend from college or something. Like it was her place to look out for him, but never in a romantic sort of way.

But friendly didn't mean privacy went out the window. Why not at least put up something that gave the illusion of privacy while she was out here?

Sabrina glanced toward the house on the other side of Tabby's. That one was farther away, with a little more land between Tabby's place and theirs. The space between filled with scrub grass and a tall sand dune, and in the neighbor's yard, trees and a fenced off garden. There was a lot of privacy on that side. Sabrina couldn't even see into the yard or tell if the neighbor even had a deck.

Huh. She'd have to ask Tabby when they talked. Now that she thought about it, it was going to bug her.

Again, she found herself glancing at Nick from the corner of her eye. Did he know why Tabby hadn't planted trees or anything to block her deck?

Not that she'd ask him. Asking might mean revealing too much. Like the fact that she was uncomfortably aware of him while she was out here. Like the fact that she couldn't completely relax, knowing he was right there. And like the fact that, if she wanted to, she could easily start a conversation with him that gave her the pleasure of listening to his voice in the growing darkness.

She rolled her lips into her mouth and shook her head. Nope. Nope. Nope. Not a good idea to do that. Her crush was already ridiculous. She didn't need that experience haunting her.

And because she couldn't relax and she really didn't want to know what his deep, sexy voice sounded like floating across the divide to her in the dark, she collected her dishes and went back inside, letting the dogs proceed her in.

Because she didn't want to be rude, though, she did say, "Goodnight. Thanks again for the table scraps warning."

He didn't look at her when he said, "No problem. Goodnight."

She shivered, her skin tingling in the wake of his rumbly voice, almost as if he'd touched her.

Yeah, that was about as much of him as she could take on her first night here.

She closed the door, cutting off the growing roar of the ocean as a large set of waves came rolling up onto the beach. Then she took a deep breath.

This summer was going to be a lot more complicated than she'd hoped. At least for her. She glanced down at the dogs. "I might need to stay inside to eat from now on. Or eat in the sunroom." She could see his deck clearly from there, too, but the barrier of windows meant she didn't have to have a conversation with him and risk embarrassing herself.

The dogs just looked up at her expectantly.

"Okay," she said with a sigh. "Nighttime treats it is. Maybe an extra one, since it's our first night together. We'll be more disciplined tomorrow."

Both dogs ambled ahead of her to the kitchen, where she got them a dog biscuit and herself a glass of wine. She needed the fortification.

But mostly, she just needed to stop obsessing about the hunky next door neighbor.

She rolled her eyes at herself.

Right. Like she had a hope of that.

<h1 align="center">CHAPTER FIVE</h1>

Somehow, miraculously as far as Sabrina was concerned, she did manage to forget about Nick for the next few days as she settled in to doing the work she'd agreed to do. Wanted to do really. She liked having her hands busy. She wasn't really a sit-around-doing-nothing kind of person in the best of circumstances. When she had things to think about—like her future and what she wanted to do with herself now that she was out of a beloved job—she *had* to have something to do with her hands. Painting walls was a very good something to do.

She loved painting. Loved watching the change to a room, the way it got cleaner and fresher with just that little application of color. She even loved the way paint smelled and the meticulousness of the prep work, getting the tape in place, setting out the drop cloths, taking down or taping over the fixtures she didn't want to get paint on.

With her phone playing a favorite playlist filled with songs she could sing along to, she spent those first few days blissfully getting paint on her hands and cheeks, walking the dogs, eating Tabby's superb frozen meals, and collapsing into bed at night too exhausted to worry.

It was glorious.

She should have known the peace wouldn't last long.

Her cellphone's incessant buzzing started on day four. She finally gave in to checking it after the fifth call. Not Tabby, as she knew it wouldn't be. They had a call scheduled for tomorrow, and even if it was something spontaneously important, and Tabby couldn't reach her on the cell after the first two calls, she'd ring the landline, because Tabby was old school and had a landline still. She mostly used it for ordering food from local places where she knew the other cooks. For all Tabby was a superb cook herself, she ate a lot more takeout and delivery than someone who didn't know her might guess. Especially in the final stages of finishing a new cookbook.

So Sabrina knew the call wasn't Tabby. And no one else would be repeatedly calling her cell with an emergency. Her friends in the city had other backup options, and they all knew she was way out here in the Hamptons at the moment anyway. Her mother—one of her more complicated relationships—was on a cruise with her aunt. Her father and his wife were visiting with his wife's kids in California. And her brother never called. He texted her. He wasn't a big phone call kind of person.

This wasn't family. This wasn't her best friend.

This was the call she'd been dreading and hoping would never come.

And the moment she was certain who it was, she sent the call, once again, to voicemail. She did look at the multiple texts that had come in with the calls. All of them from the same source.

Darren fricking Walters.

Bad enough he'd ruined her career. The fact that he now needed her help and thought he deserved it just pissed her off. She was a pretty even keeled kind of woman. It took a lot to piss her off. Darren had managed it so thoroughly she very nearly threw her phone against the wall when it rang again. Except she didn't want to take her anger out on her poor phone. It wasn't the phone's fault Darren was an asshole of the highest order.

So instead, she turned it all the way off. No music for the moment, but she could paint in silence.

She'd closed the door to the room to keep the dogs out, since Princess was a little to fascinated with the paint trays, and more specifically the paint. One doggie nose in the pale blue paint had been enough to teach Sabrina her lesson. Whatever room she was working in was a no-dog room. At least until the walls were finished and dried.

But without her phone on, she realized she wouldn't know when it was walk time. Or feeding time. And she really didn't need the dogs getting desperate and making a mess in Tabby's house because she'd had a pout and turned off her phone.

She contemplated the walls. She had two full sections done, including the floor and ceiling detail work. She could take a break here and come back and finish the third wall after lunch.

After cleaning up, she decided a walk on the beach with the dogs would work out the kinks, and her irritation with Darren's calls, so she and the dogs went out the back, spent a few minutes in the backyard to take care of the necessaries, then went for a stroll on the white sand. It was a weekday, and still early in June, so there weren't a whole lot of people on the beach at that time of day, but enough she had to keep an eye on where the dogs went. For the most part, though, they ran out ahead of her and back to her without stopping to investigate other people. Princess only got caught in one wave. Justin spent the outing running in and out of the water.

By the time they got back to the house, both dogs needed a thorough rinse with the hose. And lunch on the deck was a given so they had time to dry before coming back in the house.

"I don't know about you guys," she said as she ensured she'd gotten all the sand out of Princess's fluffy fur, "but I'm starving."

This declaration was met with a resounding bark from Princess and a tongue-lolling smile from Justin. She hadn't known dogs could smile, but Justin definitely did.

Because she was a glutton for punishment, she did turn her phone back on as she got her lunch ready. More texts and voicemails. And it rang *again* ten seconds after it was on and all the messages were downloaded.

She let out a slow breath, trying to calm her rising anger, but she still found herself snarling at the phone.

She was half considering answering, or just turning it off again, when the doorbell rang.

She wasn't expecting anyone. Maybe a delivery? Tabby hadn't warned her about one, though. She peaked out the window next to the front door. Her stomach did a little giddy dance of excitement, and she had to squash that burst of delight before she opened the door.

"Hey Nick," she said, putting on a smile she hoped didn't look too strained. "What can I do for you?"

He frowned at her for a long moment. She stared back. When he didn't speak right away, she said, "You okay?"

He shook himself and said, "I have a key to this place."

"Uh. Okay." She'd known that already. He'd used it on the very first day she was here to take the dogs out and return them. Tabby had told her he had a spare key if she ever managed to lock herself out. Why was *he* telling her this? Now. Out of the blue. "Tabby told me." She let her voice lilt up at the end, making that last sentence a sort of question.

His frown deepened. "I'm trying to ask if you want me to return it while you're here."

"Why?" Her turn to frown a little.

"I didn't want you to worry. You don't know me very well, and I have a key to the house you're living in. Thought that might…make you feel unsafe." He scowled and shoved his hands in his pockets.

He was wearing jeans again. She liked him in jeans. His t-shirt was nice too. White and stretched tight across his shoulders. He had broad shoulders. Good solid shoulders.

She blinked and focused on what he'd just said because it was probably one of the sweetest things she'd ever had a man say to her. "That's very considerate of you." Her smile felt less awkward and forced this time. "If Tabby trusts you with it, I think I can, too. But I really appreciate you even thinking about me and how I might feel about it."

He nodded and grunted something under his breath she didn't catch.

He looked so absolutely scrumptiously adorable and hot she

opened her mouth to invite him in because she couldn't seem to help herself. She knew she shouldn't. Spending any extra time with Nick was bad for her balance—which was already shaky. Better to keep a friendly distance between them so he never figured out she wanted to rip that white t-shirt off and fuck him on the hallway floor. It would get awkward when he turned her down.

Despite her better judgment, though, she still opened her mouth to invite him in, ask if he wanted a coffee or something cold to drink, or maybe some lunch since it was one of Tabby's prepared meals…

Only to stop short when her phone rang. Again.

She pulled in a deep, irritated breath through her nose.

Nick glanced behind her toward the back of the house, where her cell insisted on buzzing. "You need to get that?" he asked.

"No. Most definitely not. And if it doesn't stop ringing soon, I'm going to break it into a dozen little pieces." She said the last with a smile she was pretty sure looked maniacal. It definitely felt maniacal.

"Problem?"

"Nothing a little distance and ignoring my phone won't solve." Except it hadn't. She'd been ignoring her phone all morning. And since Darren hadn't lost her number like she'd told him too, even the distance hadn't helped.

Nick nodded, turned away from the door as if he intended to leave, then turned back. "Can I help?"

Her shoulders relaxed a little and she gave him another genuine smile. "You're really very sweet, you know that," she murmured. "There's nothing you can do. But I appreciate the offer." She sighed and waved a hand vaguely in the air. "It's a former work colleague who's now in over his head and thinks I should help him. Which I have no intention of doing. Because he's the reason he's a *former* colleague and not a current one."

She wasn't entirely sure why she told Nick that. Tabby knew of course. But she hadn't discussed the situation with anyone else. She was embarrassed she'd allowed it to happen, at least too embarrassed to say anything to her family or any of her other friends. Tabby was her closest friend, so she told her everything. Sabrina barely knew Nick, though, so sharing this should have felt awkward as hell.

Instead, it was a relief to admit the problem out loud. At least a little. And to someone who was, essentially, a stranger. Telling Nick even the vague bit she'd just admitted to felt like a weight lifted from her shoulders. Lightened the load. Just enough she could smile and shrug.

The fact that Nick's expression turned absolutely fierce as he looked back at the still buzzing phone left her even lighter and surprisingly happy. That was probably a weird reaction. But she did like that fierce expression on his face.

"Sounds like an asshole," he said. With an actual growl in his voice.

She had to press her lips together so she didn't shiver. He might misunderstand. Or worse, he might understand her reaction was pure, unadulterated pleasure.

"Want to come in for a drink," she said before she could stop herself. "Coffee? Tea? Cold soda?" She motioned toward the kitchen. She expected him to wave her off, because her offer came out of nowhere and there was no reason for him to take her up on it.

He stared at her for a moment, still frowning, and she was sure he'd decline.

But instead, he nodded and stepped into the house.

Sabrina's stomach did a happy little flutter.

Oh, that was bad. That was going to get her into trouble. At the very least, that giddy delight was going to embarrass her soon.

Shame she'd forgotten why she cared.

CHAPTER SIX

Nick shouldn't have accepted her offer. He certainly shouldn't have followed her into the house. Definitely shouldn't have snuck a glance at her ass as he walked behind her into the kitchen. Especially since the sight was now seared into his mind, and he'd have to scrub his brain with acid to remove the image.

Staring at her ass was definitely *not* why he'd come over.

He'd come here because he'd spent the last two days thinking she might feel unsafe with him having a key to her house. He was essentially a stranger to her. She was used to the city. She probably didn't want some random man having access to her home. He'd convinced himself she hated the idea, but might be too nervous to ask for the key back. The thought of her being afraid bothered him. A lot. So much so, he'd finally given in and come over to return the key.

The fact that he was checking out her ass only proved why she shouldn't trust him with a house key.

"What sounds good?" she asked as she moved behind the kitchen counter.

She did. She sounded good. "Coffee's fine."

"Not too hot for a coffee?" She smiled as she stuck a little disposable cup into Tabby's fancy coffee machine.

Her smile was going to kill him. "No." He could drink coffee in the middle of a desert. It was never too hot for coffee.

"Tabby mentioned you were a bit of an addict," she said, grinning as she put a thick ceramic mug under the machine's single brew dispenser.

He wasn't sure what to say to that. The fact that Tabby talked about him to Sabrina enough to mention his coffee habit was interesting.

He searched for some innocuous topic of conversation but was saved from having to make small talk while his brain was short circuiting by her phone ringing again. They both scowled at the little purple rectangle at the same moment. It took him a beat to realize her phone had a purple case decorated in bright, stylized flowers. Why didn't that surprise him?

"He's persistent," he said, glaring at the phone.

"He's in trouble," she said, also glaring at the phone. "And he thinks I'll save his sorry ass even though he cost me my job."

"Why would he think that?"

"Because he's an arrogant, entitled, ivy league asshole who can go fuck himself."

He tried not to react to her use of the word fuck because he was sure she'd misunderstand. Her rant was righteous, and he approved. But hearing her say fuck did something to him, and he wasn't going to recover from that any time soon.

He grunted in lieu of an actual comment.

The phone stopped ringing.

"He'll call back?" he asked.

"'Fraid so." She sighed. "I'll turn it off again."

"Want me to answer the next call?" He had no idea where that offer came from. He meant it, though. He'd happily snarl into the phone at this persistent ivy league asshole who kept bugging her. In fact, he'd relish it.

Her grin flashed, hitting him right in the gut, and he knew he'd do whatever she asked in the next moment because she was smiling at him. Her smile just destroyed him. And he couldn't even regret it.

"That would be fun to watch," she said. "And I'm very tempted.

But…" She frowned a little and glanced at the phone again when it rang. Her lips pursed, her eyebrows raised. Then she grinned again. "Go on, answer it. See what he says."

He had to take a moment to pull himself together because of her grin. Then he picked up her purple phone and swiped on.

"Hello." Yes, he'd purposefully deepened his voice. What of it?

The momentary silence on the other end was satisfying. "Who's this?" a man said, sounding hesitant.

"You're the one who called, you tell me."

Sabrina pressed her lips together, but her face was lit with her amusement and that view took up most of his thinking. He should probably concentrate on the asshole on the phone, but he was too enchanted with her joy.

"I'm trying to reach Sabrina Mitchell."

"She's busy right now." And, god help him, the ideas that flashed suddenly through his mind of how *he* could be keeping her busy in just that moment… Glorious and dangerous thoughts. Things he was safer not thinking. Because they involved a lot less clothing.

She slapped a hand over her mouth to hold in her snort of amusement. No soft chuckle. No. She actually snorted. It was adorable and he just wanted to drop the cellphone and pull her into a kiss.

He should never have come over here.

"This is important. Put her on the phone."

No please. No request. Just a demand. This guy really was an entitled asshole. "No."

Another momentary pause. "What do you mean no?"

"It's a declarative statement of negative intent. Shall I go into more detail?"

Sabrina nearly doubled over as she tried to keep her laughter silent. Which made him smile.

"No," the man said, and there was another silent pause, during which Nick assumed he was contemplating all his life's mistakes.

Nick waited him out. He was sure there were a lot of mistakes to consider in this asshole's life.

"Listen, this is very important. Life or death. To do with her job. You need to put her on the line."

"No." Was the man grinding his teeth? Nick could swear the man was grinding his teeth. Since the thought would amuse Sabrina, he said aloud, "You shouldn't grind your teeth. You'll upset your dentist."

As he'd suspected, that pushed her over the edge. She moved to the couch and dropped onto the cushions, covering her face with a throw pillow. He still heard her laughter. His own smile grew. This was fun.

There was an audible swallow. Then, "I think you're misunderstanding the seriousness of this situation. I need to speak to Sabrina. Now. It's urgent."

"For you. She's not interested in speaking with you. And if you don't stop calling this phone, I will track you down and shove your own phone up your ass. How's that for urgent? Asshole."

Sabrina's face popped out from behind the pillow. Her eyes were wide, her lips pressed tightly together, and her expression filled with delight and surprise.

And wow did he not want to be this far away from her. He pushed away from the kitchen counter before he thought better of it.

There was sputtering on the other end of the phone, but he mostly ignored it as he reached the couch. She had the pillow pressed against her mouth again, but she was staring up at him, eyes wide, looking so deliciously amused and adorable, he was pretty sure his brain was going to combust. It would be a good way to go.

"Asshole? You're calling me an asshole? Do you have any idea who I am? Who you're speaking to?"

He couldn't help his chuff of laughter then. The sound just burst out of him. "I'm not sure I've ever heard anyone say that in real life before. What a ridiculous thing to say. Makes you sound like a pathetic chump." Yes, he was pushing buttons. He couldn't seem to help it. Probably because he was currently staring into Sabrina's big brown eyes and there wasn't much he wouldn't do in that moment to keep her entertained.

"Listen you son of a bitch, when I find out who you are—"

Nick cut him off with another loud and abrupt burst of laughter.

"You're threatening me? You have no idea who I am either. But if you'd like to find out, I'd be more than happy to meet. It would amuse me."

Was that going too far? Na. This guy deserved the low level threat. He deserved an ass-kicking too, if it ever came to that.

"Tell Sabrina I'll be in touch."

The man disconnected before Nick could say anything. Which was probably for the best. His amusement had flashed to anger with that parting comment, and he was pretty sure the next thing out of his mouth would be considerably less mild.

He handed her the phone.

"That was…amazing," she said. "I wish I could have seen his face. I bet he turned purple in his outrage."

"Glad I could help. He's probably not done calling. He did say he'd be in touch."

She sighed and glared at her phone. "He's such an asshole."

"Got that impression." He hesitated, before giving in and saying, "You want to talk about it?"

A very big part of him hoped she'd say no. Because if he learned more, or spent any more time with her, or continued to stare at her, he'd be in more trouble than he already was, and he was already in big trouble with her. He had been for years now. But since he lived out here, and she lived in Brooklyn, he'd been able to keep his… He wasn't even sure what to call it. His preoccupation? Yeah, that was a safe word. His preoccupation with Sabrina at bay. Sort of.

Having Tabby remind him after every time Sabrina visited that she was off limits had helped check his…preoccupation as well.

But having Sabrina living right next door had upended all that. After just a couple of days, he was so distracted, he could barely get anything done. In only a couple of days! He'd sworn to himself he'd just leave her alone to do her thing, and he'd stick to his side of the property line and do his thing, and that would be that. But no. He'd ended up over here with some trumped up excuse about the house key. And now here he was offering to *talk* with her about a problem. It was all more than his poor brain could take. He needed to get out now while he still could.

But the part of himself he was currently labeling "preoccupied" with her wanted her to tell him everything. To reveal exactly *why* the asshole on the phone was badgering her. What he'd done to her? And, most importantly, how Nick could destroy the man so Sabrina felt better?

The determination and violence of that last part was harder to label as mere "preoccupation."

Which confirmed he was in serious trouble.

CHAPTER SEVEN

Nick hovered beside the couch, staring down at Sabrina, waiting for her to make her choice whether to trust him or not. Still sort of hoping she'd tell him her problems with the asshole on the phone were none of his concern. She'd be right. This wasn't his business. And he should probably leave now.

He wasn't going to. But he should.

Instead of telling him to mind his own business, Sabrina shrugged, her delighted smile dimming. Which made him want to punch something. Like the man who'd hurt her. That asshole's face would do nicely.

"It's…a long story," she said. "But the basics—" another sad little shrug, "—I trusted the wrong person at work. I thought he was a friend. A colleague. On the same team. And he wasn't. That misguided trust cost me a job I loved. And now I have to rethink all my life choices." She smiled at that last sentence, but the smile was forced and looked entirely too brittle around the edges.

He hated it. He hated that she felt that brittle, bitter smile. He hated that someone had betrayed her. He hated the pain in her expression down to his bones.

"I'm sorry," he said softly. "That sucks. A lot."

"Yeah. It does. But it's done now. And I'm better off out of that situation."

"That's why you're here? To…rethink your life choices?"

Her chuckle wasn't as bright and happy as before, but not as bitter as her smile had been. So… Progress.

"Yeah," she said. "I'm here to figure out what to do next. Well, and to help Tabby while she's on tour."

"Dog sitting."

"And finishing up some of the work upstairs. The painting and tiling. Detail stuff."

He realized suddenly he had no idea what this dream job of hers had been. Strangely, Sabrina's work wasn't something Tabby talked about when she talked about her best friend. She made all kinds of other passing comments about Sabrina. All the time. But she'd never mentioned her career.

He frowned a little. "What did you do? For work?"

"Oh. I'm… I was an interior designer. I know it's a little Westchester-wife cliché, but I loved the work. I was with a company that did things like swanky hotel interiors and hip new restaurants, along with our wealthy penthouse clients." She wagged her eyebrows. "Plenty of room to be creative in the business interiors, and usually enough money involved to let that creativity run free." She waved a hand at him. "You should probably sit down if we're going to keep talking about this. Oh! Wait." She popped up off the couch. "I forgot your coffee."

She hurried back to the kitchen. "How do you like it? I've got milk, sugar, some sweetener…" She lifted the mug slightly with her question.

"Black is fine. Anything involving coffee is fine, really."

She grinned. Another genuine one, and he felt his shoulders relaxing. Probably not a good thing that his stress levels lowered when her mood went up.

He settled on the couch when she brought him the steaming mug and tried to steel himself against the distraction of having her sitting so close as she dropped back onto the cushions. Justin picked that moment to nudge Nick's leg, looking for attention, so he absently scratched the big poodle's head while he sipped his coffee and tried not to stare too intently at Sabrina. He had trouble not looking at her. All the time. His gaze gravitated to her if she was in the room. But the coffee and the attention-seeking poodle gave him good excuses to look elsewhere occasionally so he didn't come off too intense.

"Coffee's good," he said. And it was. Rich and dark and strong. Tabby always had excellent stuff on hand.

"Thanks again," she said, her head ducked a little but still meeting his gaze. "For…for making Darren rethink *his* life choices."

"You're welcome." He wanted to offer to do more. But he wasn't sure what he could do for her. At least not when it came to this Darren creep. "If he calls again, let me know." Why? Why should she let him know? What was he going to do? "Maybe he and I can have another chat. That could be fun."

She snort-laughed. He smiled because she was adorable and he was truly and unequivocally a goner. Tabby was going to murder him in his sleep. He tightened his hold on the mug handle.

"I wouldn't mind seeing that again." She glanced at the phone she'd left on the couch cushions between them. "Hopefully, he won't call back for a bit."

"What's he want from you?"

"He's not as good at his job as I was," she said, her lips pursed as she rolled her eyes. "And he needs my help to get out of a mess he's walked himself into."

"You're not going to help him, are you?"

"Of course not." She scowled. "He deserves every bit of failure and disaster that comes his way."

Nick grunted in agreement. He didn't even know Darren and he agreed wholeheartedly with her statement.

"But having a multi-million-dollar job fall apart around him because he doesn't know what he's doing is making him desperate."

"Not your issue."

"Nope. Not my issue." She gave a firm nod. "I'd love him to stop trying to make it my issue, though. But at least now I shouldn't have to hear from him for a few hours." She waved a hand in the air. "Anyway. This is a depressing topic."

"We don't have to talk about it."

"Something lighter, then. What do you do for a living? Tabby's never mentioned."

Did Tabby talk to her about him often? The way she talked about Sabrina to him? Probably not since Sabrina was her best friend, and he was just a friendly neighbor.

"Architect," he said. "Mostly, I work freelance now, private clients. Less pressure. More creativity."

"The creativity is the best part, isn't it?" She sighed. "What did you do before going freelance?"

"Worked for a large firm in the city." He shrugged. "Didn't suit me after a while. I moved out here."

There'd been more to it than that. Nothing as dramatic as her situation, certainly. But he'd been approaching burnout, fast, and his change of situation had been more than necessary. Probably as abrupt as hers had been, except he'd made the choice to change. She hadn't been given a choice.

Thinking about that just pissed him off again, so he said, "Any idea what you'll do after the summer?"

He shouldn't be asking that. He shouldn't be this curious or interested in her future. "Shouldn't" didn't seem to have anything to do with what he was *actually* thinking and feeling. But really, he shouldn't want to know so much more about her.

"No idea," she said. "That's sort of the point of this summer. Figure out what I want to do next. And I needed to get out of the city." She made a face, ducking her head so she wasn't looking at him when she said, "Unfortunately, Darren knows where my apartment is, and he was making a pest of himself."

Nick's fist clenched in Justin's fur and around his mug handle. He concentrated on not breaking the coffee mug and loosening his hold on the poodle as he asked, "What did he do?"

"Nothing but show up at my door a few times, trying to get me to help him. Nothing I could call the cops on him for." She rolled her eyes. "Not that that would do me much good. But it might have been satisfying forcing him to explain himself to a cop. Anyway, he's just persistent. Not dangerous. Frankly, if he got physical, I'm pretty sure I could take him. I'm meaner than I look."

She raised her fists and pretended to look dangerous.

Nick took a sip of his coffee to hide his disbelieving snort. If she was mean, he was a fucking rage monster. Which, in this case, he might well be. At least when it came to this Darren asshole.

"You don't believe me?" she asked, eyebrows raised.

"Not that. Just…"

"I was raised with cantankerous younger brother by a mother who ensured we both knew how to punch properly so we didn't break our thumb."

"Glad to know you can throw a proper punch," he said, hiding his expression in his mug. "Not sure I'd call you mean, though."

"Don't get on my bad side and you won't have to find out just how mean I am." She wagged her eyebrows.

"Fair enough." His smile cracked though, despite his best efforts. Her answering grin was worth it.

He found himself staring at her a moment too long, studying her expressive face too closely, and realized he needed to get off this couch and out of this house. Quickly.

He set his mug down on the coffee table and stood abruptly. "Better get back. Work to do."

She stood, too, a little slower. "Of course. Sure. Sorry to have kept you."

"No problem. Glad I could help." He was at the front door before he remembered why he'd come over in the first place. "The key." He turned. She was right behind him, following so close he knocked into her. "Shit."

He steadied her with his hands on her shoulders, but the contact left him winded. Not breathless. No. Winded. Just…winded. Sure. He'd been worried about hurting her is all. Which meant he could take his hands off her now. Really, he should take his hands off her. This very instant. Now.

She stared at him, her cheeks flushing pink, and that sent his brain down paths best left unexplored because they weren't the sort of thing you were supposed to be thinking about your neighbor's best friend. Especially when said best friend was in a vulnerable situation and just needed some peace and quiet. Not a virtual stranger standing around unable to keep his own damned hands to himself.

"You okay?" he asked, then cleared his throat. "Sorry. Didn't meant to bump into you."

"My fault. I was following too close."

Why had he stopped again? He was supposed to be leaving. "Right. The key. You sure you don't want it back?"

"You can keep it. Nice to know there's a spare around in case I lock myself out." Her smile was crooked.

And instead of letting go of her shoulders, his grip tightened and he was a muscle twitch away from pulling her closer. Which was not part of the plan, not something he should do, and a reaction that probably should have surprised him more than it did.

He cleared his throat again. "Okay. Fine. I'll do that. Try not to get locked out."

He dropped his hold abruptly, spun out the front door, and stalked home without looking back.

He was never going to survive this summer.

CHAPTER EIGHT

The man was a menace. At least to her peace of mind. No one should be that sexy and that kind all at once. It was criminal. Definitely had to be illegal.

Sabrina found herself thinking those same thoughts a lot over the next few days. She painted more. She walked the dogs often. She avoided taking Darren's calls completely. She ate Tabby's excellent froze meals daily. She even talked to Tabby and her mom, once each. And in the background of it all…

Nick.

She was officially obsessed with Tabby's neighbor. And she was *not* happy about it.

She really didn't need this crush right now. She'd come out here to take a break and consider her future. And instead of deciding what she wanted to do next, what steps to take to get back to work, and what kind of work she wanted to do going forward, all she thought about was Nick!

Was he awake yet? At home? Working? Relaxing? Would she see him on his deck? Would she catch him walking on the beach?

Argh! It was so annoying.

She was approaching her thirty-fourth birthday. She should not be this overwhelmed by a crush.

To distract herself that afternoon while painting, she gave in to loud music. She was an apartment person, used to keeping her music at neighbor-friendly levels. But this was a house. She could crank the volume up as far as her Bluetooth speakers would allow and dance around without worrying about stomping on the downstairs neighbor's head. The realization was so freeing, she actually laughed as she danced while placing blue tape around the fixtures and baseboards in the guest room.

Getting the area near the ceiling required a stepladder, however, so she wasn't able to dance as well, but she still found herself grooving to Bruno Mars's *The Lazy Song* as she pressed the blue tape against the ceiling so she'd get a nice line at the top of the wall. Tabby had gone all in and gotten her good brushes to work with, which meant doing the detail painting was a lot easier.

She leaned back to study her work, her hand against the wall to steady herself as she bopped around a little to the music.

"You're going to fall," a deep voice said.

The sound startled her so much, she spun, squealed, and because she was leaning back on a ladder, she did exactly what the voice had warned. With another squeaking sound of startled terror, she toppled over backward.

She didn't quite hit the floor before very strong arms caught her.

Which was nice because she'd been anticipating a broken wrist in those startled moments of hanging mid-air. She looked up into Nick's face and shook her head, her heartbeat pounding so hard she couldn't form words. Of course it was him. And of course he'd caught her. Because…of course.

But he did make her fall first before catching her.

The reminder didn't help her to ignore how warm he was pressed against her. Or how nicely his arms felt wrapped around her waist. And it did nothing to distract from the feel of that solid body under her hands. His shoulders were broad, and her hands settled there in a comfortable way that was too familiar. Not that she'd gripped Nick's shoulders before. But something about the hold felt very secure and right. And that was just irritating.

Her heart thumped—only from the adrenaline rush, she was sure—and they were pressed so tightly together, she was certain he could feel it. Or was that his heartbeat? Hard to tell.

"Thanks for catching me," she said, a little breathless—from the fall and *only* the fall. Had nothing to do with his mouth being just… right there. "But also, don't startle me like that again since you made me fall."

He scowled down at her. The furrow in his brows was very temping. She wasn't sure why. She wanted to run her fingers across his forehead and smooth those lines. And then maybe continue exploring his face with her fingertips. All the lovely plans, the sharp angles, the roughness from his mid-afternoon scruff…

She blinked her wandering attention back to the moment.

"Sorry," he grumbled. "Thought you heard me come in."

His expression was all contrite and remorseful, and there were even two little spots of color on his cheeks, leaving her entirely too charmed to stay mad. The bastard.

"Are you hurt?" he asked.

"I don't think so."

A few moments passed. He didn't let her go. She didn't try to step away. Having his arms around her waist was much too nice. She could lean into his chest all day. He had a nice chest. Everything about him was nice. Everything about being held by him was nice.

Too nice. Maybe a little addicting.

Her stomach did a little fluttery dance-and-tightening thing that she had a hard time writing off as part of the adrenaline rush from the fall. She had an even harder time not pressing closer to him.

She needed to step away, put some space between them. Yeah. That's what she needed to do. Didn't *want* to. But…

Yeah, definitely needed to.

"You can let me go," she said, trying not to sound too disappointed by the prospect. "I got my footing back."

"Sorry. Sorry." He dropped his hold instantly and took two big steps away from her.

The speed of his retreat made her chest tight for reasons she chose not to consider. "Why are you here?"

"You weren't answering your doorbell."

"I couldn't hear it."

"I figured that out." He didn't quite meet her gaze when he said, "I used the key to get in when you didn't answer. Sorry."

Again with the apologies. At least he was capable of saying he was sorry. "Why did you come in?" she asked. "I could have been out walking the dogs."

"The dogs were at the door barking at the doorbell."

Oh. She hadn't even heard that. She winced. "Wow, guess I had my music up too loud," she said. Just as a new song started and filled the room with enough noise she winced again. She hurried to her phone and shut the app down. Then gave him a little grin. "Used to apartments. I was taking advantage of being in a house." She shrugged when he frowned at her. "No neighbors to object to the noise."

"Ah." His mouth ticked up at one side. "Can't blame you for that."

"You lived in the city. You know what it's like."

"Why I got a house."

She chuckled. Then looked around him to the door. Justin and Princess sat just outside the room in the hallway, watching the exchange. The moment she glanced at them, though, they trotted into the room, Justin going right for her and putting his head under her hand so she'd scratch him.

"Was I ignoring you guys?" she said, giving him a rub under his chin.

Princess preened for Nick, and he squatted down to pet her, which was too adorable. Why did Nick have to be so adorable? Why couldn't he be…? She didn't know. Less delightful? Less sexy? Less…everything?

"So why are you here again?" she asked. Since he hadn't actually told her that part.

He looked up at her, his mouth a tight line, those tempting furrows in his brow again. She'd never realized she could be attracted to forehead wrinkles but here she was.

He stood abruptly and turned toward the door. "Sorry. This was a bad idea. Didn't mean to bother you."

"Wait!" She rushed forward, only to bounce off his back when he did as she'd asked and stopped. She shuffled back a step. "Wait. Was it important? What's going on? You made the effort to come all the way over here. What did you need?"

He opened his mouth. Closed it again. Opened it. "Never mind."

He spun back around and left. Just…left her standing in the doorway as he stalked down the stairs.

She blinked as the front door closed. She listened to him lock it behind himself, which was baffling but sweet, and then silence.

What the hell was that all about?

"Do you two understand what that was?" she asked the dogs.

Justin pushed his head under her hand again for more scratches. Princess licked her own foot. No answers there. But they didn't seem bothered by Nick's actions either, so maybe he was always like that?

Hmm.

"Wonder if I should go over and ask what he was here for? It had to be important, right? He wouldn't have come over otherwise. Right?"

She looked down at Princess. Princess switched to licking her back foot. The pose was not lady-like even a little bit. Sabrina shook her head and stared at the stairs again as she absently scratched Justin around his ears.

Should she go check on Nick? Or should she mind her own business and stay here?

A sensory memory of his arms around her, his lovely heat, the press of his chest against her, the way his hands had flexed on her waist as she stared up at him, the warm musky scent of him mixing with the perpetual background salty scent from the ocean.

Yeah, she shouldn't go anywhere near that man again if she could at all help it. Whatever had driven him here, if he didn't want to talk about it, she needed to let it go. She couldn't risk traipsing over to his house to interrogate him. Especially right now, when her body tingled from the contact high of being that close to him.

Smarter to stay here. Finishing taping the walls. Get some painting done.

No going over to Nick's house because curiosity overwhelmed her. That was the kind of curiosity that got her into trouble.

And she was already in too much trouble where Nick was concerned.

CHAPTER NINE

Despite Tabby's excellent planning and meal prep, Sabrina did finally have to leave the house and venture farther than the beach. The grocery store called.

She'd never been to the local store, because when she visited Tabby, Tabby had already stocked her shelves and pantry. The pantry was still plenty full, which gave Sabrina a lot to work with, but she needed some fresh stuff—milk, fruit and veg, some cheese. She wasn't a big cook, not like Tabby, and while she was capable of making her own meals, she was sort of missing the easy food delivery of the city. Unlike her best friend, she didn't much enjoy thinking about food a lot. She liked eating it. She just didn't like to think about it.

Which was why, when Nick found her at the local supermarket, she was standing in front of the meat section, staring at the various cuts of beef and chicken, unable to pick anything because she had no idea what she was in the mood for.

Warming up Tabby's cooking was a lot easier.

Nick walked up beside her, also staring at the meat selection. She glanced at him from the corner of her eye. Yup, still gorgeous. Her stomach did that funny little dance, and suddenly it was a lot harder to think about food because food wasn't what she wanted to nibble anymore.

She returned her gaze firmly to the cold shelves full of plastic wrapped chicken and ground beef.

"What are you getting?" he asked without turning to look at her.

"Can't decide. Tabby spoiled me, and I don't know what to cook for myself now. I'm open to suggestions."

"Can't miss with burgers if you're a meat person."

Hamburgers actually did sound good. She grabbed a package of ground beef. "That was helpful. Thanks."

"Any time." He reached around her and picked up some ground turkey and a package of skin-on chicken breasts.

"What are you making?" She had to work very hard to ignore the brush of his arm against hers as he straightened.

"Grilled chicken. Spaghetti and meatballs." He lifted each package with the associated meal.

"Sounds tasty."

Why was she talking to him like this? She felt ridiculous. This was a ridiculous conversation. Or was it? If she wasn't so damned aware of him, standing so close, if he was just an ordinary person, wouldn't she be talking about food while standing in front of a lot of food? They were both in a grocery store. The topic seemed obvious.

"Nothing as good as Tabby's food," he said. "But I can manage."

"Yeah. Same. I mean, I can manage, but not anything like Tabby." Wow, she felt awkward. She needed to say goodbye and get back to her shopping. That would be the logical next step. "Are you finished or still shopping?"

That wasn't what she'd meant to say at all!

"Still shopping."

"Want company?"

Oh, no that was *not* what she was supposed to say. She was supposed to wish him a good day, walk away, pay for her food, and then leave. Very quickly. So she didn't spend more time with him, and risk exposing her absolutely bonkers crush. She might trip over her own feet if she spent too much more time with him.

"Maybe you can show me where the mustard is?" She really had to stop talking. Tabby surely had mustard in the house.

But if she was going to eat hamburgers, she needed mustard. It would be silly not to get some while she was here, just in case. And he was a local. He probably already knew where mustard was. Right?

She was extremely pleased he couldn't overhear what was going on in her head right then. She felt silly enough already.

He nodded and started walking, without comment. She fell into step beside him, carrying her shopping basket in front of her. She had the meat for burgers in there, an assortment of fruit, cheese, milk, and crackers. Not her whole list yet, but then again, she hadn't come with a list because she wasn't that organized.

The aisle with the mustard was empty. The store wasn't particularly crowded in the middle of a Tuesday at any rate, but without other people walking past, Sabrina felt a little too alone with Nick.

"Which kind do you need?" he asked and gestured to the shelves of different mustards.

She hadn't really considered how many types there were before, and maybe it was because the store she shopped at near her apartment wasn't this fancy, but there seemed to be a hundred different kinds of mustard on the shelf.

"I bet Tabby loves this place," she murmured.

He chuckled. "Mention the mustard shelves to her. She'll have stories."

Sabrina grinned as she hunted down the ordinary yellow mustard she liked on her hamburgers. And then, in honor of her best friend, picked out a fancy seed mustard to try. Tabby would be so proud.

"Thanks." She faced Nick. Then paused because she had no idea what to say. So what she said was, once again, extremely unplanned. "Why did you come over the other day and then run back out again without telling me why you came over?"

Oops. She hadn't meant to ask that. He'd said to forget it. She'd tried to do just that because she wasn't supposed to be thinking this much about him. But of course, she thought about him all the time. So she hadn't forgotten even the smallest detail of that incident. Especially the being-in-his-arms part, which she had a feeling was branded on her body now and she was doomed.

And the fact that he'd come all the way over and then left without actually saying why he'd been there was bugging her. Enough she'd ask him about it in the middle of the grocery store. In the condiments aisle of all places.

She should take back the question. But curiosity won out over common sense. As usual.

She needed to do something about her curiosity. It was going to get her into serious trouble one day.

"It was nothing. A stupid idea." He shrugged and focused on the mustard shelf. "I have this client…" He made a face. "This isn't really something I want to talk about in a grocery store."

"Fair enough." See. None of your business, Sabrina. "I shouldn't have asked."

"I made it a thing by running out after coming over." He looked around the aisle and let out a long breath.

A woman pushing a stroller with a shopping basket on the top of the handle swung into the aisle. She didn't even glance at them. But the fact that there *were* other people around, and Nick's thing had to do with a client, made Sabrina regret even more that she'd brought it up.

"Never mind," she said, waving away the topic. "It's work related. It's none of my business."

Although, he had come to her. What on earth could one of his clients have to do with her? Unless it had something to do with her former employer and Darren? That wouldn't be likely. She hadn't even told him the name of her former employer. But as an architect, he did work with interior designers, and her former company was one of the best in the city. Maybe it had something to do with them? She couldn't imagine another reason he might come over to discuss one of his clients with her.

"You have much left to get?" he asked.

When she frowned, he nodded at her basket. "Oh," she said, "just some onions and lettuce if I'm going to eat a burger."

"How about we finish here. Then go home and this time I come over and discuss this like a grown up instead of running away?"

She pressed her lips together so she wouldn't grin. Grinning wasn't appropriate at this moment in the conversation. But he looked so annoyed—at himself more than anything—and when he was annoyed, he was gorgeously adorable. She couldn't really resist that expression.

"Sounds like a plan," she said. "So long as you're okay with telling me. I didn't mean to press the subject. I didn't realize it had to do with work."

But what else would he come over to discuss with her? They weren't exactly friends. Acquaintances with a mutual friend, but not friends themselves.

Although, maybe they could be?

She glanced at his shoulders when he turned away and started toward the vegetable aisle. The breadth of his back stretched his t-shirt in a very nice way. His jeans did the same thing over his ass. She sighed. Then gave herself a little shake and followed him.

Friends probably wasn't an option when she kept ogling him every time he turned around. But maybe friendly acquaintances? Maybe she could manage to be friendly with him without all the edgy awkwardness? She could keep her crush to herself and still hold a conversation with him on occasion. It would make the summer easier, not having to avoid him for fear of revealing her feelings.

Her gaze dropped to his backside again, and she rolled her eyes. Right. She'd be able to spend time with him and not give herself away. Sure. That would happen.

She was ridiculous, and this was not going to end well.

That damned curiosity of hers really was going to get her into trouble.

CHAPTER TEN

Nick should have let the subject drop. He shouldn't have gone to her house in the first place, but now he really really shouldn't talk about this with her. He'd gotten another boneheaded idea, acted on it without thinking, and nearly done something he knew in his bones he'd regret.

And to add insult to injury, he'd nearly killed her.

That might be a little dramatic. The ladder had only been a stepladder. A tall one. But still. She wouldn't have broken her neck falling. But maybe her wrist. Or some other body part. And it would have been his fault because he'd startled her.

The worst part, though, at least for him, hadn't been the near disaster. Although that was going to haunt him—watching her footing slip, watching her tumble out into midair… That had been bad enough. But to make things even more disastrous, he couldn't forget the feel of her in his arms. Couldn't get the sensory memory out of his head. He'd caught her to keep her from getting hurt. He was glad he'd reached her in time. But the feel of her curvy body tight against his was an experience that would not leave him alone.

The memory had been torturing him for every second of every day since. The warmth of her in his arms, the way her body softened into his, her full breasts pressed against his chest, the flutter of her lashes as she'd looked up at him with her gorgeous brown eyes, her dark hair, pulled into a high bun that was knocked sideways, giving her a mussed look that brought to mind beds and sweaty sheets. The way her mouth had been just…right there. Lush and plump and kissable.

Torture.

And he had only himself to blame.

If he were the penance type, he'd suspect agreeing to discuss his original reason for going over to her house was his way of doing penance. For nearly getting her hurt, but also for his inability to stop fantasizing about her mouth. That's what Diego would call it. Diego was a good Catholic who believed in penance and atonement. Nick was not—either Catholic or much for penance. But he did feel like he owed her an explanation for his strange behavior.

The problem was giving her those answers meant spending more time alone with her. And that was pure madness. Dangerous.

Tabby would absolutely, without any regrets at all, murder him in his sleep if he hit on her best friend and hurt her in any way. She'd told him so. Point blank.

He didn't doubt her for a second, either, because he was just as protective of his own friends, particularly his best friend. Diego was happily married with kids now, so the protectiveness took a different shape, but still. He'd kill for Diego and his family. He completely understood why Tabby would do the same for Sabrina.

So when he found himself sitting on the deck next to Sabrina, a cold soda in hand, the sun angled behind the house giving them some nice shade as they both stared out at the rolling ocean, he knew he had to be on his best behavior. The discussion was going to be bad enough, since he had to admit to his stupid, boneheaded idea. Doing anything *but* talk was out of the question.

They sat in silence for a good five minutes before he finally cleared his throat and said, "I have this client…"

She nodded, keeping her gaze on the ocean. Which helped. If she wasn't looking at him, he wouldn't lose track of the conversation and forget why he was here.

"He's one of my biggest." He sighed. "My biggest. And if he likes the house I'm designing for him at the moment, he has the kinds of contacts with other potential clients that could secure my business for the next couple of years."

"Sounds like an important person to please," she said.

The fact that she got that without question helped him relax a little. He slumped down in the deck chair. "More like the kind of person I don't want to piss off. If my design doesn't thrill him, or the execution of that design isn't what he hoped for, that's one thing. It wouldn't be great, but it happens and it's the risks of the job. If I piss him off personally, on the other hand, I'm looking at a very difficult next couple of years. Maybe the end of my business. At least the end of my business as it stands now."

"Serious, then."

"Serious."

"What's the problem?"

"He's..." Ah, man, he really didn't want to discuss this with her. Why had he agreed to discuss this?

Oh, yeah, because he'd nearly killed her after coming over to get her help with this problem and then run away without an explanation.

He rolled his eyes. "So... Greene has two daughters. One is getting married in a few days. The other..." He felt his cheeks heating and took a gulp of his soda. "The other is a perfectly nice woman who keeps hitting on me."

He watched Sabrina from the corner of his eye. She took a drink of her own soda and kept her gaze on the beach, but when she wasn't drinking, she had her lips pressed tight together and he could swear she was suppressing a grin.

He sighed. "This is so stupid."

"Which part? The woman hitting on you, or you being embarrassed by it?"

He scowled. "That I'm sitting here telling *you* about it."

"You don't have to, you know. I shouldn't have poked into this since it's obviously private."

"No, it's my fault. I..." He was getting ahead of himself. "Anyway,

Greene invited me to his daughter's wedding. And because I'm not *always* an idiot, I accepted the invitation. A lot of his powerful friends and associates will be there. I can make a lot of contacts, get a lot of leads on potential work. But…"

"But his other daughter will be there, and you'd rather she didn't hit on you again?"

"Worse. I didn't add a plus one to the RSVP, so he wants me to accompany his daughter."

Sabrina made a little choking noise. He couldn't tell if it was a cough or a laugh. "He's trying to set you up with his daughter?"

"Yes."

"And you're not interested in his daughter?"

"No."

"Well." She cleared her throat. "That is…a situation, isn't it?"

"He loves his daughters," Nick said. "He is very very protective of his daughters."

"Wow, are you in trouble."

"Exactly!" He smacked the arm of the chair and then lifted his hand in a resigned shrug. "You get it. The whole thing puts me in an impossible situation."

"What are you going to do?"

"I…" Now the really embarrassing part. "I told him I was already dating someone. That I hadn't included her in the invitation because she was supposed to be out of town, but was back in town now, and she was my plus one, so I couldn't accompany his daughter."

Sabrina was silent for a long time after he'd finished his rushed admission.

He resisted the impulse to add more. He felt like enough of an ass already. Anything more he said would only make his embarrassment worse.

"Are you dating someone?" she asked after an agonizingly long moment.

"No."

"Who did you have in mind when you said all this to him, then? A…friend?"

"I didn't think at all." He groaned and ran a hand through his hair. "I just opened my mouth and the stupid story came out."

"Shame Tabby's not here. She'd be a really glamourous fake-girlfriend."

"Except Mrs. Greene is a huge fan of hers. She's hired her for private catering before. If I went with Tabby that would get us both into a complicated situation with clients neither one of us wants to lose."

"Wow," she said again. "You really stuck your foot in it, didn't you?"

"I absolutely did."

"No friend close enough to help? No cousin they might not know about?"

He glared out at the ocean. "Cousin? No. Women friends out here, no. And the ones who live in the city that I could have asked are all busy this weekend."

It was a little embarrassing to admit, but he hadn't made an effort to befriend a lot of people here. Outside of Tabby, most of his friends still lived in the city, and he liked it that way. He went into Queens for baseball games with Diego and some of the guys during the summer, or met up with people for dinner or concerts when he had meetings in Manhattan—all in the city, so he could come back out here and be alone. It wasn't that he didn't like people. He did. At least some people. He just didn't like them around all the time. And having that space between him and his friends was…settling.

But that wasn't something he talked about. Diego got it, of course. And he was pretty sure Tabby had figured out how much he preferred his privacy. But it just wasn't something he went out of his way to tell people. He certainly didn't intend to tell Sabrina. Especially since he felt like enough of a fool already. Admitting he'd avoided making friends out here felt…too personal.

He could sense her stare on the side of his face. He didn't turn to look at her. No doubt she'd finally put the whole thing together. He slouched further into his seat and cradle his glass in both hands. The ocean breeze wasn't doing much to cool off his embarrassment. Maybe a nice dip in the icy cold Atlantic would help. If he got really lucky, maybe there'd be a freak riptide that would carry him out to sea and away from his mortification.

Unfortunately, he didn't have that kind of luck.

"You came over to ask me to go with you to the wedding, didn't you?" she finally said.

From the corner of his eye, Nick couldn't read her expression. And he couldn't tell from her voice if she was upset or not. Her tone was remarkably neutral.

He shook his head, his attention solidly on the sandy beach and rolling Atlantic waves, because he couldn't face her as he admitted this. "I know. Dumb idea. We barely know each other. This isn't the kind of help you ask from an acquaintance."

He couldn't quite bring himself to call her a stranger, even though they didn't know each other very well. They did *know* each other. A little anyway. He knew why she was out here housesitting for her best friend. He now knew she was an interior designer. That she'd lost her job thanks to an asshat named Darren. She liked to paint. She ate meat. Drank beer *and* wine. And her taste in music leaned toward Bruno Mars and Beyonce with the volume up.

So not strangers.

But definitely not close enough friends he should be asking her to be his fake date to a wedding so he didn't insult his most influential client.

"Would never have guessed this in a million years," she murmured.

He glanced a question at her before facing the ocean again. He couldn't look at her directly for too long because he was too busy berating himself for even coming up with the stupid idea. And he wouldn't even get in to the reasons she'd been the first person to come to mind when he'd told Greene he was seeing someone. He didn't want to examine that instinctive thought at all.

"I came up with all kinds of reasons you might have come over and then left," she said. "Overactive imagination." She shrugged. "But none of them involved you asking me to be your pretend wedding date."

"What other reasons?" he asked, now genuinely curious. Plus, it changed the subject. A change of subject seemed like a good idea.

She waved a hand in the air. "You know… My music was too loud. You needed advice on a design element in something you were working on. A package had been delivered to the wrong house. The dogs had been barking. I wasn't taking them out often enough…"

"You think I pay enough attention to notice that?" He might be, but he didn't have to admit that to her. And besides, she was walking the dogs often enough.

Her grin flashed. A lethal weapon, her grin. He found himself looking directly at her. Maybe staring. He wouldn't admit he was staring either.

But he was staring.

"Not really," she admitted with a shrug. "Just digging for options."

"If a package had been delivered to me instead of here, I would have brought the package over."

"I know." She made a big swinging gesture with one arm. "I didn't say my reasons were good ones. Just that they weren't…this one."

"Fair enough."

Her bun was skewed a little to one side and all he could think about was pulling out whatever tie was holding her hair in place and turning all that glorious brown silk loose around her shoulders. Running his fingers through the strands. Maybe using her hair to tug her closer…

Nope. No. Not those thoughts. Not now. Those thoughts were what got him into trouble in the first place.

He'd known the instant he'd caught her after her fall, the moment she'd leaned against him and he'd felt all her soft curves and warm skin in his arms, that "pretending" she was his girlfriend for even one night would be a disaster. There had been a moment when he'd held her, a moment when he wanted nothing more than to lean down and claim her gorgeous mouth, devour her right there in that half-painted bedroom. It was a sensory memory, an impulse he wasn't going to forget any time soon.

Especially since he hadn't stopped imagining what it would feel like to kiss her.

"You must have been pretty desperate," she said.

He blinked a few times to get his mind back to the conversation. What was she talking about?

"To consider asking me to be your pretend date," she clarified.

Ah. Right. For an instant, he thought she'd read his thoughts. Because he was feeling a little desperate. But obviously she hadn't meant that kind of desperation. Which was good. She didn't need to know he'd been fantasizing about her mouth.

"I'll just tell Greene the truth." He waved away the issue. This was his own mess to clean up. He didn't need to drag her into it.

"He's gonna be upset?"

"Yes. And that will be my problem to deal with."

"What would happen if you did show up with a date?"

"I would hope he'd stop trying to fix me up with his daughter." He sighed. "I've never had this kind of issue before. I handled it pretty crappy."

"Never? This has never happened to you before?"

She sounded so incredulous, he glared at her. "No. Why would you think it had?"

"No client has every hit on you? No colleague gotten too friendly? Or made wrong assumptions? Nothing like that?"

"No," he repeated. Emphatically.

"Wow." She huffed. "Lucky you."

"Has that happened to you before?" The anger that jumped through his system in that moment was something he'd have to examine later. It was instant, instinctive, and…dangerous.

"Nothing too bad." She waved a hand idly in the air. "You know, just the usual crap from the usual sorts of people."

This was normal for her? "That's…appalling. You get hit on a lot by people you're supposed to be working with and for?"

"Nothing too serious."

"Did that Darren asshole hit on you?"

"No," she said with an eyeroll. "I'm not his type."

"He's gay?"

"No. I'm just not…blond and breasty enough for him."

He tightened his jaw so he wouldn't comment on that last statement. And he very carefully kept his gaze on her eyes, resisting every impulse to look at her breasts, which, if memory served—and it did—were perfectly perfect breasts. And Darren was an idiot.

"But, you know, sometimes, especially with certain types of clients…" She shrugged. "They feel entitled."

"How the hell did you handle that?" He had to clear his throat because it had dropped into a rumble of anger, and he didn't want her to think he was angry at her. He would happily strangle all the "clients" who'd made her uncomfortable, though.

"I don't know. The usual, I guess. Deflect. Get out. Avoid. Always have someone with me when I met with those particular people."

The usual? "That sounds exhausting."

She titled her head, giving him a look he couldn't interpret. "It is, actually."

The moment stretched out, a long silence filled with a weird sort of connection Nick didn't fully understand. He had a new respect for her, for all the people who had to deal with that level of nonsense from colleagues and clients. He'd managed to escape that for his entire career until now. Which made him one lucky sonofabitch.

"Greene won't take you rejecting his daughter well, will he?" she asked quietly.

"No. But I'll deal with it."

"It would make your life easier to have a date at the wedding, though?"

"It would." He shrugged. Maybe he could pretend to be sick that day. Sabrina had said that was one of the techniques she used—avoid. He could just avoid the whole situation. It would cost him a valuable networking opportunity. But better that than piss Greene off.

"Okay," she said.

"Okay?" He shook himself out of his thoughts. "Okay what?"

"Okay. I'll pretend to be your girlfriend for the wedding."

He opened his mouth, but nothing came out. She was…agreeing to his dumb plan? She was going to help him?

Turned out it was good he hadn't managed to get any words out, because she grinned and her smile short circuited his brain, so he forgot what he wanted to say anyway.

"I owe you for helping me out with Darren the other day."

"I don't want you to feel obligated—"

She cut him off with a slight hand gesture. "Not obligated. Just… willing to help a friend in need."

Friend. Could they be friends?

"It'll be fun," she said with another devastatingly sunny grin.

Sure. Fun. No problem at all. In fact, problem solved. She'd be his date. They'd let everyone think they were a couple. Greene would stop trying to fix him up with his daughter. Anya would leave him alone. And he wouldn't lose a valuable and influential client.

Easy.

His gaze dropped to Sabrina's mouth. His muscles tightened. And his heartbeat started thumping a little harder. He tightened his grip on his nearly forgotten soda glass.

Maybe not so easy.

Chapter Eleven

Sabrina shuffled through Tabby's closet while Tabby looked on from the video app on Sabrina's phone where it was propped on the dresser. The bedroom was in disarray, most of the furniture pushed to the center of the room to accommodate the painting, but Tabby hadn't even commented on that since they'd started the video chat.

"Thanks for letting me borrow something," Sabrina said, glancing from the closet to the phone. "I didn't exactly come prepared for a formal wedding."

Tabby shook her head, her thick blond hair pulled up into a high, smoothed bun that gave her already long, elegant face even more grace and sophistication. She'd put on her event makeup already, the understated rose eye color and plum lipstick complimenting her dark brown skin and hazel eyes. Tabby was one of those people who was just striking. Impossible not to look at twice. Which made her goal of getting her own TV cooking show that much more likely. The camera loved Tabby's face.

She gave Sabrina one of her serious *looks*, the looks she'd been giving Sabrina since college whenever she thought one of Sabrina's plans would not end well. "I still can't believe you actually agreed to this."

Sabrina couldn't either. She'd been questioning her sanity ever since. What the hell had she gotten herself into?

"He was stuck. What else could I do?" She pulled out a sleek and sexy black dress, held it up. Then shook her head. "Nope, too much."

"I like that one for you," Tabby said. "You'd look hot."

"For a wedding? I don't want to look hot. I just want to look appropriate." Okay, a part of her wanted to look hot for Nick. But that wasn't the point of this fake-girlfriend-date, so she'd stick to appropriate.

"Listen, Nick's a great guy," Tabby said. "You know I love him like a brother. And the Greenes are difficult. I've worked for the wife a few times, catering events."

"Nick told me. Said Mrs. Greene was a big fan."

Tabby smiled. "I'm good at what I do."

"Yeah, you are."

"But that's not the point."

"What was the point?"

"I know Nick was in a fix, and this really could cost him. I think what you're doing for him is great. I'd have done the same thing in your place."

"He said he would have asked you if Mrs. Greene wasn't such a huge fan."

"And I would have said yes if I wasn't also worried about upsetting the Greenes and ruining perfectly good business connections. That's still not my point."

"I haven't heard anything like a point in all this." She pulled out a sundress with thin straps and a pretty flower pattern.

"Too yellow for your complexion," Tabby said.

Sabrina wrinkled her nose. Yeah, Tabby was right. Yellow made her look sallow. She put the dress back.

"My point," Tabby said, emphasizing the word, "is that agreeing to something like this isn't…you."

"You think I'm such an ass, I wouldn't do a friend a favor?" That actually hurt.

"That's not what I'm saying. Nick isn't your friend. You barely know him."

Sabrina frowned at the phone. Tabby's expression wasn't exactly a frown, but she wasn't smiling either. "What?" Sabrina asked. "You're trying to get to something and taking the long route."

"You've agreed to pretend to be Nick's girlfriend. You don't know him very well. And you've had a thing for him since you met him."

Sabrina's eyes widened. She opened her mouth to protest, then snapped it shut. "How long have you known that?"

"Since I watched you make moon eyes at him when I introduced the two of you."

"I didn't make moon eyes."

"Babe, you've been soft on him from the beginning. And I'm worried you're going to take all this…"

"What?"

"Too seriously."

"You're afraid I'll think it's a real date or something? Because, yeah, no that's not happening."

"What makes you so sure?"

"It's just a wedding. And for him, a business event in a lot of ways. It's not like we'll be doing something that could easily be confused for a real date. Weddings are…crowded and noisy and there's a lot of schmoozing involved. None of that is conducive to unintentionally revealing my crush to him."

She turned back to the closet so Tabby wouldn't see her expression. She wasn't sure how to feel about this. Tabby had a point. Sort of. Sabrina was worried herself that she'd get swept up in the occasion and forget this wasn't real. But she didn't have to admit that out loud.

"You've just gone through some seriously bad shit thanks to a man," Tabby said. "I don't want to see you get hurt again. Even if it's you doing the hurting to yourself."

"By crushing on a man who doesn't return the feelings?" She kept her back to the phone, discarding another two dresses while she waited out Tabby's silence.

"Not exactly what I meant," Tabby finally said.

"True enough, though."

"Nick is…"

"What?"

"He's kind of a loner. I'm not sure he's suited to anything long term."

"What makes you think I'd want long term?"

"You're a long term kind of girl, and we both know it."

Sabrina rolled her eyes even though Tabby couldn't see her. Unfortunately, Tabby was right about this, too. Sabrina wasn't a casual relationship type of woman. She didn't date much because she didn't want to waste time on someone who wasn't looking for a long term thing. She'd been in a few relationships before. None of them had lasted less than two years.

And none of them had lasted longer than four.

She stared into the closet as she considered that.

Then she shook herself hard. She wasn't here to reassess and figure out her romantic life. She was staying at Tabby's to reevaluate and fix her work life. Romantic life could wait.

"Try the gold one," Tabby said.

"Gold is too flashy." But she pulled out the dress anyway.

It wasn't all gold. Just the details along the hem, down one side of the skirt, and the thick strappy sleeves were embroidered in gold thread. The rest was a light bronze silk that felt like heaven in Sabrina's fingers. The skirt fell to just above the knee on Tabby, which meant it would fall a few inches below the knee on Sabrina. But the cut of it was generous enough to fit Sabina's figure, and because it was a wrap dress, she could adjust it to fit across her waist and hips without any annoying bunching.

As she studied it, she decided it was a pretty nice dress for a wedding. Especially a summer wedding at the beach.

She held it up in front of herself and faced the camera finally, letting Tabby see how it looked.

"That's the one," Tabby said. "Elegant and still appropriate for an outdoor wedding. You'll look amazing."

Sabrina let out a sigh and looked at the dress. "It is gorgeous."

"Trust me. I have better taste in clothes than you do."

Sabrina chuckled. They actually both had pretty bad taste in clothes, or at least they had in college. But Tabby had made an effort to rectify her shortcomings in the fashion department because it helped when she was on book tour or had to glam up to impress the rich and famous so they'd give her catering work. And when Tabby glammed up, she was a truly impressive sight. Sabrina had made a few attempts to increase her fashion sense, too, but she'd only managed the standard Little Black Dress look and hadn't advanced to the Bronze Silk with Gold Embellishments stage yet.

"You have shoes for this thing?" Even though Tabby was five inches taller, they had the same size feet. Something that might have bugged Sabrina if not for the fact that Tabby loved shoes and always had the best ones, which she let Sabrina borrow all the time. It was the one area of fashion they could both get into, even in college.

"There should be some neutral sandals on the rack. They'll go nicely and work for the beach. Flats. No heels. You'll end up on your face."

"Yeah, never had the opportunity to perfect my walking-on-the-beach-in-heels skills."

Tabby snorted out a laugh. Then she sighed. "You sure about this?"

"Yes, yes." She tossed the dress onto Tabby's bed in the center of the room, then faced her friend. "I'll be fine. The wedding will be fine. Nick will be fine. It'll all work out. Nothing to worry about. Just a single afternoon and evening of pretending so Nick can save face and get out of an awkward situation. If I can help a fellow human out of a business jam, I'm happy to do it. Especially after what I just went through."

Another long sigh.

Sabrina raised her hands. "I swear. I have no illusions here. I will not confuse this for a real date."

"I'd argue more, but I have to go. My escort will be here soon to take me to the next event."

Tabby was currently in Paris for a huge food festival, where she'd do some cooking demonstrations and sign books. And frankly, Sabrina was jealous. Not of the book signing part. Tabby could keep that level of celebrity. But she was definitely jealous of the food.

"Have a croissant for me," she said, moving closer to the phone so she could end the call. "Thanks again for the loan of the dress and shoes."

"Any time. Keep me updated on the date night."

"Fake date night."

Tabby ignored her interruption. "And take care of yourself. No falling in love with my neighbor. He'll break your heart."

"No falling in love." Sabrina put her hand over her heart. "I swear."

She was pretty sure she could keep that promise. She didn't fall in love easily. And she knew better than to fall for Nick when he wasn't interested in her that way.

Falling in lust, on the other hand… Well, that was another matter entirely.

Because *that* she'd already done.

Chapter Twelve

Sabrina checked and rechecked her makeup in the mirror in the downstairs bathroom as she waited on Nick. He wasn't late. She was just stupid early. And way too anxious.

She had the house air conditioning up higher than usual, to keep her from overheating in Tabby's fancy dress. The dress wasn't actually that hot to wear. In fact, it was perfectly comfortable and cool and would work on the beach today. Her nerves, on the other hand, kept her agitated, and too warm, and she was going to wear through her deodorant before Nick even showed up. Which wasn't the look—or scent!—she was going for.

Her look, if she did say so herself, would do well for the day. She'd pulled her hair up into a twist pinned to the back of her head, a style that would be much cooler for the outdoor event and had the bonus feature of looking elegant. The bronze dress suited her pale skin tone better than she'd feared—it didn't wash her out or make her look sallow—and her light makeup did the rest of the work making sure everything worked together. Minimal jewelry because she hadn't thought to bring much with her while she was here. Just some small diamond studs in her ears, which had been a present from her mother when she left for college, and she wore the little studs all the time.

As she assessed her makeup—again—she tried to convince herself this would all go just fine. No need to worry, no need for all the nerves. *She* wasn't the one getting married. *She* wasn't the one with business contacts on the line. All she had to do was sit quietly watching the ceremony, then make small talk at the reception with a bunch of people she didn't know. She could do small talk. She had done small talk in her career. If she channeled that energy, she could carry this off without hyperventilating.

One thing she could actually bring to the table was that she did like talking to people. She liked getting their stories, getting to know them, imagining their decorating choices… She could do the chat-with-strangers part of the day pretty easily.

The problem was chatting to the not-quite-a-stranger who was taking her to the wedding and whom she had a thing for despite her best efforts.

But Tabby was right. She'd get hurt if she let those feelings overwhelm her. Nick wasn't interested in her that way, and he wasn't a relationship sort of man according to Tabby. And Sabrina liked relationships, even if she hadn't had that many. So even if Nick *was* interested in her, she wouldn't be able to just have a summer fling with him.

Would she?

No. No. She glared at her image in the mirror. "First, he's not interested, so get your head out of his pants. Second, you are not a summer fling kind of woman. Been there, tried it, had the heartbreak to show for it. Not gonna do that again."

It had happened years ago, in college, between junior and senior year. She'd fallen hard for a boy during an internship they were both doing at a design company. They'd dated, had a great time, spent all their free time together, she'd tumbled head over heels, and he'd left at the end of the summer without a backward glance. He'd looked confused when she'd wanted to keep in touch, but had shrugged that off as well as her feelings.

She'd been young. She'd overestimated his feelings and told herself stories about the seriousness of their relationship that didn't reflect reality. Tabby had been there to talk her through it all, and hold her and feed her ice cream while she cried. And later, when she had more perspective, she'd accepted that the whole "relationship" she'd built up in her head had only been in her head.

After that, she'd been determined to never do anything like that again. When she got involved with a man, she made sure after the first few dates, when things looked like they might get serious, that *he* was as serious about things as she was. If he wasn't, she left.

And that way of living had served her well all these years. Or. Sort of well. The fact that she was single and her last relationship had ended more than two years ago with no real dating prospects since, maybe didn't reflect so well on her "only do real relationships" plan.

She considered that as she wandered out to the living room to check her purse. Again. Yup, wallet, keys, cellphone, lipstick still inside the little neutral cream bag Tabby had loaned her.

She returned to relationship thinking. All her past relationships, the few there'd been, hadn't gone the long haul for…reasons. She'd insisted on an actual relationship and not just casual dating right from the start. She'd tried hard to build the kind of relationship she thought she wanted, too. Monogamous, together as often as they could be, enjoying each other's company, doing things together as a couple, traveling together, spending all their spare time together. That's what couples did, right? They loved each other so much, they spent most of their time together and committed to each other.

That had been the problem with her parents' marriage. They drifted apart, stopped spending time together, and finally they'd split. It had been mutual, but still hard on her and her brother. Now, her dad was in a good marriage that really worked for him. His wife and he were inseparable. And he was still friends with Sabrina's mom. Sabrina loved the relationship her father had now. That's what she'd been *trying* to form with the men in her life.

But in the end, where had that gotten her? Three exes. Two of whom she was still friends with because they were nice men. They'd just reached a point where they had to accept they weren't working as a couple any more. Things had felt a little…stifled. So they'd gone their separate ways but amicably. The third ex—well, he'd been a jerk who'd cheated on her, so he'd gotten chucked to the curb at her earliest convenience.

But if she left him out of the analysis, her dating history was: (1) meet a nice guy, (2) tumble into a relationship that took over her life because she committed every moment of every day to ensure she was *with* her boyfriend, and he was *with* her, (3) end said relationship when things felt stale and over for both of them.

(4) Do it all over again when the next nice man she thought might be serious about her stumbled into her life.

Hm. She sat down on the couch, straightening her skirt so she wouldn't wrinkle it, even though she wasn't sure this silk would wrinkle, and thought back through those relationships.

Nice. Comfortable. Time-consuming. Mutually content for a while. But...

Lacking. For both of them. That was why she could stay friends with both men after they'd broken up. Neither she nor them had felt that...spark? Was that the right word? That *something* anyway that meant this was it, for the rest of their lives, and she wouldn't be happy if she didn't have this other person around.

She'd tried for that spark. Devoted all her time to the relationship. To trying to ensure it worked. Done all the things she was *supposed* to do in a good relationship—spent all her spare time with him, made sure the relationship came first, insisted he give her all his spare time and attention, too. Made sure each relationship looked like what a real relationship should look like. Like her father's current marriage. And the men had gone along with her requirements, adapting their lives to fit this image of a relationship she insisted on.

In the end, none of it worked. For either of them. She'd just ended up feeling constrained and...bored.

Maybe she'd been too focused on the "only a relationship" plan. What had it done for her? Gotten her a few nice friends and an empty bed.

The doorbell rang, disrupting her thoughts. She'd have to consider this epiphany later, when things were quiet again. Because she felt like she was on the verge of something. She just wasn't sure what yet. And while she'd come out to Tabby's house to figure out her career future, figuring out the things holding her back in her personal life would be a nice bonus.

All that internal analysis melted away when she opened the door for Nick and got a look at him in his suit.

Thinking? What was thinking?

He looked ridiculously handsome in the dark gray suit, over a crisp white shirt and a deep blue tie. The jacket fit perfectly, tailored to his shoulders without stretching fabric or looking too bulky. His hair was still a little damp from his shower. He was clean shaven. And he smelled like some sort of spicy soap she could just bury her face in and live happily for the rest of her life.

She opened her mouth to ask what his soap was before realizing that was a weird question and snapped her mouth shut.

Several swallows later, as she tried to wet her throat, she managed to squeak out, "You look great."

Had there ever been a more egregious understatement in the history of understatements? Probably not. Great wasn't the word. He was just…the sexiest thing walking and she had no idea what do to with her hands in that moment. She wanted to fidget. She wanted to touch him. She wanted to push him against the wall and bury her nose against his neck while she stripped him out of that perfectly tailored suit.

None of which she was going to do because this was a work thing for him and she was supposed to be helping him get through the wedding, not prevent him from getting to the wedding because she'd gone all brain-addled and lust-crazy seeing him cleaned up and wearing a suit.

She'd never realized she was such a sucker for a man in a suit. She worked with men in suits all the time.

Nick in a suit was an entirely different experience.

"You look great, too," he said, his voice deep and gruff.

He stuffed his hands into his pockets, and that should have messed up the lines of the suit and made him look less scrumptious, but all it did was add another layer of suave sexiness. Her brain was going to melt. Had melted. She couldn't find any words. There were some there, she was sure. She knew words. She just…couldn't access any at that moment.

After a silence that went on too long, he said, "Are you ready or…?"

"Ready! Yes. Ready." She snatched up her purse, gave the dogs a scratch under the chin. "Be good while I'm gone." Hey words! And followed Nick out to his car.

She didn't quite trip when he held the car door for her, but her knees wobbled as she slid into the old, well-preserved BMW. The scent of his soap made her tingle in all sorts of places, and that only got worse when he climbed into the car next to her. Wow, she'd never realized the scent of soap could do such intense things to her libido.

She had to work at not fidgeting as they pulled away from the house. And every time she glanced at him, her heartbeat kicked up speed and her body tingled with awareness. She shifted against the soft leather seat, which didn't help, and pressed her thighs together, hoping to ease some of the tingles there. Didn't work. She was wet and achy and her body so jumpy with anticipation she nearly moaned watching him grip the gearshift and moved the car into drive.

That was probably an overreaction to watching a man's hands do ordinary things like drive. But he had such excellent hands. Strong, broad, long fingers…

She swallowed and turned to stare out the window. That didn't protect her from his diabolically delicious scent, but at lease she didn't have to look at his hands and imagine those long fingers on her skin, pinching her nipples, running over her stomach, moving lower…

That wasn't helping.

Argh. How the hell was she going to get through the entire day with him when he was doing all this to her without effort? Just a nice suit and a delicious smelling soap.

She was in a lot of trouble.

Chapter Thirteen

Nick was in a lot of trouble.

He'd never had such a horrible idea in his entire life as this idea to ask Sabrina to be his fake-girlfriend at this wedding. He should have just pretended to be sick and avoided the whole thing. Or he could have broken a bone to get out of it all. That would have been a lot less uncomfortable.

Not that Sabrina wasn't the perfect escort. She was friendly, she chatted easily with the strangers surrounding her, and she handled the questions about their relationship like a pro. It hadn't occurred to him to come up with a story. But then one of the many Greene relatives they were introduced to as they settled into the rows of seats set out on the beach had asked how long they'd been dating. And he went blank. Sabrina filled in with a few easy, purely fictious details that left him slightly in awe of her cunning.

Also a little nervous that she could lie so easily. But significantly more awed.

The problem wasn't that she wasn't playing her part perfectly—better than he was at that moment. The problem was that he couldn't stop staring at her, couldn't stop mentally stripping her out of that gorgeous dress, couldn't stop fantasizing about mussing her perfectly arranged hairstyle and then licking every delectable part of her body.

His brain was so preoccupied with fantasies of where and how he wanted to fuck her, he could barely concentrate enough to make casual conversation. Most of what came out of his mouth were grunts and half formed sentences designed to discourage conversation.

And since one of the big reasons he'd accepted the invitation to the wedding was so that he could network and schmooze other potential clients, not being able to carry on a conversation was a definite disadvantage.

The day turned out perfectly for an outdoor wedding, which was good for the bride and groom he supposed. Sunny. Warm, but with a nice cool ocean breeze blowing through the area under the giant, open-sided tent. The set up for the ceremony included rows of chairs under the tent, then a raised dais under another open-sided tent. There were flowers and bunting and plenty of gauzy material floating in the breeze. All very wedding-y.

Beyond the setup, the Atlantic rolled onto the white sand and back out in a never ending background rumble. If he concentrated on the waves, he didn't focus so much on the woman sitting next to him. He might even be able to carry on a conversation. They were still at least ten to fifteen minutes away from the ceremony starting. Guests were still being seated. Wait time had never felt more excruciating.

Focus on the ocean. Focus on the waves.

Sabrina brushed against him, her thigh pressing against his, as she scooted closer to make room for someone moving past them to reach their own seat.

He fisted his hands in his lap and tried not to make it too obvious that his brain had just exploded. So much for focus and concentration. Even the cool breeze and prospect of the icy Atlantic couldn't cool off the heat rushing from that point of contact between their thighs right to his dick.

He let out a slow, deep breath. Which might have helped if the inbreath hadn't brought her scent to him. She didn't seem to be wearing a perfume he could identify, so maybe it was just the soap she used? Maybe her shampoo. The scent—something spicy instead of flowery—got stronger when she leaned her head closer to him.

"You okay?" she murmured near his ear.

Ho boy was that a mistake on her part if she expected him to think. He felt the brush of her breath down his spine. The sensation left him barely capable of a grunt. He hoped she'd translate the noise as, "Yes, I'm just great. Thanks for asking."

"Because you seem pretty tense," she continued, still leaning much too close to him, her arm and thigh pressing into his.

He stared at the frigid Atlantic waters and tried to think cold thoughts. "Fine," he mumbled.

At least it was a word. Those seemed to be in short supply at the moment. Unless the word was "fuck" or "lick" or "suck" or "devour." Those words were ricocheting through him loudly. Those were words he could get behind.

Wait. No.

They weren't here on an actual date, and Sabrina wasn't trying to drive him crazy, and this wasn't going to end with him taking her to bed. He wasn't even going to kiss her at the end of the night. This wasn't a date. Tabitha would kill him if he hurt her best friend. Which meant Sabrina was off limits. Which meant he had to get his mind out of her panties and back to the situation, the *reason* they were doing this in the first place.

His work. His future. His livelihood. Those were important.

Not that he remembered *why* they were important just then with her breath on his cheek and her spicy scent swirling around him, invading his senses like a marauding pirate.

Pirates showed up on beaches, didn't they? That's what she was. A pirate. Stealing all his self-control.

The older couple sitting in front of them both turned a little in their seats and smiled at him and Sabrina.

"You're a lovely couple," the woman said.

What was her name? He was pretty sure they'd been introduced. She was one of the Greene relatives, or something close. And by the sparkling diamonds in her ear lobes and on her fingers, she was one with enough money to maybe want the help of an excellent architect one of these days. Someone who he should talk to, charm. Ensure she and her husband remembered him later when they went looking to build a summer home they could share with their many grandchildren. Or dogs. Or whatever.

Except he couldn't remember their names. Because Sabrina was still leaning against him. All he could think about was how soft he bet her skin was. He couldn't feel it through the barrier of his suit, which covered a lot more of his skin than her dress covered of hers, but that didn't stop him from trying to imagine the feel. As silky as her dress, but warm.

He blinked at the woman when she raised her brows at him.

"Thank you," Sabrina said to fill the silent gap.

He might just be in love with her.

"How long have you been together?" the woman asked.

"Geraldine," the man said with an eye roll.

Geraldine! Nick gave himself a mental forehead smack.

"They don't want to talk about themselves," the man continued. "They want to talk about the wedding. Or the upcoming NFL season, am I right?" He winked at Nick.

Nick made an attempt to smile. He was more of an NHL guy in the winter, but if Geraldine's husband wanted to talk football, he could talk football. Anything that distracted from questions about his fake relationship with Sabrina.

"Oh stop." Geraldine waved her heavily jeweled hand at her husband. "It's a romantic day. I'm allowed to ask about romantic things. You boys can save football for the reception."

From the corner of his eye, Nick saw Sabrina grin. That grin. The one that hit him right between the eyes and left him breathless. Probably good he wasn't looking directly at her. He was breathless enough already.

"You're here for the bride, right?" Sabrina said.

Another perfect deflection. He might have to marry her.

"I'm her godmother," Geraldine said, tilting her chin up. "We've known Bianca since she was a baby. To see her getting married is a dream come true."

"You must be very proud," Sabrina said.

Nick had no idea why Geraldine should be proud of her goddaughter for getting married, but it seemed to be the right thing to say because Geraldine preened under Sabrina's comment.

"Oh, we are. Beautiful girl. Lovely couple. I'm sure they'll be very happy."

"What do you do for a living?" Geraldine's husband asked Nick.

He sucked in a breath so he could get words out. Bad idea. That pulled in more of Sabrina's scent. He managed, after clearing his throat, to say, "Architect. Designing James and Eugenia's new home."

He hoped going with the casual reference to the Greenes, using their first names, fit the setting and didn't come across as too familiar. Should he have been more formal? All his schmoozing skills had abandoned him. Not that he had a lot to begin with, but what he did possess seemed to have checked out the minute Sabrina opened her door.

"Did you hear that, Harold," Geraldine said, waving her bejeweled hand at her husband again. "He's an architect! Just the person we've been looking for."

Words Nick had come all the way here to hear. And if his "date" hadn't been unintentionally torturing him, he might have even gotten excited about the possible work.

"Hey, isn't that a coincidence," Harold said. "We've been saying we need to do some work on this old house we have up the coast. Bought it years ago and did nothing with it. Needs a complete rebuild. Could do with an architect."

"And what about you?" Geraldine asked Sabrina. Skipping right over the part where Harold gave Nick his next job. "What do you do, dear?"

"Interior design," Sabrina said.

She stiffened a little next to him, and he heard the very faint strain in her voice. He wanted to ask her about that. Did her reaction have to do with leaving her last job? With the Darren asshole? Was she rethinking being an interior designer?

He pressed his hand against his thigh. Later. He could ask her later.

Right now, he was supposed to be encouraging Geraldine and Harold to give him a job.

"Well, isn't that perfect," Geraldine said. "Is that how you two met? Do you work together?"

"No," Nick said before he thought better of it. "I mean, we don't work for the same company. I'm freelance."

Did that cover his abrupt denial or make things worse?

"We met through a mutual friend," Sabrina said, smoothly.

"Oh, that's lovely. How romantic. Did this friend set you up on a blind date?"

Sabrina chuckled. "No. I think she would have discouraged the relationship if she'd known it might happen."

Nick turned to stare at the side of her face. Tabby *had* absolutely discouraged anything happening between him and Sabrina because she was protective of Sabrina and didn't want her hurt. Did Sabrina know that? Had Tabby said something to her? And was Sabrina using that fact to build this story because it was true and so easier to remember? Or was she trying to remind him to keep his damn hands to himself because Tabby would kill him otherwise?

He didn't *think* it was the latter. She was smiling at Geraldine, not even looking at him. She probably—he hoped—didn't even realize he'd been thinking about her nonstop since… Well, if he were being honest, she'd been lurking in the back of his mind since they'd first met. But really, he'd only been thinking about her to the point he hadn't been sleeping well for the last couple of weeks, since she'd moved into Tabby's place.

She wasn't warning him off, she was just spinning a story with enough truth they could both remember if someone else asked them these things. That was all.

But the reassurance didn't keep him from shifting uncomfortably in his seat.

He was saved from further conversation, and his own brain, by the first strums of music from the string quartet set up to the left of the dais.

"Oh, it's starting!" Geraldine clapped her hands together and her eyes got misty.

Harold handed her a tissue, before he turned in his seat to face the aisle.

Sabrina grinned at the couple, then grinned at him.

A smile that fried his synapsis, making all further conversation impossible.

Yeah. He was in a lot of trouble.

Chapter Fourteen

The ceremony was beautiful. Sabrina had always liked weddings. And she spent most of the ceremony admiring the way the planners and couple had laid out the details. The perfectly folded white bunting over the tents. The white lilies and hydrangeas providing pops of purple and pink. Big ribbons of purple and pink gauze hiding and tent poles. The subtle detail of the microphone setup for the minister— set unobtrusively off center, so the guests could hear everything over the rolling noise of ocean and breeze. The way the bridesmaids, wearing soft, silky dresses in shades from plum to carnation, and groomsmen, in their light gray suits and their ties perfectly matched to the bridesmaid opposite, all lined out to the side of the dais, while still remaining underneath the larger of the two tent overhangs. The bouquets held by the bride and bridesmaids were delicate and fragrant, even against the salty tang of ocean air.

The sheer floral, gauziness of it all against the white sand and cresting waves was a thing of perfection as far as Sabrina was concerned. Even the ocean had presented itself more blue and lush today.

The bride herself looked like she'd stepped out of a bridal magazine, complete with perfect makeup, elegantly upswept blond hair, a dress that probably cost more than Sabrina's apartment in Brooklyn, and a serene smile. The groom also looked confidently handsome in his gray suit, a shade just a bit darker than his groomsmen, and a deep purple tie that matched the details in the bride's bouquet and hair ribbons.

Romantic words spoken, the ceremony ended in a kiss and a cheer and general good feelings. Sabrina grinned and leaned into Nick. "That was beautiful."

He grunted something that sounded like agreement.

She pressed her lips together so she wouldn't chuckle. She wasn't sure if he was so stiff and uncomfortable because he'd rather be schmoozing with the guests than sitting through the romantic stuff, or because he was just uncomfortable with their fake relationship situation. But whatever was bothering him, he'd spent most of the afternoon grunting. He'd managed a few short sentences with the nice couple sitting in front of them and that was about it. Mostly, he'd sat very stiff and still beside her, his jaw tight, his fists clenched against his thighs.

The fact that she knew this in such detail, that she'd been paying way too much attention to him throughout the ceremony, was not lost on her. She was hyper aware of him, his heat, that damned delicious smelling soap, the way his hair curled a little against his neck as it dried fully. Every little muscle twitch and hand gesture drew her attention and captured her entire imagination. Keeping her mind on the ceremony, on the conversations with other guests before the ceremony, had been an act of will.

But she was supposed to be here helping him, not ogling him and daydreaming about getting in his pants. She'd agreed to this out of… well, she supposed friendship? They weren't really friends. Not really. But something coming close to friends anyway.

She could play the social part just fine. She enjoyed chatting casually with all the guests around them. The couple in front of them, Geraldine and Harold Roland, were a particular delight.

The real trick had been pretending to be in a romantic relationship with Nick without letting the whole thing go too far. No holding hands, even though a couple might. No kissing him casually on the cheek, even though that was extremely tempting every time she leaned in to talk close to his ear. No leaning against him and smiling up at him during the vows. If they'd been a real couple, those were all things she'd probably have done. Gestures so easy to fall into as they pretended. But each step she took into the role of "girlfriend" made it very difficult for her to keep the line between what was real and what was pretend.

Tabby had been absolutely right about one thing. Nick would break Sabrina's heart if she wasn't very careful. No falling in love. No forgetting this was a bit of playacting. No letting herself go too far down the rabbit hole of real emotions.

And still, when the clapping was done and everyone had cheered the bride and groom back down the aisle, as they moved away from the ceremony tents, down red carpet runners to the reception tent, Sabrina reached out and grabbed Nick's hand.

She hadn't meant to. It was a casual gesture she would have made on any normal date, with any normal boyfriend. And it was perfectly in fitting with their act. But the minute she took hold of his big hand, felt his fingers tighten around hers, she knew she'd made a huge mistake.

His hand felt absolutely perfect around hers. The heat and strength and slightly rough brush of his fingertips. The way he squeezed once before loosening, but didn't pull his hand out of hers…

Too close to real.

Too close to stealing her heart.

She mentally smacked herself in the arm. They were just holding hands. They weren't declaring undying love or any such nonsense. Other couples were holding hands as they navigated the carpet runners over the beach and found their seats at one of the forty huge round tables set up on a low platform under yet another giant, open-sided tent. Other couples smiled at each other as they wove through the reception area and greeted people they knew. This hand holding thing was perfectly in line with their act.

The soft brush of his thumb over her inner wrist meant nothing.

Just a touch. A shift of his hold on her. The fact that that soft caress made her shiver and her thighs clench was nothing to worry about.

When she squeezed his fingers, she was simply reassuring him that everything was fine. This was working. They were good. No one had pointed at them and shouted, "Fakes!" He could relax his jaw a little. No need to crack teeth. They were getting away with this and everything would work out.

That was all the hand holding meant. Nothing more. Just a way to reassure him they were making this work, and adding to the image that they were an actual couple.

So she shouldn't feel quite so bereft when he finally let go of her hand to hold her chair for her as they sat at their assigned table.

The table was large, covered in a soft white cloth, and topped with a full place setting in front of each straight-backed white-cushioned chair. The dinnerware was made up of delicate white and gold filigreed China, silver cutlery, and crystal glasses. The center piece was an elegant flower arrangement with thin gold wires twinned through it that sat low to the table so she could see the person sitting across from her. Everything maintained the color scheme of mostly white with purple and pink accents, and an occasionally, but restrained, flash of gold.

Sabrina admired the restraint. Given the obvious amount of money that went into this wedding, there was always the chance the planners would go over the top. The understated elegance appealed to Sabrina's personal aesthetic.

There were enough guests that the tables were full, but nothing felt crowed. In fact, she would have preferred to be a little more crowded, at least with Nick. That was a very bad idea. A distracting idea. But she missed having him pressed close to her side because of the seating arrangements. At least with the space, she might be able to think a little more clearly.

Also eat without bumping into him.

She kept sneaking glances at him throughout the meal, though. The food was as outrageously excellent as the décor was elegant. Each course—there were seven—a delicious explosion of perfection that would have thrilled Tabby. But Sabrina could only partially concentrate on the food, because Nick kept drawing her attention.

When he lifted his wine glass to drink. When he leaned back to let the servers switch out his plates. The way he devoured everything put in front of him with admirable concentration and yet still managed to carry on a polite conversation with the older woman sitting to his right. Sabrina couldn't seem to look away. Not for long. She was mesmerized watching him do the simplest things.

Tabby was right. She shouldn't have done this. She was going to shift from crush to full on obsessive behavior if she wasn't more careful.

She made an attempt to carry on her own appropriately polite conversation with the other people at the table. The couple to her left were distant cousins of the groom, down from Connecticut, and a little on the snobby side, but she'd dealt with their type before. She got them talking about themselves and that made the conversation easy as that seemed to be their favorite topic.

There were several older, single people around their table, and a very nice young woman sitting almost exactly opposite Sabrina who kept giving her surreptitious eye rolls every time the snobby couple expounded on their latest vacation to someplace glamorous, or the size of the yacht they were considering buying, or some other obnoxiously boastful thing. And while she couldn't carry on a very good conversation with the young woman because the whole table was between them, and the low level hum of all the conversations going on under the tent backed by the sounds of the rumbling Atlantic made that impossible, she did feel they bonded over their shared exasperation with the snobby couple.

Meeting people she could talk with—or exchange understanding glances with—made the meal go smoothly enough. Despite her distraction with Nick. She hoped everyone else just assumed their relationship story explained why she couldn't stop looking at him. They were *supposed* to be a couple after all, so she wasn't acting out of character for the roll she was supposed to be playing.

Just out of character for their *real* relationship.

The nice thing about the self-obsessed couple, though, was that they didn't ask her questions about her and Nick. No "how did you meet?" or "how long have you been together?" or "where do you live?" sorts of questions to be navigated. From what she could overhear of Nick's conversation with the older woman to his right, she hadn't asked much about their supposed relationship either.

Probably a good thing since he seemed to freeze up and revert to mostly grunts at those sorts of questions.

"What do you do for a living, dear?" the older woman asked Nick just then.

"Architect," he said with a smile. "I'm designing a new house for James and Eugenia."

"Well, isn't that something," the older woman said. She leaned a little around Nick. "And you?" she asked Sabrina. "Are you an architect, too?"

"I'm an interior designer." She forced her smile and tried not to flinch. For her, these questions were the hard part. They didn't used to be. She'd always been proud to tell people what she did. Proud of the work she'd done over the years.

But now, she wasn't sure what she did anymore. She didn't technically have a job. Not now. Not thanks to Darren. She wasn't even sure if she'd stay in interior design going forward. If she'd switch gears to something else. What else that might be.

Her own questions about her career, her own uncertainty, made discussing her career much more difficult than discussing her fake relationship with Nick. That part was just making up stories, which she was good at, and sticking as close to the truth as possible—Tabby did actually introduce them. They had known each other for several years. The fact that they hadn't been dating in all those years was the only part she had to skim over.

Her departure from her job and her uncertainty about her future were all still so raw, though. She didn't have ready stories or easy half-truths there. And she was so thrown by trying to answer the question, "What do you do for a living?" that she wasn't quick enough to deflect from the conversation.

"How about you, Mira?" Nick asked. "What do you do?"

Sabrina could have kissed him for switching topics and pulling attention away from her failed career. She could have kissed him anyway, but in that moment, she actually thought she might follow through with the impulse.

The older woman, Mira, grinned up at Nick and said, "I'm retired now. But I was a dancer." Her expression shown with such pride, she practically glowed. "I danced on Broadway."

And that was so fascinating, Sabrina fell into asking questions about Mira's career, which Mira was more than happy to answer. Not just answer. Mira was a storyteller, and she went on to delight them with tales of old New York, stories of being a chorus line dancer back in the day, of actually having an understudy role in A Chorus Line on Broadway. All the people she met over the years. The affair she had with one of Broadways' leading men years ago. The affair she had with his wife.

Sabrina completely forgot about her own worries and let herself get swept away by Mira's amazing life and loves. And it was a glorious life. And Mira was a fascinating person. A lot more interesting than the self-obsessed couple next to Sabrina. Hell, even they leaned in and listened to Mira's stories. The entire table was rapt, and it made the rest of the meal a delight.

When the time for dessert and speeches rolled around, Sabrina actually pouted that Mira had to stop telling stories.

"You should write books," she whispered to her before leaning back in her seat to watch the speeches.

She exchanged a passing look with Nick. He was smiling, relaxed. The most relaxed she'd seen him since that afternoon when he'd picked her up.

As the best man stood, tapping his champaign glass to get everyone's attention. And the servers wove through the tables, refilling glasses for the toasts, Sabrina leaned into Nick and murmured close to his ear, "Thanks for distracting everyone from my job."

He glanced at her from the corner of his eye, not actually facing her. "You're welcome," he murmured. "You looked…unhappy with the question."

"Mmm." She didn't want to discuss her career feelings right now. But the fact that he'd picked up on her discomfort, despite her trying to hide it, was either very sweet, or a reflection of her piss-poor acting skills. If the latter, that didn't bode well for their ability to pull off this fake relationship charade.

Since he'd come to her rescue twice now, though—first with Darren and now with the uncomfortable "what do you do for a living?" question—she decided to see Nick as just a sweet man trying to help her feel better.

She bumped her shoulder against his in thanks, but what she really wanted to do was kiss him.

She considered that. If she kissed him on the cheek, no one around them would comment on the gesture, or even think twice about it. They were supposed to be a couple after all. And if he asked her about it later, she could say she was just playing her part. She was very tempted. He was so close and warm and his soap scent mixed with the smell of salty ocean and the bubbly glass of wine he held in one hand, making her feel bubbling and a little giddy.

Had she had too much wine? She might have had too much wine. She hadn't been paying close attention. She thought she'd just been sipping at her drink, but the servers refilled constantly so maybe she'd had more than she assumed.

Because as she stared at the side of Nick's face, she very much wanted to press her lips against his smooth cheek, soak in a little more of his warmth.

She pressed her lips together instead and faced the dais and the best man mid-speech.

But the idea of kissing Nick remained a lingering temptation, hovering near the front of her mind.

Chapter Fifteen

The speeches were nice. No big scandals revealed. No shocking or disastrous admissions. Nothing that might have thrown a pall over the event. The bride and groom continued to glow radiantly in the waning orange-pink sunlight. Both the ocean breeze and the heat died back as the sun got lower. The evening promised to be a perfect night for dancing and celebrating.

And all Sabrina could think about was the man next to her.

Even amidst the general noise and animation following the speeches, when the dance floor opened up and the band began to play and everyone started leaving their tables to wander around and visit people at other tables, her focus continued drifting back to Nick.

It was a real pain in the ass.

"Do you want to dance?" Nick asked.

"No," she said firmly.

Actually, she sort of did want to dance. But she was afraid to let herself relax that much. It was a fast, upbeat song, not a slow dance, so she wouldn't have to worry about that at least. Still, dancing felt like it might make the wine in her system sparkle too much, and that would make her relax her guard too much, and before she knew it, she'd be kissing Nick and revealing her years old crush and thoroughly embarrassing herself.

So, no. No dancing. No relaxing her guard.

Nick scanned the crowd, leaning back in his chair, taking in all the people under the smaller tent where the dancefloor and band were centered. There were still a lot of people under the dining tent, but few enough now it was easy to see everyone. She wondered if he wanted to go schmooze some potential clients, and was leaning in to ask, when a deeply sexy female voice made her pause.

"So glad you could make it, Nick," the woman said.

Nick's shoulders went stiff, but he turned to face the woman with a smile that Sabrina wanted to call a grimace. She faced the woman, too. And the family resemblance to the bride was unmistakable.

The infamous sister who'd been hitting on Nick. The reason Sabrina and Nick were pretending to be a couple.

Sabrina wasn't sure why she hadn't looked out for this woman before now. She'd been so distracted by Nick—and trying not to reveal how distracted she was by him—she'd forgotten to ask where the sister was or who she was. Of course, Sabrina had seen this particular woman throughout the day, even without knowing this was *the* sister, because she'd been part of the wedding party. Not, strangely enough, one of the bridesmaids, but she'd been at the head table with the rest of the family. And she did bear a striking resemblance to the bride, though a little younger and with maybe a slightly broader face.

So it wasn't so much the woman's looks that startled Sabrina. Oh, she was definitely beautiful, just like her sister, in that sophisticated, rich blond sort of way. Maybe a little too standard in that look. There seemed to be a lot of women here who possessed the same general straight blond hair, perfect makeup, slim figure appearance.

But that wasn't the thing that really struck Sabrina. What struck her was the way the woman looked down at Nick with a sort of…Sabrina wanted to call it proprietary hunger. That seemed pretty dramatic, but yeah, that was the look. Hunger. And possessiveness. All glimmering in her blue eyes. She even had the temerity to put a hand on Nick's arm, giving it a little squeeze as she greeted him, and she wet her lips.

Wow, that wasn't blunt and over the top. Sabrina wasn't sure whether to scowl or laugh. Nick, for his part, held himself very still as he greeted the woman, not reacting at all to her touch. If he'd flinched, Sabrina probably would have stepped in sooner. But she knew this was a delicate line they had to walk. No offending the client's beloved daughter while at the same time sending said daughter packing.

Nick said, "Nice to see you, Anya. Thank your parents for inviting us."

Sabrina watched the woman closely as the "us" hit. She flicked her gaze to Sabrina, taking her in in an assessing, full-body sweep of a glance. Her expression stayed fixed and polite, but not what Sabrina would call friendly.

"Anya Greene." The woman introduced herself, without extending a hand for a polite handshake. "Sister of the bride."

Sabrina smiled, all friendly and unaware of the underlying tension even though she was extremely aware of the underlying tension. "Sabrina Mitchell. Lovely to meet you. Your sister looks stunning and the wedding is amazing."

Anya blinked very slowly, and her smile stiffened at the edges. "Thank you. Have you met the family yet?"

"Not yet." She maintained her friendly expression, but it was getting hard under Anya's focused stare. The woman was not going out of her way to make Sabrina feel comfortable.

"I'll make the introductions when they come off the dance floor. I'm sure my father would love to meet you."

"Groovy," she said, mostly just to see what Anya would do.

Another slow blink. Then she focused the full force of her attention on Nick again and Sabrina found herself taking a deep breath. The woman had some serious intensity. Under other circumstances, Sabrina was pretty sure someone like Anya would have intimidated the hell out of her.

Even in this current circumstances it was a close thing.

"Nick, do you have time to talk privately?" Anya asked.

Well, that was pretty bold, right in front of Nick's fake-girlfriend and everything. Anya still had her hand on Nick's shoulder, too. If

Sabrina had been his real girlfriend, she'd be getting pretty annoyed right about now. As his fake-girlfriend, she was still getting annoyed.

"I'm sorry," Nick said, all formal politeness, "Sabrina and I were just getting up to hit the dance floor. She loves to dance, so I can't disappoint her."

Sabrina did love to dance. She wasn't sure he really knew that, but at least she could assure him later he hadn't been lying. And escaping to the dance floor now seemed a lot less dangerous than spending any more time in Anya's presence. She wasn't even sure what it was about the woman. Her intensity was just…uncomfortable.

She supposed, if she was Nick's real girlfriend, she might have felt some jealousy. The woman *was* gorgeous, even if it was a sort of standard-rich-white-woman gorgeous. And she definitely still had her eye on Nick. But Nick was so stiff and formal with her, jealousy wasn't the thing here. No, this feeling was definitely more discomfort.

Working in Manhattan meant Sabrina had come into contact with a lot of rich people. Some of them were really nice. Some were snobby and entitled. Some were indifferent and distant. Some were mean. The variety had given her a good perspective, so now she tried not to judge an individual by their on-paper demographic. Their individual behavior, especially toward the people working for them, spoke more than their bank accounts or general appearance.

Anya was a difficult one to judge, though. The hunger and possessiveness toward Nick were there, and that should have put her into the entitled category. The intensity of her attitude could have set her in the snobby or even mean category. Yet Sabrina was hesitant to assign any of those labels. Maybe she was just trying to be fair, and not assume the worst. She didn't like those "mean girl" games that encouraged knee-jerk dislike of other women.

Still, there was something about Anya that left Sabrina…uncertain.

She shook off the confusion and stood when Nick did, keeping her friendly smile in place. "Nice to meet you," she said to Anya.

Anya's gaze flicked to her. "You too." Then she was staring at Nick again. "Perhaps we could speak later."

That wasn't a question. Sounded suspiciously like an order.

Nick grunted something that served as an answer without actually committing himself to anything, took Sabrina's hand, and led her toward the tent with the band.

Sabrina kept her mouth shut until they were well away from Anya. Then, "That was weird and interesting."

"Anya can be intense."

"Oh yeah. There's more to all this, though, isn't there?"

"Not sure what you mean."

The music had shifted from a fast dance song to a slower song and people coupled up to sway together. Not exactly the kind of dancing Sabrina had intended to do with Nick. Slow dancing meant close contact and physical touching and all the things that were going to get her into trouble. But she couldn't beg off now because Anya was probably watching them.

Nick pulled her into his arms, his gaze distant as he stared at nothing in particular. His distraction helped immensely because the minute she was pressed close to him, her body tingled and tightened and her breathing got a little rougher and her pulse sped up and she was pretty sure her skin flushed because she felt hot all over. And, thank all the deities in the heavens, he didn't notice any of that because he was thinking about something else. That gave her a moment to catch her breath, to calm her pulse, to focus on ignoring how warm and solid he felt. How their slow sway to the music left her feeling languid and sexy and desperate to melt against him. There wasn't much space between them as it was, but she carefully kept that inch of air. To do otherwise would blow all her ability to hide her lust. And that would be bad.

Plus, grinding against him during a wedding where he was trying to charm clients seemed a bit over the top.

Close call, though, because she really wanted to grind against him.

She clenched and relaxed her jaw a few times, trying to settle her jumping hormones and impulses. He looked distracted and upset. She should discuss that with him. Discuss the encounter with Anya. Yes. That would keep her mind off the way his thighs kept bumping against hers and calling her full attention to the lower halves of their bodies.

"So, Anya, huh. Kind of a weird exchange," she said, keeping her voice as low as the music allowed, so he could still hear her but the others swaying next to them couldn't.

"Mmm," he said.

Not much of a response. To be fair, he had spent a lot of the day grunting his answers to questions. She tried again. "Want to talk about it?"

"Mmm."

He nodded, but wasn't looking at her, so she wasn't sure whether to take that as a yes or no.

"She's…pretty."

Was that a weird thing to say? Anya Greene was, objectively, a very attractive woman. A little plastic, a little ordinary, but ordinarily gorgeous all the same. Sabrina wasn't a very good judge of these things, though, because she much preferred interesting, unique, even a little flawed. That design aesthetic had been one of her major selling points over the years, it had worked for her. So she sometimes had a little more trouble finding ordinary pretty interesting enough to judge if other people would find it attractive as well. She was pretty sure, though, Anya was the kind of woman most men considered attractive.

"Mmm," he said again.

Okay. "This conversation is a bit like pulling teeth."

He frowned down at her.

She grinned. "There he is." She let her grin fall away and said gently, "If you don't want to talk, that's fine. We'll hide in the dance until she goes away."

His expression softened, the scowl easing. "I'm not sure what to say about her. I'm not sure what to do about her."

"She seems a little…possessive maybe? I'm not sure. There was a lot of proprietary touching in that exchange. If I was really your girlfriend, that would have been weird. Maybe offensive. Like she was challenging me? I'm not sure. But it was weird."

"Mmm," he muttered again.

"Back to that, huh?"

His self-deprecating grinned was so charming she nearly tripped over her own feet. And the urge to kiss him returned with a vengeance. If he wasn't careful, she would follow through on that impulse. And then where would they be? Really, he should put that grin away. There were children around.

"Sorry," he said. "She's…complicated things a lot on this job. I thought introducing a 'girlfriend' into the mix would force her to return things to a more professional level. But…"

"That didn't seem to be the case."

"Exactly."

"Well, either she doesn't believe I'm your girlfriend—" and since she wasn't that was pretty astute on Anya's part, "—or she doesn't care. And the not caring part is the real issue. Means she's going to keep hitting on you, or…whatever the hell it is she's doing."

His snort was half-amused, half-annoyed, and all adorable.

No. Not adorable, Sabrina. This wasn't a cute and adorable situation. He was upset and his business was in jeopardy over this woman. No time to get caught up in being charmed by her fake-boyfriend.

"You going to talk to her? In private, the way she asked?"

"That doesn't seem like a good idea, does it?" He looked very serious again, his brows creasing. "I'm not sure what she'd want to talk about in private that could possibly be innocent."

"The job? A new job maybe?" Hopeful and very unlikely, but she felt obligated to at least voice the possibilities.

"Doubt it. Her father is the one who hired me, the one with the influence."

"Maybe she thinks if she gets you more work, you'll…I don't know. Be grateful?"

Ew. That was the kind of thing Sabrina had dealt with early in her career. A man, a former boss, thinking if he arranged a good job for her with a client that could make her career, that she'd owe him for it, and that she'd show her "gratitude" by fucking him. Something his wife would have objected to, and Sabrina objected to a lot. She'd quit. Still done the work for the client—because the client knew talent when they saw it—and gotten another job on the back of that work.

A job she was now out of thanks to Darren.

"If that's what she's thinking," Nick said, "she's going to be disappointed."

"Disappointed enough to cause you problems, though, right?"

"Mmm."

"Did you notice the way she got all tight and sour when I mentioned how beautiful her sister and the wedding were?"

"She did?"

"Yeah, she did. Her fake smile got even more…fake. Like she wanted to snarl instead of smile."

"I didn't notice."

"Maybe it was just my imagination, then. I don't know her so I could be reading her wrong." But Sabrina didn't think so. That flash of tension, that hardening around Anya's mouth, that had been a real reaction, even though Anya had tried to hide it. Whatever it meant, it spoke to some difficulty. Maybe between the sisters? Maybe just the whole wedding thing?

"She wasn't in the bridal party either," Sabrina said, another thing she'd found strange once she'd thought about it. "With that many bridesmaids, I would have though the bride's sister would be in there somewhere. Maybe not her main bridesmaid, but still, somewhere in the group."

Nick frowned a little, his gaze moving inward even as he looked down at her. Probably good he wasn't looking at her. She found his scowl adorable and went right back to wanting to kiss him.

"Now that you mention it, she wasn't involved in a lot of the wedding planning. At least not from what I picked up from Mr. and Mrs. Greene. They talked about the wedding a lot around our meetings. And Anya's name never came up in that context."

"Sibling rivalry? Sisterly problems? Jealous of the sister getting married? Just don't like each other? Lot of possibilities there."

"None of which are my business," he pointed out.

True, but, "Some of those issues could lead to… I don't want to call it desperation because that might insult you."

He tucked his chin and gave her a look and she had to press her lips together so she didn't laugh. "You think she's only hitting on me as some sort of revenge against her sister?"

"Not exactly." She rolled her eyes, attempting to be casual and to dispel some of the lust his teasing tone sparked. "But some women can get weird about their sisters and weddings and things. Maybe she's feeling competitive and looking for her own groom?"

"I'm not interested. Why fixate on me?"

"Cause you're extraordinarily handsome. Any woman in her right mind who is interested in men would want you. Why shouldn't Anya?"

Something moved through his expression. And Sabrina's stomach tightened and tingled in response to that look. She couldn't have named it, but her body reacted to it. She realized too late she probably shouldn't have admitted out loud that she thought he was handsome. He'd be ridiculously unaware if he didn't *know* he was handsome, but her admitting that *she'd* noticed seemed a dangerous thing to have done.

His gaze dropped to her mouth and against her will she licked her lips. His hands tightened around her, a flex and release that left her breathless. And then her gaze was on his mouth. And she was leaning in a little more closely, that inch of breathing space between them evaporating.

"Are you in your right mind and attracted to men?" he asked, his voice deeper than it had been a moment ago.

The sound caressed down her spine, leaving a shiver of tingles in its wake. "Attracted to men, yes," she muttered around her now dry throat. "In my right mind? Right now, not even a little bit."

"But you still think I'm handsome?" he murmured, his arms tightening until she was flush against him.

"Mmm."

Yup, she'd made a big mistake.

Chapter Sixteen

Nick's world narrowed down until the only thing filling it was the heat of Sabrina pressed tight against him. The way the ocean breeze wrapped around them and blended with the smell of her shampoo, driving him closer to crazy. The soft lights under the tent warming her skin. The music languidly mixing with the waves in the background. And the deliciously plump temptation of her mouth.

So fucking tempting.

His hands fisted against her lower back, gripping the silk of her dress before he could stop himself. Would the silk rip? He could replace the dress if it did.

He couldn't drag his gaze away from her mouth. When she licked her lips again, he leaned down. She pressed up, her breath brushing his cheek, and that almost broke him.

Why wasn't he supposed to kiss her? He was sure there had been a reason. Otherwise, he wouldn't have resisted this long. Something important, right?

Tabitha. Her best friend. His neighbor. The woman who would kill him if he got involved with Sabrina.

Nick watched Sabrina's eyes drift half closed as her arms tightened around his neck. Death didn't seem so bad just then. Not with Sabrina so close, her lips just right there, her little sigh humming in the air between them. He felt that hum where her breasts pressed tight against his chest, and the faint sensation went right to his cock.

A kiss wouldn't be too bad, right? Just a kiss. Nothing they couldn't walk back from. Nothing too significant.

Just one kiss.

"Nick!"

A hard smack on his shoulder had Nick blinking and jerking upright, away from Sabrina. For just a moment, he imagined it was Tabby about to kick his ass for almost kissing her best friend. Then he realized the voice had been a man's.

"Good you could make it! Sorry it's taken me so long to work my way around. Busy day. Busy day."

Nick let out a slow breath and forced a pleasant, professional smile. "Mr. Greene," he greeted the boisterous older man. "Thanks again for inviting us."

"Of course. Of course! Glad you could make it." Mr. Greene turned a meaningful look on Sabrina.

"Yes, uh, James Greene, this is Sabrina Mitchell." He stopped just shy of saying "my girlfriend" because he couldn't get his mouth around the false words when he'd just been thinking about ripping her dress off as he devoured her mouth. "Sabrina, father of the bride, James Greene."

"Lovely to meet you, Mr. Greene," Sabrina said.

Was her voice huskier now? Sounded a little huskier. Her friendly smile seemed a touch wobbly around the edges, too. And she was blinking a lot.

"Call me James," Mr. Greene said, also clapping Sabrina on the shoulder, though a bit more gently than he'd done with Nick. "Great to meet you, great to meet you."

"The wedding has been perfect," Sabrina said, her social skills returning faster than Nick's. "And your daughter is an absolutely beautiful bride."

Mr. Greene's chest puffed up with pride. "She is, she is, my Bianca, isn't she? Beautiful girl. Chose a good man, too. Good provider." He looked between the two of them. "Maybe another wedding in the near future, eh? Maybe? One can hope. One can hope."

Nick had to bite the inside of his cheek to keep from responding to that. Sabrina made a little choking noise. She covered it with a cough.

Fortunately, Mr. Greene was deep into the Dom Perignon and didn't seem to notice their reactions. "Well, I won't keep you young people from the dancing. Just wanted to stop and say hello. Doing the rounds, you know. Host and all that. Great to meet you." He gave Sabrina another shoulder squeeze, winked at Nick, then moved on to another couple dancing nearby.

Nick let out a long, slow breath. He couldn't look at Sabrina again. Not yet. If he did, he might fall down another rabbit hole of fantasies about her mouth.

"He seems like a nice man," she said, clearing her throat a little.

"He is. He's also quite drunk."

"Can't blame him. After the stress of planning a wedding, I suspect he and his wife deserve to get plastered."

Nick chuckled, but the laugh was distracted and half-assed. He was still having trouble calming his body down. His skin was tight and hot, and Sabrina was still too close, still in his arms. Her mouth still just right there. And he couldn't even put space between them yet because his arousal was a little too obvious. A cold plunge in the ocean seemed like a good idea. Might help.

He glanced at Sabrina from the corner of his eye. Or might not.

How had they gotten to this point? They'd been having a perfectly reasonable and very unsexual conversation about Anya, and then suddenly he was intensely aware of Sabrina swaying against him and the next thing he knew he was inches away from kissing her.

The most amazing part, though, was that she'd been about to kiss him, too. He was sure of it. And that was…unexpected.

They swayed together until the end of the song, and he tried to think sobering, cold thoughts full of baseball statistics and a swim in the Atlantic. It worked enough that when they eased apart, he could release her. Reluctantly, but he could manage it.

For a moment, they stood in the middle of the dance floor as a faster song started, just staring at each other.

"Wanna talk about it?" she asked.

"Probably shouldn't," he said.

"Probably shouldn't."

They were going to have to talk about it.

He really didn't want to talk.

He led her off the dance floor with a hand at her lower back, trying not to feel the way the silk moved over her warm skin. They made it all the way to the edge of the dance floor before Anya stopped them.

Nick didn't groan aloud, but it was a close thing. Somewhat to his surprise, Sabrina moved a little in front of him, putting herself between Anya and him. And she leaned back against him, pulling his arm around her waist as she smiled up at Anya. The gesture was the sort of thing a slightly tipsy girlfriend might do. Casual. A little possessive. Definitely flirty.

And entirely too comfortable.

He tightened his arm around her before he could stop himself. She didn't object, just cradled the arm at her waist and leaned her weight into him.

"Do you have time to talk now?" Anya said. "In private."

"We were just going to get a drink," Nick said, hoping another excuse would fly. "Thirsty after the dance."

Tiptoeing around Anya set his teeth on edge. If James Greene wasn't such an influential client, he wouldn't do it. He'd been clear from the start he wasn't interested in her romantically. He didn't understand why she kept pushing.

And frankly, he wanted to stay with Sabrina. Wanted to think about the fact that she'd been as ready to kiss him as he was to kiss her. He'd thought this spark was one-sided. That he'd been struggling to resist her because Tabby would kill him, and Sabrina wasn't interested anyway. But if she was interested…where did that leave them?

He was kind of hoping it left them with at least a kiss in the near future. Maybe more.

But he couldn't work through all that while Anya was standing there staring at them, or staring at him. She was pointedly ignoring Sabrina. Which was pretty fucking rude since Sabrina was supposed to be his girlfriend. At least as far as Anya knew.

Without meaning to, he felt his neutral expression dipping to a frown.

"This is important, Nick," Anya said. "Business."

"Then we can discuss it on a call on Monday," Nick said, trying to keep the bite out of his voice. "I'll call."

There weren't any emergencies in his line work that couldn't wait until Monday when other offices were open so he could solve any problems that had come up with permits or contractors or supplies. None of the possible "emergencies" needed to be handled on a Saturday night during a wedding. And if there *had* been a problem with the new construction, Mr. Greene would have mentioned it earlier. The man might be deep into his drink and giddily happy to have one of his daughters married off, but James Greene was a savvy business man. If there was something they had to deal with, he'd have mentioned it, at least in passing.

Anya's gaze flickered, an expression he couldn't read passing through her eyes, before she said, "Please. This is important."

Sabrina's arms tightened on his around her waist. A reassuring gesture. Then she eased away from him. "I'll go get us another glass of wine."

She held his gaze for a moment, her face turned away from Anya, and mouthed, *I'll be right back.* Then she moved toward the nearest server with a tray full of champagne flutes.

Giving Anya a few minutes to speak to him without actually abandoning him to the woman. He watched Sabrina walk away, watched how she kept looking back, keeping an eye on him even as she stopped the server.

Something inside his chest did a funny tightening.

"Nick," Anya said, drawing his attention.

"What's so important?" He kept half his attention on Sabrina, where she hovered a few tables away, watching their exchange, but he focused enough on Anya to see her frown at his tone.

"Is that woman really your partner?"

"Yes. Why are you asking?"

"You've never mentioned being involved with someone before."

"I don't often talk about my private life with my clients." Was that clear enough? Could he be any more blunt?

"I thought I was more than a client."

"Why?"

Another one of those flickering shifts in her gaze. He didn't want to be rude. He'd been trying to remain neutral and avoid this conversation. If he pissed her off now, and she went to her father about it, all this would have been for nothing. But he was having a hard time keeping the irritation from his tone.

Anya didn't say anything for a long moment. The tension made Nick want to fidget.

"I should get back to Sabrina," he said, but gentled his voice. "Why don't you tell me what the emergency is, and we'll deal with it on Monday." There. That sounded at least a little professional and conciliatory, didn't it?

"My sister getting married was the emergency," Anya muttered.

"I...don't understand."

"Of course you don't." She sighed and waved a hand vaguely in the air. "I was hoping... Well, it doesn't matter now."

Nick frowned. Sabrina was right. There was more here than just Anya hitting on him. But for the life of him, he had no idea what. "Anya, what's going on?"

"Have a good night, Nick," she said, and walked off without looking back.

He stood blinking at the spot where Anya had disappeared in the crowd as Sabrina returned, holding two glasses of champagne.

"You look like you need one of these," she said, handing him the drink. "What happened?"

"I... I have no idea." He looked down at her and frowned. "She didn't say much. Asked if you were really my girlfriend."

Sabrina winced. "Shit. What did you say?"

"That I hadn't mentioned you before because I don't talk about my private life with clients."

"Ouch. How did she take that?"

"I couldn't tell. I…" He shook his head. "You were right. There's more going on here than I thought. But I have no idea what. She said the wedding was the emergency. What the hell does that mean?"

Sabrina's brows rose. "Huh. No idea." She glanced in the direction Anya had gone. "But it sounds…complicated."

"Too complicated for me to be in the middle of it," he said. "Especially since I have no idea what's happening."

Absently, without looking at him, Sabrina rubbed a hand over his arm. "Well, hopefully, this is the end of it. You being in a relationship seems to have ruined whatever she wanted from you. Maybe it was a family issue? If it's tied to the wedding?"

Her hand on his arm distracted him and he almost missed what she'd said. He really didn't want to think about Anya and her family just then. He wanted to think about that almost-kiss on the dance floor and what it meant and if maybe they could dump the almost part. Soon.

"Not sure what I have to do with their family issues," he grunted, shifting a little so he was closer to her. She didn't step away. Or take her hand off his arm.

She sipped her champagne thoughtfully. "I'm pretty curious now, myself."

"I don't care."

She finally looked up at him. Her dark eyes reflected the overhead fairy lights illuminating the tent. And she looked extremely kissable. Would she taste like champagne now?

"Not even a little?" she asked.

He blinked, and it took a moment to remember what they'd been talking about. "No. So long as it doesn't affect the job I'm doing for Greene, the familial machinations are none of my business."

"Hmm." She glanced away again.

Which was good because he couldn't. At this angle, he found himself studying the curve of her jaw, the way her neck slopped into her shoulder. There was a spot, just there, he thought might be warm and in need of a kiss. He blinked again when he realized he was leaning over, ready to press his lips against her skin. Slowly, he straightened.

But he wasn't concerned about Anya and her family issues any more.

Now, all he wanted to do was get Sabrina alone.

And see if she really did taste like champagne.

Chapter Seventeen

Unfortunately for Nick's desire to get Sabrina alone, they got swept up into introductions, and greeting the bride and groom, and all the other social conversations inherent at a wedding. And since he was supposed to be at this wedding to charm future clients, Nick managed to drag his attention away from Sabrina to do the rounds.

But she remained in the periphery of his awareness. When they got separated, he found himself following her with his gaze, making sure he always knew where she was. When they were together, he was acutely aware of her presence and had to exert a lot of energy focusing on other people and what they were saying to him.

By the time they were ready to leave, he was exhausted from all the effort.

When Sabrina shifted a little in the seat of his car and her dress rode up just enough to give him a glimpse of her thigh, he tightened his hands on the steering wheel. He wasn't *that* exhausted.

He couldn't stop thinking about that almost-kiss on the dance floor, either. So when he parked the car in front of her house to walk her to her door, the simmering possibility of that almost-kiss hung in the air between them.

"You could have parked in your own driveway," she said, smiling at him as he walked her up the two steps to the small front porch.

"This isn't any trouble," he said. He hadn't been thinking clearly enough to remember that he could have parked in his own drive anyway. They paused under the portico, the security light at the front door casting them in a yellow light.

Sabrina looked up at him, keys in her hand. "This was surprisingly fun."

"Surprisingly?" He raised his brows in mock offense and she smiled and his breathing sped up.

"You know what I mean. Weddings can be...strange events sometimes."

He couldn't really argue with her on that. Mostly because he didn't go to enough weddings to know. He'd been Diego's best man, and that day had been hectic but lots of fun. His two other married friends had also had great weddings.

She shifted a little, a move that brought her closer, and he lost track of the conversation. She was warm, and flushed, and standing very close. His gaze dropped to her lips.

"I hope it worked," she said.

Worked? Oh, right. Anya. Pretending this was a real date. Real relationship. He'd nearly forgotten that part. Especially the part about how this was supposed to be pretend.

He'd also forgotten why kissing her was a bad idea. Couldn't begin to recall why he'd been resistant to kissing her. Didn't really matter just then, because she was staring up at him and he heard her breath hitch a little when he leaned down. That soft sound did something to him. Something he couldn't even name. But he wanted to kiss her more than he'd wanted to do anything else in his entire life.

"Nick?"

"Hmm?"

"I..." She swallowed and angled closer.

"You what?"

"I forgot what I wanted to say."

"Tell me when you remember."

"Okay."

"I really want to kiss you," he murmured.

"That seems like a really good idea, doesn't it?"

"Really really good idea."

"You should do that."

"Do what?"

"Kiss me."

So he did. Without touching her in any other way, he closed the last few inches between them, watching her eyes drift shut, feeling the brush of her breath against his face, the faint sigh she released. He pressed his lips to hers in a gentle caress.

She tasted like champagne.

He sank down into the kiss, first just soft pressure, then deeper when she sighed again and opened to him. The sweet taste of her as he swept his tongue against hers, the play and dance of their lips. He angled his head, changing the contact just a little, deepening the kiss, and she followed him, languid and lush. She was all soft and sweet and bold, no hesitance, no restraint, no rush.

He flexed his hands, desperate to touch her and yet not wanting to break the spell. All of his focus was on the sounds of her soft breathing and warm sighs, the gentle murmurs as he changed angles again for a new kiss, the way she leaned into him and rose up just a little on her toes to meet him for each brush of lips, each deepening taste.

She was the first to give in to touching more than mouths, bringing her hands to his waist and easing closer, until they were flush against each other. The contact, pressing into her from chest to thighs, sent his mind reeling. He was completely sober, having switched to water and coffee hours ago because he was driving. She'd cheerfully done the same, claiming solidarity with her ride home. Still, he felt light headed and dizzy. Buzzed. Both solidly in the moment and like the world was spinning away and it was only the two of them here. He brought his arms up around her, one hand resting against the silk dress on her lower back, the other around her shoulders, pressing her closer until there wasn't any space between them. Just her warm, lush heat and his desperate need to feel all of her at once.

He ran one hand up to cup her neck, and she moaned softly into his mouth when he brushed his fingers along the silky warmth of her skin. So soft. Her breathing hitched when he brushed his thumb over her pulse, just at the point where her neck and jaw met. Another little catch when he did it again. And she ground against him.

The growl that rumbled up from his chest didn't quite sound like him, but he felt every bit of it, having her so eager and in his arms. He wanted to glide his lips over that soft soft spot he'd just found and see how she reacted to that. Find all the other places that made her breath hitch, made her moan, made her sigh.

Easing back from the kiss took an act of will. And they both let out a quiet groan that would have made him laugh if he wasn't so busy ensuring he had the strength to let her go. He didn't immediately. He just couldn't seem to take his hands off her. He brushed a thumb over her cheek, tucking a strand of hair that had escaped her elegant hairdo back behind her ear. Everything about her was soft and silky. The feel of her hair running through his fingers made him want to sink his hands into the mass, release all the pins and clips and whatever was holding the hairstyle up, let all that silk fall around her shoulders.

Caught up in the thought, he forgot for a moment he was supposed to be letting her go, letting her go inside.

She held his gaze, and he could feel her heart beating hard against his chest. Or was that his heart? Hard to tell.

Finally, with another of her soft sighs, this one sounding resigned, she pushed gently to put space between them, and he reluctantly let her go.

"Goodnight, Nick," she said, her voice breathy and faint.

The sound ran down his spine like lightning, sparking off his nerves with delicious electricity. An image of her sounding just like that, in a dark room, tangled sheets, more sighs, a lot less clothing…

He cleared his throat. "Goodnight."

Another long pause, and then she turned and opened the door. She smiled at him as she closed the door between them, only breaking eye contact at the last moment.

He took a few deep breaths, letting his pulse calm and his body relax. Well, not relax. That wasn't happening for a while yet. But he gathered himself enough to get into his car and drive the hundred feet to his own driveway. To get safely inside his own house.

But knowing she was right next door, knowing what she tasted like now, remembering her sighs and moans and those little breath hitches…

That followed him into a restless, mostly sleepless night.

Chapter Eighteen

The kissing had been a terrible idea.

Not a terrible kiss. The kiss had been incredible. Mind blowing. Lush and sexy and overwhelming. Sabrina had gone to bed thinking about it and hadn't stopped reliving it all morning. She could still practically taste him. And she very much wanted another kiss. More than one. More than just a kiss.

Which was the reason it had been a terrible idea.

Tabby had warned her. Don't get sucked into the idea that the wedding was a real date. Had she listened?

Well, actually, she sort of had. She'd tried anyway. She'd even switched to water and coffee when he did so she'd stay sober and not let her guard down. Especially after nearly kissing him on the dance floor. They hadn't danced again, which was safer, and they'd spent time apart socializing to be good guests. She'd spent some time talking to Geraldine Roland, the bride's godmother who they'd met during the ceremony, who told her all about her non-profit work and the activity center the non-profit was building for neurodiverse kids and adults, which sounded perfect. She'd met the mother of the bride eventually, talked with the bride herself once, though very briefly and in passing, hadn't talked to the groom at all outside of introductions, and never saw Anya again after she'd stopped Nick at the edge of the dance floor.

That was a strange, strange situation. And that, all on its own, should have been enough to keep her hormones under control.

But nope. She'd slipped into the dark interior of his car, let the night seep in around her, let his scent get into her head all over again, and suddenly she was thinking about his arms around her during their dance. The way his hands had felt against her back, the way his body had felt when she pressed into him, the way he'd leaned down so close, like he wanted to kiss her. And how she'd gone up a little on her toes, like she'd kiss him back.

She might have convinced herself she'd imagined that part. Imagined his focus on her mouth and the intensity in his eyes. After all, he hadn't seemed even a little interested in her before this. But then they'd stopped at the front door. She'd looked up at him. He'd looked down at her. And…

Well, she'd given in to something she'd wanted to do since Tabby introduced them.

Now everything was messed up. She had one more thing to worry about. And she had no idea how to deal with this escalation in her crush when what she was supposed to be doing was *fixing* her life.

She took the dogs for a long walk on the beach the next morning to try and straighten out her head. Trying to convince herself she and Nick could just pretend that kiss had been a product of their weird sort-of date night and move on as friends without complicating things.

The biggest problem was, she didn't want to do that. She wanted more. Even though she wasn't in a position to start a new relationship. Even though he wasn't a relationship sort of man. Even though she had no idea what she was doing with her life after this summer was over.

Which was exactly the problem Tabby had warned her about.

She let the dogs back into the house through the back door, their nails clicking over the polished wood floors as they headed right for the kitchen for breakfast. She followed, slower, still deep in thought. The fresh air and ocean breeze hadn't helped much. She still felt off kilter, upside down, and inside out all at once. Breakfast and coffee didn't help either.

She had to call Tabby.

She so didn't want to call Tabby. She didn't want to hear the "I told you so"s and she didn't want to upset her friend. But she needed to talk about this with someone. Someone who actually knew Nick.

She rang Tabby's cell, got the voicemail, and left a message. It was late afternoon in Paris. Tabby was no doubt busy with book tour stuff. Sabrina kind of hoped she was too busy to call back today. She desperately wanted to talk, but she also desperately wanted to hide from what had happened. Well, no actually what she desperately wanted was for what happened to continue happening. Which was the problem.

She'd watched for Nick while she was on the beach. Glanced at his deck when she'd walked up to the back door. No sign of him yet this morning.

And maybe that was for the best. She couldn't bear the thought of him just waving her off after last night. Even though she knew that's what they both should do. But it would hurt.

Damn it.

She buried herself in painting for the rest of the morning, being meticulous about the ceiling lines and details so she didn't have to think about Nick. The distraction worked pretty well because when her phone rang, she realized it was well past lunch and she'd completely lost track of time.

"How did you guys let me go this long without a trip to the kitchen?" she asked Justin and Princess. They were still sitting in the hallway, watching her paint. She'd had to put a barrier up in front of the door to keep Princess from coming in to investigate the paint, so their good behavior wasn't just because they were good dogs.

She wiped her hands on a paint rag and swiped her phone on, speaker on so she didn't have to handle the phone much with her still dirty hands.

"What happened?" Tabby asked unceremoniously. "You sounded stressed in your voicemail."

"I'm not interrupting some important book related stuff, am I?" She wasn't really stalling. She was just…stalling.

"No. I wouldn't have called yet if didn't have time to talk. I have a feeling this will take some time."

Sabrina sighed. And told her everything.

"You kissed him?" Tabby said at the end. "You stood at my front door, shaking your keys instead of going right inside. And you kissed him."

"Well, it was a mutual kiss."

"Stone cold sober."

"Stone cold sober. No excuses." Not that she would make excuses for the kiss. She'd meant every minute of it. What she couldn't quite get over was the fact that Nick seemed to have meant every minute of it, too.

"He's…" Tabby hesitated. "He's a nice man."

"He is."

"But he's not a relationship man."

"I know. You've warned me."

"And you are a relationship woman."

"We've talked about this already." Just a couple of days ago, as a matter of fact. She sighed. "I know all the reasons it was dumb, Tab. I know I'm gonna get hurt."

"Because you want to do it again."

Not a question. She still said, "Yeah." She sat a little straighter on the couch where she'd slouched for this call. "But I mean, maybe he doesn't and so there's no real issue here. If he wants to forget the kiss happened," and yeah, that would hurt, but it would also make things simpler, "then I could go right back to crushing on him from a distance while I got my life together." Her professional life anyway. "No harm, no foul."

"You really think you can go back to just passing acquaintances without it breaking your heart?"

"I'm not in love with him for god sake. He's a crush." Granted, a big one. Still. "And the kiss was…" She couldn't lie to Tabby. "Okay, the kiss was hot. I'm gonna have trouble getting over that."

Tabby snorted.

"But I will."

"You will be living next door to this man for the rest of the summer."

Sabrina glanced down at the dogs. Princess—who wasn't supposed to be on the furniture—was contently sound asleep at one end of the couch. Justin sat looking up at Sabrina, resting his chin on her knee while she absently scratched around his ears. Tabby was right. It wasn't like she could just leave and go back to her apartment in Brooklyn. And not just because the building didn't allow dogs. She couldn't kick her subletter out. She'd be a real shit if she displaced her friend's sister just because she couldn't keep it together around a man.

"I know," she said. "I don't need to run away. It's fine."

"If it was fine, then why did you call me?"

"So I could confess. You're my confessor. Didn't you know that?"

Another mildly sarcastic snort.

"And I needed the reminder that I should let things go now. Not try to…do anything more about the kiss. Just let it go."

"Yes. That's exactly what you should do."

"I could consider it just a summer fling," she said before she could stop herself. Then she winced. Knowing exactly what Tabby would say.

"You are not a summer fling kind of girl. You know that. I know that. I do not want to go through this again with you. It hurts me when you get hurt, and I don't want to have to kill Nick. I like him."

"Even if I get myself hurt, it'll be my own fault. No need to kill Nick. It's not like I'm going into this with my eyes closed."

A little dazzled, though, maybe. She'd always been able to keep this crush in check because she assumed none of the lusty feelings were returned. Now that she knew he didn't mind the idea of kissing her, she kept wondering if he'd mind the idea of more, and that just led her down all kinds of fantasies that would definitely end in Trouble.

"Don't go *into* anything at all and then you won't get hurt," Tabby said. "It's not too late."

"I know. I know." Except it was probably too late. "And I know I'm not usually a summer fling kind of person."

"No usual about it. Girl, you will get to the end of the summer trying to figure out how to move out to the Hamptons. I don't want a roommate again. I love you, but I love my space to myself even more."

Sabrina chuckled. "I'm not going to beg to move in. Besides, what the hell would I do out here? It's not like there are jobs just dropping at my feet."

If she hadn't had to leave her last job in disgrace, then maybe she could have leveraged that into a freelance career in interior design for rich people. But even that wasn't likely. She'd get bored with that work eventually. Plus, interior designers for rich people were probably a dime a dozen out here.

All of that was moot, though. She eventually had to go back to the city and make something of herself. She was only out here for the summer so she could figure out what that new self would be.

And that new self would not include a relationship with Nick.

Just a shame that thought had to hurt a little.

Chapter Nineteen

The kiss had been a terrible idea.

Not at the time. At the time, Nick couldn't have done anything else but kiss her. Not when she looked up at him all lush and beautiful and sleepy-eyed. Not when she'd risen on her toes to meet him half way. He kept replaying that moment, when her eyes drifted shut, when that little sigh escaped her as he finally settled his mouth to hers.

But now…

Now he could barely keep himself in his own house. He was edgy, pacing around the place, telling himself he absolutely could not go over there. Not even with the excuse to talk. He didn't want to talk. He wanted to drag her up to her bedroom, strip her naked, and fuck her until they were both exhausted. Nap. Probably eat. Then start all over dragging her back up to the bedroom. The only talking he wanted to do was in bed. And maybe in the shower.

He certainly didn't want to talk about why kissing had been a bad idea.

And that was because he was having so much trouble convincing himself it *had* been a bad idea. Why was he supposed to keep his hands to himself around Sabrina again? He knew there was a good reason—

and that the reason had something to do with her best friend killing him.

But they were both adults. They could manage a little chemistry without losing their minds or getting carried away. Right?

This didn't have to turn into a big deal. No one had to get hurt. And if he didn't hurt Sabrina, Tabby couldn't justify killing him, and when Sabrina went back into the city at the end of the summer, everyone would be just fine.

Right. Just fine.

He collapsed onto his couch and dropped his head onto the back cushion, running his hands through his hair.

He'd never minded before when the women he'd dated left. In fact, he'd usually been relieved. He wasn't good at having long term romantic relationships. He didn't go out of his way to avoid them, necessarily. They just didn't seem to last for him, and he never felt bad when they ended. Just relieved. Relationships took up too much of his time. He liked having time alone. He loved his work. And that focus didn't seem to mesh with the women he'd dated in the past.

So he wasn't sure why the idea of Sabrina going back to the city bothered him. Of course she would. She lived there. It wasn't that far away, couple hour's drive. No big deal. She came out here to see Tabby all the time. Not like there was a continent or ocean between here and the city.

But why exactly was he thinking about the distance between him and Sabrina after the summer? Why did he care?

He tugged at his hair and groaned. This was the reason Tabby warned him away from Sabrina. She probably knew he'd lose his fucking mind and end up a jabbering mess because he didn't recognize his own fucking thoughts.

And Tabby wasn't here to talk him down.

He leaned forward and grabbed his cellphone off the coffee table, checked the time. Diego would be up. Sensible man. They'd talk baseball and work and Nick would get out of his spiraling thoughts and be able to think clearly again.

Diego answered on the second ring. "What's her name?"

"No hello? No long time no talk? That's the greeting I get?" Nick scowled and slumped back in his couch. "I could be calling to talk baseball."

"We've been texting about baseball all week. Why would you call about that?" Diego sounded amused.

In the background, Nick heard a crash and a shout. Diego shouted something back. Then came back on the line. "Kids dumped over a Legos table, broke a bunch of stuff they'd built. There will be tears."

"Your life makes no sense to me," Nick said.

Diego chuckled. "I love it."

"I know. That's what makes no sense to me."

"Said the perpetual bachelor. So what's up? Why are you calling me on a chaotic Sunday morning?"

"Baseball. Work." Stuff that doesn't have to do with Sabrina.

"What's her name?" Diego asked again, still sounding amused even with more shouting going on in the background.

"You need to deal with that?" Nick asked.

"Na. Jessy's got it. You're avoiding my question."

"No, I'm not," Nick said.

"Then why don't I know her name yet?"

"I just said I called to talk baseball."

"The Mets suck this year. What's there to talk about?"

"Maybe I got tickets and wanted to invite your sorry ass to a game?"

"Did you?"

"No."

"What. Is. Her. Name?"

"You suck."

Diego chuckled. "You wouldn't have called me if you didn't need to talk. You're a texting kind of a guy. I appreciate that by the way. Don't get me wrong. I prefer texting too. Life with kids is too unpredictable for a lot of phone calls."

"I bet," Nick said as another shout in the background resulted in some more crashing. "You sure you don't need to deal with that?

Sounds like Jessy has her hands full. I can call later. Or not at all. No big deal."

"You need to talk. I'm here for you, bud. Just…" He put a hand over the phone and Nick heard some muted conversation. Then he was back. "All set. She's taking them down to the park to work off some energy and get over the Legos apocalypse."

"It's not a big deal," Nick said as he stared up at the ceiling, watching the fan slowly circle. It wasn't a big deal. He was just making things into a bigger deal than they needed to be. One kiss. After a fake date. Not a big deal. She wasn't calling or knocking on his door, trying to hound him into anything. This was fine. She hadn't sicced Tabby on him. Obviously, Sabrina wasn't bothered by what had happened. No reason for him to be.

"You ever going to tell me this woman's name?"

"What do you think about the lineup for tonight's game?"

"I think you're an asshole, but mostly to yourself. So, let's try it this way. How did the wedding go yesterday? Anya still complicating things?"

"Wedding was fine." He didn't want to talk about the wedding. That meant talking about Sabrina. That wasn't why he'd called Diego.

"No issues with Anya?"

"She stopped to talk to me a couple of times but then mostly left me alone."

"That's…unexpected. Why?"

"Why did she leave me alone? Maybe she finally had enough of my sparkling personality."

Diego snorted. "Wouldn't be surprised. I've never understood why women don't realize you're a grumpy bastard to be avoided at all costs."

"Not that bad," Nick grumbled.

"Don't get me wrong. I love you. But in my experience, most women like more than the occasional text from the men they're seeing."

"Not seeing Anya. I'm working for her father. Maybe she finally just took the hint."

"She's not the reason you're calling, is she?"

"What makes you say that?"

"She's a work problem," Diego said, sounding thoughtful.

Nick made a face even though Diego couldn't see him and glared at a spot on the ceiling. What the hell was that? A spider?

"You have a different huffy tone when you're having work-related problems. Women-related problems is a whole different sort of irritation."

"How the fuck can you tell the difference in my irritation from my voice?"

"We have been friends most of our lives," Diego said with a snort. "You think I can't tell the difference between you being pissed off about work or pissed off about a woman?"

Nick launched off the couch and started pacing the room. He shouldn't have called Diego. He should have taken a cold shower, locked himself in his office, and buried himself in work. That would have been a better choice.

Not that he seemed to be the poster child for good choices these last few weeks.

"I don't want to talk about it."

"This Tabby's friend?"

Nick stopped pacing to glare at the phone. "What?"

Diego paused. "Huh. What happened? Thought Tabby had warned you off that one. Put the fear of God in you."

"Diego…" Nick tried for a warning tone. Most people crumbled under that tone.

Unfortunately, Diego was not most people. "This is about Tabby's friend, isn't it? Sabrina. What happened?"

"What makes you think this has to do with Sabrina?"

"Cause you bring her up all the time."

"I do not. I barely know the woman."

"Dude. You mention her as often as you mention Tabby even though Tabby is your neighbor and you rarely see Sabrina."

"That…can't be true." He scrubbed a hand over his head again. He didn't really talk about Sabrina to Diego. Did he? He didn't remember doing that. Why would he? Until this summer, with her staying next door for this long, he'd have had no reason to even mention her to Diego.

"Ah, man. You've got it bad for this woman, don't you? Does she hate you? Is that the problem?"

"No, she doesn't hate me. Why the hell would you say that?"

"I don't know. Just guessing since you're not telling me anything yet. Does she love you?"

"Shut up."

"Yeah, right, why would she, huh?"

Nick's scowl deepened.

"Except, Nick, why wouldn't she?"

"What the fuck are we talking about?"

"Your denial, I think. And you are really good at denial so this is taking some work on my part."

"I shouldn't have called you."

"Of course you should have. So what's happened with Sabrina that's got you so wound up? She walking around Tabby's house naked?"

Nick tripped over his own feet and nearly swallowed his tongue at just the thought. He cleared his throat. "Even if she was, how the hell would I know? I'm not fucking looking in her windows and spying on her like a fucking stalker. Fucks sake."

"You're cursing a lot so we've hit a delicate subject. Hmm."

"Shut up. I'm hanging up now."

"Fine. I'll talk to you when you call back still not wanting to talk but needing to talk, and we'll get to the bottom of the problem."

"Fuck."

Diego chuckled. "Just spill, Nick. You'll feel better."

"Jessy teach you that?"

"She's been good for my personal growth."

Nick snorted.

"You didn't call to talk about baseball and work," Diego said.

"I did actually."

"Then only to distract yourself from your real problem."

"You suck."

"I know you love me."

"I kissed her." The words tumbled out before he could stop himself. And then so did the rest of the story, all of it, from Sabrina's arrival to his stupid idea to invite her to the wedding to the wedding itself.

Diego was quiet through it all except for a few well-placed grunts and murmured words of understanding.

When Nick finished, he collapsed back onto the couch. "And now I can't stop thinking about her. And I want to stop thinking about her."

"Hate to tell you, but you've never stop thinking about her since you met her. If you had, I wouldn't have known her name. Hell, you dated two different women for months whose names I never knew because you barely talked about them."

That couldn't be true. Why would he talk more about a woman he barely knew than he did about women he was actually dating? Diego was just being an ass.

But he was right about one thing. Nick hadn't been able to keep Sabrina out of his thoughts for very long since meeting her. More than two years of having her hovering somewhere in the background, aware of her every time she came to visit Tabby. He couldn't believe he'd let that preoccupation slip out to Diego. But he couldn't deny the preoccupation had been there.

He rubbed a hand over his face. "So what do I do?"

"I'd suggest talking to Sabrina," Diego said. "Women like when you talk to them."

"Fuck off."

"They do. Jessy swears to me they do. Well, maybe they don't like when *you* talk to them."

"I'm hanging up."

"Is Sabrina interested in you?"

"I hadn't thought so, but…"

"But she didn't slap you away when you kissed her."

She most certainly had not. In fact, she'd told him to kiss her. The memory started his nerves humming again. He glanced toward his front door.

"So why don't you talk to her," Diego said.

"What the hell am I going to say?"

"That you want to marry her and have lots of sex and babies."

"Jessy's made you watch *Love Actually* too much."

Diego chuckled. "It's her Christmas movie. I can't deny her. The fact that you picked up the movie line means you've watched *Love Actually* too much, too."

"You're not helping."

"I think I am. You need to find out where Sabrina stands in all this. She interested or not?"

He continued to stare at his front door. "Tabby will kill me," he said, but absently now.

"Only if you hurt her friend. Don't do that, and you should survive."

"How do I *not* do that?"

Diego was quiet for a long moment. The silence left a hollow feeling in the pit of Nick's stomach for some reason.

"You like her?" Diego asked quietly.

"Yeah. I like her."

"How do you feel when you think about her leaving at the end of the summer?"

"I don't know." He hated the idea. He couldn't understand *why* he hated the idea, but he did. He just wasn't ready to admit that out loud yet.

Apparently, with Diego, he didn't have to. "I think the big issue here isn't you hurting her, Nick. I think the big problem is gonna be her hurting you."

Nick sighed. Wouldn't that be just his fucking luck.

Chapter Twenty

By the time she got off the phone with Tabby, Sabrina was half convinced she should just let last night go. Try to pretend it didn't happen. Maybe Nick would be good with that, too. After all, he was the one that didn't really do relationships. According to Tabby.

Sabrina laid on the floor in the bedroom she was painting and considered that. She only knew Nick didn't do relationships from Tabby. Maybe Tabby was just saying that to keep her from getting hurt. Maybe Nick wasn't that kind of guy?

Or maybe she was making excuses to pretend this wasn't going to get her hurt.

She sighed. Thoughts of Nick had at least taken her mind off her career troubles, but since she was here to concentrate on recovering from her career troubles, this seemed counterproductive.

She rolled onto her side and looked at the dogs laying just outside the bedroom door in the hallway. "Princess, you're a girl, right?"

Princess sat up. When no treats were forthcoming, she spun in a quick circle before dropping back down again into a fluffy ball.

"I'll take that as a yes. So, what do you do when you have these kinds of issues? Do you talk it out with the man or just…let it go and try to move on so you don't get hurt?"

Princess rolled onto her back, her stomach in the air and let out a little yipping bark. That was her scratch-my-tummy pose.

"Not helpful," Sabrina said. "How about you, Justin? Any sage advice?"

Justin stood as if he intended to come into the room, but she had drop sheets and open paint cans around the room and the last thing she needed was Justin stepping in fresh paint and tracking it all through the house.

"Stay," she said. "Sit."

He stayed and sat just like Tabby had trained him, his tongue lolling out to one side as he stared at her.

"Not really helpful on the personal side either, but thanks for minding," she said.

She rolled back to stare at the ceiling. Maybe going somewhere else would be a good idea. Nick was entirely too close right now, just next door. Too easy to head over there to talk about last night. Or maybe not talk. Maybe more kissing. Maybe naked kissing. In bed.

She shook her head hard and rolled to her feet. Time to clean up and go do something that didn't involve Nick fantasies. Some place she could clear her head. She had no idea where that place would be, but she needed to get out and around other people so she could distract herself from her own circling thoughts.

* * *

She ended up at an open-air farmers market a half hour drive away. The place was packed with people wandering between stalls filled with fresh vegetables, baked goods, local dairy, and honey stands. There was even a stand with locally made wines. That stand drew her in immediately. The bread and baked-goods also called to her.

The market was set up in a long narrow park area surrounded by roads in the middle of one of the many villages dotting the coast. The air inside the market had a strange mix of yummy baked foods and the more ordinary town smells of cars motoring by and heat off the sidewalks. The day had grown hot, despite the breeze, and she was sweating under her t-shirt, hopping from shady tent stall to shady tent stall to avoid the sun.

At a fresh pressed fruit juice stand, she bought a bottle of combined berry and carrot juice that tasted remarkably good and refreshing in the heat. And she picked a shady spot on a park bench to drink her juice and eat one of the cookies she'd bought at one of the three baked goods stalls she'd visited.

This was just the kind of thing Tabby loved. Wandering farmers markets, looking for fresh ingredients to experiment with. Sabrina loved these kinds of things too, but for very different reasons. She was never inspired to cook more. She was, however, inspired to eat things with lots and lots of color.

The breather, the getting away from the house and from Nick so nearby, helped a lot. She didn't stop thinking about him, but she also wasn't obsessively glancing at the doors and windows, wondering if she should go over and talk to him. That was definite progress.

Now if she could just turn her thoughts to the fractured life she'd left in the city and figure out a way to fix that, she'd be batting a thousand.

She was contemplating another berry juice when a woman in the crowd waved at her and hurried over. It only took a moment for Sabrina to recognize Geraldine Roland from the wedding.

"Well, this is a surprise," Geraldine said, "I thought all you young people would still be sleeping off the wedding."

Sabrina grinned. "It's good to see you again so soon."

"I never miss the market. They have the best eggs. I won't tolerate eggs from anywhere else."

Sabrina tried not to laugh. But she was really delighted to see Geraldine again. They'd had several really nice conversations last night. "Where's Harold? Doesn't he like the market?"

"He loves it of course! He's arguing with Ken Nunez about the price of his strawberries. He loves nothing better than haggling. So does Ken." She sat on the bench next to Sabrina and shaded her eyes as she looked out over the stands. She was wearing a pair of oversized sunglasses, but the shading gesture seemed automatic. "They'll be at it for half an hour."

She smiled at Sabrina again. "And how about you? You enjoy the market?"

"It's my first time here, but it's lovely." Sabrina raised the remaining chunk of her cookie. "Especially the baked goods."

"You young people and your metabolisms. Oh to have a fast metabolism again." She patted Sabrina's arm, but before Sabrina could respond, she said, "And where's that handsome architect of yours? I don't see him. Doesn't like the market, does he?"

Sabrina froze. Shit. She hadn't considered she might have to answer questions about her and Nick after the wedding. Hadn't thought what might happen if she ran into some of the guests she'd met. But she obviously couldn't say she had no idea what Nick was doing because she was actively avoiding him. Geraldine thought he was her boyfriend. For the sake of Nick's career and reputation she had better keep up the charade.

"He had some work to do this morning," Sabrina said, attempting to sound casual as she cleared her throat and tried not to choke on her cookie.

"On a Sunday? He's very dedicated, isn't he?"

"Oh, he is. Very much. Comes with freelancing. No regular hours." She scrambled to recover from her shock, hoping the words coming out of her mouth made sense. Yesterday, she'd gone into the situation knowing it was an act and prepared to play that role. But this conversation had caught her completely off guard. She really hoped Geraldine didn't hear the panic tightening her throat.

"Do you freelance as well?" Geraldine asked, appearing oblivious to Sabrina's discomfort. Thankfully!

Only she'd managed to bring up the other topic Sabrina wasn't prepared to answer questions about. "I'm…in between situations. I was working for a company in Manhattan. But I'm considering a change to freelance."

Was she? She hadn't actually thought about it seriously before this very moment. Did she want to try freelancing? Having control of her career sounded nice. No more Darrens to deal with. No more bosses who didn't support her. No more "there's no I in team" bullshit. But the risks...

She wasn't even sure she wanted to remain in interior design.

"Well, you let me know what you decide," Geraldine said. "I need someone who can do the interior for the center we're building, and I love supporting young business people."

"Thank you," Sabrina said, meaning that on several levels. The potential job was probably just Geraldine being nice. Still, Sabrina appreciated the thought. But even more than that, the fact that Geraldine didn't ask *why* Sabrina left her last job was a huge relief, and she was grateful Geraldine didn't push for that answer.

"How did you and your handsome man manage with you working in Manhattan?" Geraldine asked.

"It's not that far away," Sabrina said, forcing a smile. "And sometimes he had to be in the city for work. I could come out for the weekends." Boy, was she spinning a tale now. She had no idea how people managed a relationship living that far away. It wasn't like living across the country or anything. Not even living in a different state. It really wasn't *that* far. A few hours drive, depending on the traffic. She came out here to visit Tabby, and when they weren't visiting in person, they talked all the time.

But that was her friend. She and Tabby could go for weeks or months without seeing each other in person and it didn't do a damned thing to their friendship. But with a romantic relationship... Well, what was the point of one if you didn't see the person regularly? Shouldn't you want to be with the person you were romantically involved with a lot?

Maybe?

She'd never even considered a relationship where you spent a lot of time away from the person you loved. That wasn't the image of "relationship" she'd tried to cultivate in the past. Could something like that even work? Maybe it did for some people. But she wasn't sure it was something she could do.

Except she'd just told Geraldine that's what she and Nick did, so she better pretend she was that kind of person now.

"Sounds a little hard on a relationship," Geraldine said, giving her knee a pat. "But you young people do all kinds of things that would never have occurred to my generation. Or more likely most of us wouldn't have followed through with those ideas so easily. The young people tell me polyamorous relationships aren't as taboo as they used to be." She winked, as if confiding a secret. "I have to say, though, from my perspective, being married nearly fifty years, that sounds like a lot of work."

Sabrina grinned, trying hard not to bark out a laugh. "I haven't tried it, so I wouldn't know."

"Well, you seem happy enough with that handsome architect. He seems like a keeper."

"Nick is a good man."

And she was pretty sure she was telling the truth. He wouldn't have offered to help her with the Darren stuff if he wasn't. Tabby said he was. After spending most of yesterday with him, watching him with other people, Sabrina was inclined to agree.

But him being a good man, a nice man, didn't solve the problem of her wanting to jump into bed with him, knowing that their idea of "future" wasn't the same.

She should probably talk to him about that.

She really really didn't want to talk to him about that, though. Not after one fake-date and a very hot kiss. Talking to him about whether he did relationships or not after *one* kiss seemed super presumptuous and also rushing things and maybe even reading more into the kiss than was there. With the distance between them, it was easier for her to believe she'd blown the whole thing out of proportion. That she'd read more into that kiss than was there.

Something she, unfortunately, did a lot.

Geraldine brought her back to the conversation with her next comment. "I wish Anya would find a good man. She's had such a tough time."

"Anya," Sabrina said carefully. "Sister of the bride, right?"

"You met her yesterday?"

"I did."

"She's a beautiful girl, like Bianca, but…" Geraldine waved a hand in the air. "Less of a people person, shall we say. A little more brusque. Not that that makes her any less lovely. She's a very sweet girl. Just not her sister."

"You said she'd had a tough time lately?" Would that explain why she kept coming after Nick? Explain some of the underlying strangeness of the interactions she'd witnessed between Nick and Anya?

"Oh yes. Something about her sister's wedding has really upset her. Probably not having a relationship herself. You know how sisters can be. Very competitive. I was that way with my own sister. Though I married better than she did." Geraldine flashed a smug smile that spoke volumes for the sibling rivalry she had going with her sister. "Always has been a lot of competitiveness between Bianca and Anya," she continued. "I think the wedding just made things worse. Put a wedge between the sisters."

"Jealousy?" Sabrina asked, trying to tread lightly.

"Oh, I'm sure. They don't talk to me of course. I'm only as old as the pyramids. What would I know, right?" She pursed her lips, and Sabrina could swear she *heard* Geraldine's eye roll, even though she couldn't see it through the older woman's sunglasses. "But Anya has never warmed up to Brad, and it's strained the relationship between the girls. Eugenia even told me Anya avoids Brad. She refused to be part of Bianca's wedding party. That caused all sorts of tension." Geraldine tisked. "Such a sad situation."

"Very difficult, I imagine," Sabrina said, hoping Geraldine would continue.

Peeking into the tension between sisters leading up to the wedding was fascinating in and of itself because Sabrina was maybe a little too curious about the drama of it all. But how this all related to the difficulties Nick was having with Anya also caught her. What if the trouble between Anya and her sister and Brad-the-groom had somehow motivated Anya to go after Nick?

Or was she trying to make excuses for Anya's behavior? Find reasons for it? The reasons could be as simple as Nick was gorgeous and Anya wanted him for herself. Sabrina completely understood that feeling.

"I think Anya just wants to be married too," Geraldine said. "It's hard to be the sister who isn't married. I married second, too, so I understand. I married better of course. My sister's husband was horrible to her."

"But Bianca's husband isn't horrible, right?" Sabrina smiled as she spoke, making a joke of the question. But a part of her brain caught the idea and wondered if that had anything to do with Anya's reaction to him. Except everyone at the wedding had seemed fond of Brad. Geraldine seemed to like him. And Mr. Greene certainly considered him a good husband for his daughter. So again, maybe she was inserting drama where she didn't need to. Maybe it was as simple as Geraldine said—Anya was just jealous and wanted to be married?

Sabrina didn't quite understand that motivation. She loved being in relationships. And she wanted that forever love. But she wasn't jealous of her sibling's relationship. Her brother had been with his boyfriend for a hundred years now—or at least it felt that way—and they'd been married for the last three years, and that hadn't had any impact on Sabrina's life at all. So while objectively, she knew other people got jealous when their siblings got married, she never got that at a visceral level. Other people's relationships had nothing to do with her own future relationship.

Unless that other person's relationship was with Nick.

She almost gasped out loud at that thought. Whoa. Nick wasn't her future. And his relationships didn't matter to her own future. And wow, she had to stop doing that to herself or she was going to get hurt without Nick having to contribute to the process at all.

Back to Anya and Bianca. Easier to think about.

"Brad is a descent fellow," Geraldine said. "Maybe a little…loud for me personally. I like my quiet, friendly, laid back men." She smiled fondly and searched the crowd again. Sabrina followed her gaze to see

Harold standing at a nearby juice stand, chatting with the person behind the colorful, bottle-lined table.

Sabrina smiled too.

"But he's a descent fellow. He'll make Bianca a good husband. Good provider."

"That's exactly what Mr. Greene said." *Good provider.* Why did that sound so…cold?

Geraldine waved a hand in the air. Her large, impressive selection of jeweled rings sparkled in the bright sunshine. The giant diamond on her ring finger in particular caught the light and prismed it out into a rainbow of colors across her sunglasses.

"They'll be happy, I'm sure," Geraldine said. "Oh, to be young again."

"I don't know," Sabrina said, glancing toward Harold as Geraldine's gaze went back to him again. "You make ageless look fun."

Geraldine snorted. "You're allowed to call me old. I am. I don't go in for all that dancing around the facts language." She sat up a little straighter. "But yes, getting old with the man you love can be lots of fun." She winked.

Well. Sabrina could get behind that idea. In fact, she aspired to it. But only with her "Harold." No lesser love would do.

She tired not to let her thoughts drift back to Nick. But they did. And she wanted to groan again. She wasn't in love with him. He certainly wasn't in love with her. They'd helped each other out with work situations and had precisely one kiss. One amazingly hot and impossible to forget kiss. But still… A single kiss didn't mean future and growing old together. And she had to stop romanticizing him this way.

Maybe she was dehydrated. It was really hot out now.

"I think I need some more juice," she said. "Thirsty after those delicious cookies. Do you need anything?"

"No, no, but if you're heading to the juice stand, I'll go with you and collect my Harold. He'll talk Lorraine's ear off if we don't rescue the woman soon."

Before they parted ways, Geraldine insisted on getting Sabrina's contact information, for the center's interior design project. Sabrina gave her her cellphone number but didn't think much would come out of the exchange. Geraldine was sweet to consider her for that kind of work, but Sabrina wasn't an expert in designing interiors for neurodivergent people, many of whom required special sensory considerations. Geraldine would more likely go with someone expert in the field. And well she should. Still, it was nice of Geraldine to even consider her as an option.

Now if she could just consider what her own options were for her career.

And stop obsessing about Nick.

CHAPTER TWENTY-ONE

On the drive home, Sabrina worried over Geraldine's parting goodbye.

"Say hello to that handsome architect of yours."

Geraldine wasn't the only wedding guest who lived out in this part of the island. Sabrina, and Nick, were likely to run into more of them at random moments. And, like Geraldine, they might bring up her and Nick's supposed relationship, even in passing. Nick lived here. Word of his "relationship" might pop up in other aspects of his life, too.

They had a potential problem.

She'd assumed the charade would be a one day thing and they'd go back to just living their lives over the summer. No big deal. But he could hardly tell random wedding guests he bumped into that his "girlfriend"…wasn't. Word of that would get back to Mr. Greene. And Anya. And while Sabrina thought the Anya situation might be more complicated than they knew, having Sabrina and Nick's "relationship" revealed as an act wouldn't endear either of them to the Greenes. Which would be very bad for Nick's business and defeat the purpose of them pretending to be a couple in the first place.

She had to talk to Nick about all this.

But she was afraid to knock on his door. Afraid she'd forget why she was there and do something stupid—like try to kiss him again. She didn't want to have a conversation about the kiss. She just wanted to sort out how they should react if they bumped into people from the wedding. She didn't want to deal with him calling their kiss a mistake.

That was the crux of it all. The thing she'd been running away from all day. She didn't want him to apologize and say it was a mistake. Yes, it would be better for them both to just move on. Probably. But she didn't want to hear that from him. She didn't want to have the memory of him calling that super hot kiss a mistake mixing with her memory of the super hot kiss.

So she sat in her car in Tabby's driveway for a good ten minutes before she got out, took her purchases inside and put everything away, then stood in the hallway staring at the front door for another ten minutes, debating with herself. The dogs waited patently with her, Justin staring up at her, Princess cleaning her paws.

Finally, she pulled in a deep breath. "Put on your big girl pants and go talk to him," she told herself sternly.

Justin pushed his head into her hand so she'd scratch him.

"Right." She gave both dogs a parting scratch, then headed out, walking around the short hedge that separated her driveway from Nick's and up to his front door.

She realized as she raised her hand to knock, she'd never seen the inside of his house before. In fact, she'd never been to his front door before. Her stomach did a funny tightening dance thing that made her regret that second large juice she'd picked up at the farmers market. Or maybe it was that cookie she'd shoved into her face before leaving the market?

Waiting for Nick to answer the door took several seconds longer than she had anticipated and her imagination went wild in those few moments, creating all kinds of reasons he wasn't answering the door— from him not being home, a mild reason, to him having a girl in there and he was naked and had to get dressed before he answered, a much less likely but much more painful scenario—none of which helped calm her nerves.

Why was she so nervous?

She pressed a hand to her stomach, debated whether to knock again or just leave, then heard the lock click. She pulled in a deep breath as the door swung open.

Nick filled the doorframe and her brain short circuited. He looked gorgeous, as always, all warm male, dark hair curling around his neck in a way that made her want to run her fingers into the strands to test the thickness. He was wearing a t-shirt, nothing fancy, but it drew her attention to the muscles in his shoulders and arms, and sparked a sensory memory of having his arms around her. Her knees went a little weak. His dark eyes were narrowed and his hands were shoved in the pockets of his cargo shorts. His jaw was tight, like he was clenching his teeth.

That wasn't good.

Guess she wasn't the only one feeling the next day tension.

Yet he looked so amazingly yummy, even tense, she didn't know what to do with herself. She wished her long summer skirt had pockets —all skirts should have pockets, damn it!—because she wanted to do what he was doing and shove her hands in some handy pockets to keep from reaching for him.

No, not his pockets, Sabrina. That would defeat the purpose.

When she could find words again, which took long enough it was a little embarrassing, she said, "I think we might have a problem."

Because if she didn't say something and get this conversation going, she was going to do something ridiculous, like turn around and run away. Or maybe push him against the wall and kiss him again. Close call. Could go either way.

He opened his mouth, she watched his shoulders hunch, and she just *knew* he was going to bring up last night, so she rushed in before he could and said, "I ran into Geraldine Roland at the farmers market. She was the bride's godmother, sat in front of us at the wedding?"

Nick frowned a little and nodded.

She realized he hadn't spoken yet. That was good. His voice did funny things to her and she needed to get this out.

"Anyway, she casually brought up our 'relationship' while we were talking. Just…asked where you were, that kind of thing. And I realized that we might run into more of the people we met last night that think we're a couple. We should…talk about that. How do you want to handle it? Because it's not like we can tell people we aren't really a couple. That will defeat the purpose of the whole thing, right? And word will reach the Greenes. So, yeah, we should talk about how we want to deal with this."

She pressed her lips together so she'd stop talking. She was rambling, not even sure she was making sense, and having a hard time concentrating as she looked at him. She let her gaze move away from him, trying to look at anything but him, so she could think enough to have this discussion.

He still smelled faintly of whatever soap or aftershave or whatever he'd used yesterday, and she just wanted to sink her face against his neck and breathe him in. And she was not going to do that. But she really wanted to do that.

Nick cleared his throat. "You should probably come in."

"If I'm not bothering you," she said, her heartbeat hammering. "We can talk about this later if you're busy. Just…we need to talk about it at some point. But doesn't have to be right now." She winced. More rambling. Way to look like a grownup, Sabrina.

He stepped to the side and gestured her into his house. "I'm not busy. We can talk now."

About the way they'd handle their "fake relationship" with wedding guests. Only that. Not the kiss. They were not going to discuss the kiss.

They weren't going to repeat the kiss either.

Her hormones had other ideas about that last part when she brushed past him as she stepped inside. He was so close, so warm and solid and…close.

She pulled in a sharp breath. Mistake. More of his scent. Was she blushing? She felt all hot and antsy. It was hot out. Of course she was warm. Didn't explain her need to fidget, though. She needed pockets. Skirts should always have pockets. Something to do with her hands that didn't involve putting them on Nick. Which was what she really wanted to do.

She tried to focus on his house instead of him. He was an architect. Had he designed the place or just taken what was here? It was a nice house, as much as she could pay attention to it. Open and airy. Hard wood floors. Walls painted a cool pale blue in the hallway by the door. Couple of rooms in the front she didn't look at too closely. A big, airy open living room at the back of the house. She spotted a gallery-style kitchen to the left. And the glorious view of the Atlantic through the wall of windows at the back of the house was truly impressive.

But most of the details went past her. She was much much too aware of the man walking behind her, and the way her heartbeat was hammering.

He offered her a seat on a large L-shaped sectional couch that faced a huge flat-screen TV hung on the wall. No fireplace here, like at Tabby's, she noticed. Probably good. Fireplaces gave her romantic thoughts. She was having enough lusty ones as it was. She didn't need pretend romance as well.

He cleared his throat. "Want something to drink?"

"I'm good. I overdid the juice at the farmers market."

His smile flashed briefly. She shoved her hands under her thighs to keep them to herself. For a long moment, he hovered at the side of the couch, and then finally sat, but he sat on the farthest end from her, the short part of the L-shape. She sat at the opposite end of the long part of the L-shape. All that space between them was good. She knew it was. She didn't like it. But she knew the distance was good.

"So," she said. "Problem with wedding guests. Since I assume you don't want word reaching the Greenes that we lied about being a couple, how do you want to handle things? I mean, I suppose it'll only be an issue over the summer while I'm still out here. Or when I come to visit Tabby. Otherwise, I doubt I'll ever see any of the guests, right? And then you can tell them anything you want. Whatever works for you and keeps things calm with the Greenes. But, I should have a story for when I run into people and they ask about you, right? I mean, I managed with Geraldine, but I almost froze, almost said something wrong. Don't want to risk that again. Right? So..." She pressed her lips together.

Lot of rambling going on here. She needed to stop that. Her nerves were probably obvious enough as is, she didn't need to make things worse by rambling. Except she'd already rambled a lot. Couldn't take it back now.

"I hadn't considered the fact that we'd run into the guests outside of the wedding," he said, frowning. "Sorry to have put you in that situation. I don't want you to have to keep lying."

"It's fine." She tried to go for a casual, we-are-friends-and-this-is-what-you-do-for-friends attitude. She hoped she succeeded because she wasn't having "just friends" thoughts and it was hard to focus. She wanted to crawl across the couch and climb onto his lap and just…

Nope. Not going to finish those thoughts. Concentrate. Geraldine. Farmers market. Potential business disaster for him. That's the *only* reason she was here right now.

"Still, when I suggested all this, I only thought it would be a day," he continued, scowling fully now. "One day out of your life. I didn't think it would turn into a full summer project."

A niggling, shaky part of herself wondered if he was also referring to the kiss. To that momentary indulgence. Was that also only supposed to be one night and not a full "summer project."

Of course it was, Sabrina! she scolded herself. That part of the night wasn't supposed to have happened at all. Which meant of course it wasn't supposed to happen again. Definitely not for an entire summer. Certainly not *beyond* the summer.

"I don't mind," she said, clearing her throat. Why did her voice sound so breathy? That was weird. "Really. I don't mind playing along for the duration if it'll keep you on the Greenes' good side. Well, everyone's good side but Anya of course. Oh, wait, Geraldine talked about that a little too. She said there was a lot of drama—my word, not hers—leading up to the wedding. That Anya had never warmed to Brad, and there had been some fighting of some kind. That Anya refused to be a part of the wedding party. The tension could have something to do with the way she acted with you at the wedding, right? I mean, there *was* more going on there. Not just her hitting on you, but something else, right?" She winced. She was saying "right" a lot.

He stared at the coffee table that rested inside the L of the couch, a rustic, sturdy-looking piece she might have noticed and admired sooner if she could keep her mind off Nick for more than twenty seconds. Actually, she hadn't had her mind off wanting him for even twenty seconds since walking up his driveway. She really needed to get her mind off wanting him. If she didn't, she was going to do something stupid soon. Like that earlier idea of crawling onto his lap, pulling that t-shirt off over his head, leaning in and…

Nope. Nope. Nope. Bad Sabrina. Sit. Stay.

She wondered if Justin and Princess found those commands as difficult to follow as she was finding them in that moment. Poor dogs.

"She did say something about the wedding being the emergency," he said quietly.

"Right?" She bit her tongue at using that word *again*. Really, she had a bigger vocabulary than this. "That was a strange thing to say."

"Yeah."

"Geraldine just thought she wanted to be married too. A sibling rivalry thing."

"And she thought I'd be her future groom?"

Sabrina shrugged. "Maybe?"

"We never had anything but a work relationship. Why would she think that?"

"You'd have to ask her. But I got the impression from Geraldine you were in the middle of something more complicated than just Anya thinking you're hot." She winced again. She'd put a little too much emphasis on the "you're hot" part of that sentence. Because he was. And she was getting distracted again.

She shifted on the couch and tried to find something better to do with her hands than sit on them. Except the better thing that crossed her mind was putting her hands on Nick. Which she wasn't going to do. So she sat on her hands again. She probably looked like an idiot.

He nodded a little, but vaguely, as if he was deep in thought and not listening closely to what she'd just said. Probably good. She wasn't entirely sure what she was saying made sense since her brain was trying to carry on this conversation while at the same time fantasizing about stripping him naked and fucking him on the couch. Hard to concentrate with those images running through her mind.

After a moment, he met her gaze and his sigh sounded pained. "You're…nervous here," he said. "I made you uncomfortable last night. The kiss…"

"Nope. Don't have to talk about that. We're good. I'm good." She forced a smile. "Not uncomfortable at all."

Well, she was, but not for the reason he seemed to assume.

His gaze narrowed. "You're fidgeting like you want to bolt for the door."

"No, no. Not why I'm fidgeting. Not fidgeting." She was totally fidgeting. "I'm fine. No need to talk about it. Everything is good."

"You're sure…"

"Good. All good. We're good."

"Diego said you'd want to talk about it," he murmured.

"Diego?"

"My best friend."

Something in her softened in a dangerous way. "You talked to your best friend about me?"

"Called him to talk about baseball," he said, his tone a grumble.

"But ended up talking about…me?"

Was that good or bad? One of the first things she did was call Tabby to talk. She'd *had* to talk to someone about the kiss. Had he felt the same way? Or did it just slip casually into his otherwise sports-related conversation? And how did she ask that without sounding needy and too hopeful?

He fell silent for a long moment, but this time staring at her instead of the coffee table. Finally, he said, "I don't want you to…get the wrong idea."

"I don't. Didn't. I'm fine. We're fine. Momentary thing. No problem. No need to discuss it." *Please don't say it was a mistake. Please don't say it was a mistake. Please don't say it was a mistake.*

"Just… I feel like an ass now because you're so obviously upset about it."

"Not upset. I promise." That was most definitely not what this was.

"Sabrina, you're practically jumping out of your skin in your hurry to leave. I never meant to make you uncomfortable. I shouldn't have—"

"Stop. Don't say it. If you apologize, I'll scream." Wow. She hadn't intended to say that out loud. Well, in now. "We were both involved last night. I'm not jumpy because I want to leave."

"Really?" His voice dripped with sarcasm and that tone just made her teeth clench. "Then why can't you sit still?"

Argh! "Because I can barely stay away from you. I want to get closer. Not run away, you ass." She sucked in a breath. Shit. Had she really just said that out loud? Damn damn damn damn.

She closed her eyes and dropped her head forward. Well hell. Way to give herself away.

What had she just done?

"Sorry," she said, her eyes still closed and her head down. "Sorry. I didn't mean to…"

"No." His voice was a hard hiss that had her looking up at him again, even as she flushed. "Don't you dare. Don't apologize either. Just… Don't."

She swallowed. "I know… I know you don't…" Don't what Sabrina? What was she going to say? "I know you weren't interested in me before the wedding, and that was just a momentary thing, probably brought on by all the wedding atmosphere?" Did she really just say that out loud? "And that wasn't why I agreed to go to the wedding with you. I swear. I hadn't meant to…" She rolled her eyes. "I'd intended on keeping my crush to myself, so I wouldn't make you uncomfortable. So maybe I'm the one who got carried away by all the wedding atmosphere. But I swear I really had just meant to help you and not… put you into a situation you don't…want."

That was one of the most difficult things she'd ever forced herself to say out loud. Even harder than her confrontation with her boss over Darren. She felt vulnerable now, an exposed nerve just waiting for the wrong word to set off a cascade of pain. But she couldn't regret the words. She couldn't have him thinking he'd done something wrong kissing her. She couldn't bear the thought that he thought *she* was the injured party here.

"We were both fully involved in that kiss," he said, his voice very deep now.

"Yes." There hadn't been any ambiguity. They'd both wanted that in that moment.

"What makes you think it wasn't something I wanted, then?"

She waved a hand in the air, unable to meet his gaze. "You'd never been interested in me before last night. Makes sense it was just the night in it. Not a mistake." Never that, even if this conversation did hurt to have now. "But not exactly something you would have wanted to happen."

"You're wrong about that, you know."

"About which part?" She glanced at him from the corner of her eye. "You think it was a mistake?" She didn't want to hear him agree with that. She really really didn't want to hear him say the kiss was a mistake.

"No. I don't think it was a mistake. But you're wrong about my interest before last night."

"Meaning?"

"Meaning… I've wanted you since the first time we met."

She sucked in a sharp breath. Her head felt a little floaty and her heartbeat hammered so hard she was sure he could hear it.

"I thought I was the one keeping my un-returned interest to myself. Not the other way around."

She blinked. "You didn't think I was interested in you?"

He nodded.

"I was kind of obvious."

"You weren't. You were very good at hiding your interest."

She wasn't sure whether to preen under the compliment or wince at the misunderstanding. "You weren't obvious either. You've mostly avoided me these last few years."

"Self-preservation."

She nodded. She got that. She'd been avoiding him out of self-preservation, too. Thinking she'd get hurt if he knew she wanted him, because he didn't return the feelings.

Except…

This whole time, he did?

"Well fuck," she muttered.

"What?"

"We've wasted a lot of time."

Chapter Twenty-Two

Sabrina rose from her spot on the couch and finally gave in to the impulse that had had her sitting on her hands. She didn't exactly sit on Nick's lap—tempting as that was—but she did sit down next to him, facing him and holding his gaze.

He held very very still. But he didn't move away from her.

"If I kiss you right now, will you be upset?" she asked.

"No." His voice had gone even deeper, a little rough.

The sound caressed her spine and her stomach danced in response. "I've wanted to kiss you for a long time," she murmured. "And I was afraid you'd say last night was a mistake."

"It might have been," he said, without looking away from her.

"Why?"

"Not sure I'll be able to stop now."

"Stop kissing?"

"And more."

"I like more."

His nostrils flared and he pulled in a deep, slow breath. "You sure about this? Could be…complicated."

"Could also be fucking fantastic," she whispered, her gaze dropping to his mouth.

His low growl went right to her pussy. Her body coiled, tightening in anticipation. She wasn't sure who leaned in first, him or her, but they met halfway.

No gentle teasing this time, though. No exploration. They came together in an explosion of need that swept her up so fast she was breathless. And didn't care. She tasted him, devoured him, sank into his scent and heat. Lust chased away all thought of regret, or consequences, or complications. She wanted him so bad she could barely stand it. And knowing that feeling was returned was a kind of power, a kind of relief that only fed her lust.

She wrapped her arms around his neck and sank into him, crawling up over his lap without hesitance. He cupped her ass, pulling her close, and she ground against him, delighted by his groan, the way his hands tightened on her. He ran one hand up into her hair, loosening the band that kept it up in a ponytail until she felt the band give. Her hair spilled around their faces, and in the heat and darkness created, they were surrounded by the scent of her shampoo and his soap, whatever it was, and that only fed her hunger.

He cupped her head, threading his fingers into her hair, cradling her gently even as his fingers flexed and tightened. He squeezed her ass with his other hand, and she moaned in to his mouth. When he pulled his mouth away from hers to kiss her jaw, her neck, she sighed. Closed her eyes, filled herself with sensation. Shivered when he hit a sensitive spot. Gasped when he bit gently on that spot. Moaned when he sucked that spot. She rubbed into him, grinding against the solid wall of his chest. Delighting in the thick press of his cock against her lower stomach.

"Too many clothes," she muttered as he pushed aside her tank top strap and bra strap at once to kiss her shoulder.

"Agree," he said against her skin. "Way too many clothes."

She glanced past him at the wall of windows. There was some privacy provided by the rolling dunes and grass at the edge of his property, but people on the beach could still see in if they paused in just the right spot and bothered to look.

A very surprising part of her didn't actually care. She wanted him naked now and wasn't particularly concerned with an audience. In fact, the thought turned her on a little more—which was a complete surprise to her. She hadn't had exhibitionist tendencies with previous relationships. But she was so impatient, so desperate, everything else seemed a lot less important than stripping off the last of their clothes and getting to finally explore him.

He pulled back from kissing her neck to glance at the wall of windows too. "Upstairs?"

His voice was gravely and rough and she just wanted to live in that sound. "If you insist." Though she didn't want to get off his lap.

His chuckle traveled through her chest and thighs. She tightened around him, trying to relieve some of the pressure that was building. It didn't help. She needed his hands on her. His mouth. Now.

"Condoms are upstairs," he said, moving her hair aside to nibble at the delicate part of her neck again, at a spot where her jaw and throat met.

She groaned. "Important point. Good point." She wasn't sure if she was making sense. She couldn't really think. All her attention was focused on the feel of his lips on her skin and the heat and hardness of his cock between her legs. "Too many clothes," she grumbled again.

He tightened his hold on her, his fingers digging into her ass, and then he loosened his grip and patted her hip. "Up. Upstairs."

She slid off him, her knees wobbling a little as she stood up. He caught her up in another kiss that did nothing to help her knees but went a long way toward making her forget her own name.

He walked her backward, around the coffee table, guiding her and half lifting her as they stumbled through the living room to a set of stairs she hadn't noticed coming in. She barely noticed them now except as an obstacle they had to maneuver while continuing to kiss and caress. She couldn't take her hands off him, though, so she stumbled up the stairs awkwardly, running her fingers up under his t-shirt to feel his heat and the slick slide of his skin. His muscles bunched and flexed beneath her fingertips.

She kicked off her sandals as they went, the sounds of them thumping down the stairs a vague reminder they could fall if they weren't careful. She didn't really care. She tugged at his shirt and pushed it up high enough she could get her hands more fully onto his skin. He pulled back enough to sweep the t-shirt off over his head and toss it aside. She approved, wrapping herself around him again, soaking up all his heat and resenting her own shirt and bra still irritatingly in the way. She slid one hand around his neck and ran her other hand up his chest, her fingers caressing through his chest hair. His heart hammered against her palm.

They somehow managed to reach the landing without tripping or falling back down the stairs, and once there, Nick paused and pulled her in so close their bodies were pressed together thigh to chest. Ah, she loved that. So hot and hard. She forgot where they'd been going and just sank into him, kissing him like it was more important than breathing.

In the midst of that kiss, she somehow lost her bra. It was on. Then it wasn't and his hands were up under her tank top, cupping her bare breasts, and her thighs clenched so tight she thought she might come just from having his fingers pinching her nipples. Still didn't want the shirt in the way. She was a little desperate to feel her sensitive nipples rubbing against his chest hair. But taking the shirt off would mean breaking the kiss and she wasn't ready just yet. In a minute. She'd pull back enough to get rid of this last bit of material in a minute.

She ground against him. And in a sweeping move that left her a little dizzy, he spun her up against a nearby wall and leaned into her. So hard. So close. She groaned and wrapped one leg up over his hip. Her skirt was too long, the material got in the way, but it was also loose and flowy and that meant it didn't prevent her from wrapping him up in a one-legged hug. One of his hands moved from her breasts to her hip, curving back over her ass, urging her even closer.

They were up here for a reason, weren't they? They'd braved the stairs obstacle for… Bedroom! Bed. Condoms. Naked.

Yes. Naked sounded right. Perfect.

"We need to be naked," she muttered against his mouth before sinking into the kiss again.

"God, yes," he breathed. His hands tightened on her, squeezing, and she was pretty sure her legs wouldn't hold her up much longer.

Abruptly, he pulled back, leaving her reeling forward and dizzily disoriented. For a terrifying heartbeat, she thought he was going to stop and say this was a mistake. Instead, he took her hand and fast walked to an open door. She sighed in relief when she saw the big bed in the middle of the room. That was about all she paid attention to, though, because he'd spun her around into a kiss again and she was only too happy to sink back into the bliss of having his mouth on hers.

She bumped against the bed, not entirely sure how they'd gotten that far into the room, and gasped and giggled at the same time when they both tumbled onto the mattress together. His weight on her was delicious. But she still had her tank top on and it was in the way. She wiggled the shirt off over her head. She barely had the material past her hands when his mouth closed over her nipple. She arched up under him, moaning. Ah, yes. Finally. Finally. The wet warmth, the hard suck, the brief rough bite. She finished freeing her hands from her shirt and wove her fingers into his hair so she could hold him just there. The rub of his chest hair against her abdomen added an extra layer of delicious friction that left her breathless and desperate.

He left her breast, his mouth traveling along her stomach and she released her hold on his hair so she could help him slide her skirt and panties off. Everything went in a rush of material and desperate hands. And then she was naked beneath him and so happy with that state of affairs she could have burst.

He was still wearing his shorts. Those needed to go. Soon. But since his mouth was now at her hip bone, his tongue sliding down the slop of her lower abdomen, his breath brushing her wet curls... She forgot everything else. Just...everything went out of her head except the sensation as his tongue flicked against her clit, gently, his fingers spreading her as he licked into her. Then he gripped her thighs, his broad shoulders pushing her wider open. She felt his gaze on her, but her own eyes had closed. She didn't remember doing that. Only that her entire being was focused on sensation, on his mouth hovering over her pussy, the heat of his breath, the way his fingers dug into her thighs, the way her lower body clenched in anticipation and of his next touch.

Breathless. She was panting. She didn't care. More. She wanted more and more and more, and she was too breathless to speak, but she still nudged her hips up, reaching for him, begging without words.

He didn't make her wait. His mouth closed over her, he licked into her, his tongue finding her swollen clit like the bright little beacon of joyous, overwhelming sensation it was, and he sucked and licked until her entire body wound so tight, so high, so fever pitched, that when she came, she actually screamed—or close to it. The sound was strangled by the overwhelming release, the quake of coming ripping through her body.

She jumped when he gave her a final lick and had to force him up because she was so oversensitive now she could barely stand it. That wouldn't last long, she wanted him inside her too much to wait, but she needed a minute.

"Just a minute," she muttered. How much of this was she saying aloud? She couldn't remember. Her brain had definitely taken a vacation and left her body doing its thing all on its own. Which was fine. Her body was *very* happy with what it was doing.

Nick kissed his way over her neck, then kissed her mouth, gently, languidly. Like they had all the time in the world. She wasn't sure she did. Her minute was almost up and she was feeling desperate again. But she sank into his kiss because there was nowhere else she wanted to be. Right here. In his arms. Tasting herself on his mouth as they kissed and he held her close and her body rippled with the aftereffects of her orgasm.

"You still have your shorts on," she murmured, pushing at the top of his pants. She'd almost forgotten they hadn't managed to remove all the barriers yet. Something about being fully naked, and one orgasm in, while he still had some of his clothes on was...surprisingly sexy. But she wanted him naked now. "These have to go."

He grinned down at her. A grin that made something in her chest swell and shot her through with pleasure. She wasn't going to think about that too closely since it felt a little too much like her heart getting involved. No no, heart. Not this time. This was just sex. Epically spectacular sexy times, but not…anything else.

She shut her brain down again—which wasn't as difficult as she might have thought because he rose enough to shuck off the rest of his clothes. And having Nick finally *finally* naked in a bed next to her was the only thing she wanted to think about.

She ran her hands over his warm skin, down his chest, down farther. His stomach muscles clenched as she got lower and she loved listening to his sharp gasping breath as she brushed her fingers against the top of his cock. And what a lovely cock it was, thick and hard and just right. Perfect. She wrapped her fingers around him, watching his face as she did, watching his eyes close and his jaw clench tighter. Watching the color rise in his cheeks as she stroked, slowly, hard, using the moisture beading at the tip of his cock to smooth her strokes.

All of it. This moment. She wanted to memorize this moment. She wasn't sure she'd get many of these with him. If she were lucky, maybe the rest of the summer. But this could be it. And she wanted this to last and last. She took his cock into her mouth, wanting to taste him, watching his reaction. His sharp hiss, the way his breathing sped, made her smile. She ran her tongue down his length, pulled him deep into her mouth, gentle gentle strokes, licks, one hard suck… She didn't want to make him come like this, so she didn't play too long. But she enjoyed making him tremble.

When she lifted away, crawling up the length of him to kiss him, his arms came around her hard and so solid and warm. His heat seeped into her. His kiss was fierce, hers a little frantic, and her heartbeat hammered knowing she'd brought him to this. Knowing they'd got here together.

She didn't try to help him with the condom. Her hands were shaking more than his and she was afraid she'd push his hands aside to take him into her mouth again. She was desperate for all of him, now, at once. Which left her too overwhelmed by all the things she wanted from him, with him.

Feeling him finally, finally slide into her, though… Ah, that was a homecoming. Friction and heat. He felt so good. So right. She let that thought fleet through her mind unexamined as she settled around him, under him, meeting him stroke for stroke as her body wound tight again. For as long as she was able, she kept her eyes open, watching his face, watching him watch her. She'd never seen anything sexier than the darkening of his eyes, the tight clench of his jaw. She cupped his face in her hands, kissing him when she couldn't keep her eyes open anymore. And then there was nothing but the feeling coiling in her core, the heat and pressure building, the delicious slapping of skin against skin as he moved harder, faster, and she went higher and higher.

She had to drag her mouth from his as her orgasm broke over her again, shattering and glorious and shivery sensations rolling through her. She might have called his name in the end, she wasn't entirely sure. She just knew this was him. For him. With him.

Only him.

His orgasm hit as she was still feeling hers race through her. And that was perfect, too.

For long moments, only his breathing and hers filled the room, pants and gasps as they both came back down. He held her close, she wrapped around him. Her limbs were weak and shaky, but she needed her arms around him, needed to hold this moment close for as long as possible.

As her breathing slowed, the heat in the small room finally got past her addled thinking. She was sweaty, and not just from the sex. She glanced up and realized he had a ceiling fan light in the room, but the light was off and the fan was still. Another wall of windows would probably give another spectacular view of the Atlantic, but the shades inside the windows were lowered, which had plunged the bedroom into a soft light, just enough glowed through the shades to see by but dark enough to feel intimate. Their own personal cave of sex.

She grinned at that image, kissing him on the shoulder because she could.

"I need a shower now," he muttered into her hair.

She chuckled. "Me too."

"Join me?"

Well, that was an offer she couldn't refuse.

Her brain wanted to start working again, start thinking again. But she wasn't ready to have this bubble of wonderful sensation and satisfaction end yet. So she stood on shaky legs and let him lead her to the attached bathroom, and she enjoyed the sight of him naked in the muted light, and she refused to think yet. Not yet. Just a little bit longer to enjoy the bliss of this moment.

She could always think tomorrow.

Chapter Twenty-Three

Nick couldn't remember the last time he'd felt this good after sex. Not just sated and satisfied, but…content. No restlessness to get up and go back to other things. No need to just shut down and go to sleep. Although he was sated enough now he could take a nap. So long as Sabrina was with him.

When more of his blood flow reached his brain, he'd probably worry about that a little. Right now, he didn't care.

Watching her reaching into his shower, still naked, her ass perfectly displayed, he couldn't begin to care about anything else. There was a part of him that barely believed she was here, like this, and that this moment wasn't just some fevered dream he'd concocted after the kiss. It wasn't like he *hadn't* considered just this scenario before. Living out the reality was infinitely better, though.

He cleaned up the condom and himself, listening to her hum as she got the shower to the right temperature.

"This water pressure is fantastic," she said, her voice echoing off the tall, tiled walls inside the shower stall. "My apartment has crap water pressure. It's like standing under a dripping fossette on the worst days."

"Nothing your landlord or super can do?"

He turned, leaning against the counter next to the sink to watch her. He liked this view a lot. And even though he wouldn't be getting hard again for a bit thanks to the epic orgasm he'd just had, he still felt a surprising amount of heat watching her get *their* shower ready. Enough he thought he might manage to get hard sooner than expected. Made him feel a bit like a horny teenager again. He didn't mind.

She looked back at him over her shoulder and rolled her eyes. "All I hear is it's a building issue, old pipes, have to replace them all, too expensive, need an assessment, et cetera. Lot of excuses. No fixes."

"You could move?"

"And give up my rent-controlled place a block away from a subway station? Ha. Never."

For some reason, that hit him wrong. Why? He wasn't sure. Why did he care that she wasn't interested in giving up her apartment? Weird.

He came up behind her, and she leaned back into him when he wrapped his arms around her stomach. There. That was better. No thinking needed.

"Although," she said, "I might have to move if I can't figure out what to do about work. I'd hate that."

She sounded so sad, and he hated *that*. He was about to offer a platitude, which wouldn't have helped, when she patted his hand and said, "Sorry. Not the moment for that stuff, huh?"

She grinned at him over her shoulder again, and his brain lost what little blood it had regained for thinking. All that blood rushed right back down to his cock. Not hard yet, but hell if he might not be again soon.

Steam puffed out of the hot shower. "Not too warm for that?" He nodded to the steam.

"You want a cold shower?" she asked, raising her brows as she turned in his arms to full face him.

He might need one, but, "No. It's just a hot evening. I'm surprised you don't want the water a little cooler." They'd worked up quite a sweat. He needed to remember to turn on the overhead fan. Maybe open a window to let the breeze in. They might scare the neighbors—

she wasn't quiet when she came and he loved that so much—but the breeze would feel good.

"Even in the middle of summer I hate cold or cool showers. If it's too hot for you, though, I can turn the temperature down." She was still grinning, so it was hard for him to think straight.

"I'm good. Whatever makes you happy." He meant that. On more levels than he cared to consider. But to prove it, he edged her back inside the shower. "We're wasting water."

"Offset by taking our showers together," she murmured, her eyelids lowering a little as she looked up at him.

He closed the shower door behind him, letting the darker interior of the stall encompass them. He'd tiled the shower in dark blue and hadn't installed lights inside the stall because he liked a cave-like feel for his shower.

Liked it even better with Sabrina in there with him.

The warm wash of water over his back as he held her, the water slicking down over and between them, felt like a little bit of heaven. Her dark eyes glittered in the shadowed shower-cave. He tightened his hold on her, pressing her so tight, he felt her breathing in his bones. Yeah. He could live like this.

She rose on her toes for a kiss he was happy to return, long and languid and lazy this time. Hot enough with her wet naked body sliding against his he felt his cock stir again. Once all that blood reached his brain later, he'd be a little amazed at what she did to him. Right now, no chance he could manage coherent thought.

Right now, all he wanted was her.

AFTER, THEY MADE THEIR WAY BACK TO THE BED AND COLLAPSED IN A heap, still damp from the shower, the wetness on his skin a cool contrast to the warm room. Nick was so loose-limbed and relaxed now, everything felt perfect and right and he didn't want anything to change.

He pulled Sabrina close, hoping to hold off reality a little longer. Or the outside world reality anyway. He could keep this reality, of having Sabrina in his bed, forever.

But there was a world outside this room, unfortunately. And she had a best friend in it who had very specifically warned him *not* to do this.

"Tabby is going to kill me," he murmured, his head resting on Sabrina's shoulder.

Except, he hadn't been alone in getting them here. Sabrina wanted him, too. Had wanted him for as long as he'd wanted her. He still hadn't quite gotten over that truth.

"I won't let her," Sabrina said, her voice quiet and content, "don't worry."

She drew lazy patterns over his back with her fingertips, which was soothing.

"Might not have a choice," he murmured.

"Why?"

"She told me if I ever…made a move on you she'd kill me. I think this qualifies."

"Na. I made the move on you."

He lifted his head to see her grinning, which had the duel effect of making him exceptionally happy and also ruining his ability to think again. He was starting not to mind so much. "Mutual moves were made, how about that?"

"Agree." She chuckled.

He liked that too because they were so close he felt the laugh vibrating from her body to his and that was a sensation he could get used to.

"Don't worry about Tabby," she said. "She's just a little overprotective. Had to watch me go through a few breakups, as friends do." She shrugged. "And she knows me and men. Maybe a little too well. But don't worry."

"About Tabby killing me or that there are men in the world dumb enough to break up with you?" Luckily for him, or he wouldn't be here with her. But he still considered those other men pretty fucking stupid. Having Sabrina, being able to hold her and kiss her at will, and then letting that go…? Stupid.

Another delicious chuckle that made her lush curves bounce. Mmm. That was distracting. In a good way.

"About Tabby killing you. I won't let her. I promise."

"I'd appreciate that." He felt like he had a lot to live for at the moment.

"I appreciate your comment on my exs. Although, to be fair, I'm still friends with two of them. Nice men. We just…ran out of steam. Know what I mean?"

He did, actually. That's how most of his relationships ended, when he somehow managed to find himself roped into one. Some of those ends were a little more acrimonious than others, but all of them happened because his need for time alone ended up building walls between him and anyone he was seeing. And in the end, they were too distant to bother trying to maintain a relationship. He'd never really minded that before. But Sabrina sounded a little sad and resigned when she talked about it.

"Not meant to be," she continued with a little sigh. "That kind of thing. I'm afraid I have a problem…requiring relationships." She winced. "But don't worry," and now she was rushing to get words out. "You don't have to worry about that here. Tabby told me you don't like them. I'm not trying to force you into anything. I promise. This is great. And we have a summer for more of this if you're still interested, because I am, by the way. But I promise, I'm leaving at the end of the summer. So you won't have to worry. Tabby won't kill you. And wow, I can't quite believe I said all that out loud after one evening of sex."

Her cheeks were a bright red now, which he might have found amusing and delightful if her words weren't hitting him like boulders and making him progressively angrier.

Except… She was right. He didn't like being in relationships. He didn't do them well. Never had. Was always relieved at breakups. And lived out here so he could avoid having people in the middle of his life all the time. Why was her acknowledging that pissing him off so much? It was only the truth.

"To be fair," she said, "I've usually had the 'relationship' conversation before sex." The bright pink color in her cheeks wasn't fading. "But again, no need for you to worry. I get it. I'll be heading back to the city at the end of the summer, and we can call this a happy summer fling. No problem. Casual is just fine with me."

What made her think it was fine with him?

What made him think he *wasn't* fine with casual when he'd always preferred that before?

Tabby knew that about him. It was the reason she'd warned him off Sabrina. And he couldn't blame her. He'd tried to keep his hands to himself for the same reason. Neither of them wanted Sabrina hurt.

But now all of that seemed…upside down. Wrong-headed. He wasn't sure why. Just that every time Sabrina talked about leaving, he got annoyed. Irritated. Even a little angry. But because he wasn't sure *why* he was angry at the thought of her leaving, he kept that part to himself. He'd have to unpack that more when he wasn't lying in bed naked with her naked next to him.

If he had any say in the matter, she'd remain naked in bed next to him for so long he'd forget why this conversation was irritating him so much. That wasn't practical. They had to eat eventually. But he could pretend.

Until her stomach rumbled.

She gasped, put a hand to her stomach, and laughed all at the same time. "Guess all this exercise has left me a little hungry." She rolled to face him, snuggling close and wrapping her arms around his neck. "Want to order take out?" Her eyebrows rose and she hurriedly said, "Or would you prefer I leave now?"

"Take out," he said firmly, tightening his hold on her. And never leave.

But he didn't say that last out loud either.

Because the fact that he'd even thought those words left him reeling.

CHAPTER TWENTY-FOUR

Sabrina spent the next few weeks deliriously happy and absolutely not thinking about the future. She didn't want to think about the future. The future of her career, the future of her life, but most importantly, she didn't want to think about the summer ending. She didn't want to think about that moment when she'd have to say goodbye to Nick and know that was the end of...

Whatever this was.

No. No labels. Just enjoyment and fun and some of the best sex of her life and that was all she was going to think about.

She didn't push spending time with him. She had lots to finish in Tabby's renovations and was pretty busy with that most days, doing work she enjoyed. She kept her music up and sang and danced while she worked. She wanted him to know he had space, and she understood exactly what this...not-a-relationship was—that it was Not A Relationship—so he could relax, too.

He surprised her, though, by making an appearance every evening without fail. Sometimes even as early as the late afternoon. Either with bags of take away or an invitation to go to dinner with him. Sometimes for a walk on the beach with the dogs. Most of the time he texted ahead of arriving. Once, he just showed up and surprised her. But he was there at her door. Every night.

She'd sort of assumed after the first week, that pattern would fall by the wayside as he got back into his normal life and routines. But no. Throughout the second week he arrived every night, too. They'd have dinner, talk, walk the dogs, sit on the deck watching the ocean, talk some more, and invariably end up stumbling up the stairs to her bedroom, stripping clothes off as they went.

That part…well, she couldn't get enough of him. Some days, they barely got to the takeout bags because he'd show up at the front door looking all delicious and sexy and fresh from a shower, smelling more delectable than the food, and she'd drag him up to bed without waiting to eat. After the first time they'd done that and the dogs ate the food out of the bags Nick dropped on the floor in the entryway, though, they usually took enough time to put the food up on the hallway table before stumbling up the stairs. Justin could still reach the bags there, but he knew better than to drag them down. She had a feeling Princess wouldn't have been so reticent if she'd been the taller dog.

Outside of the sex, though, she was, for some reason, surprised at how much they talked. Especially about the little things. Daily life. His current project, and the one he was bidding for. Her progress on Tabby's second floor, the work she was going to do in the guest bedroom once she was finished in the other rooms. They talked about Tabby's book tour, and his friend Diego's family, and baseball, and some of their favorite restaurants in the city. She told him stories about the rich people she'd worked for, some of the houses and apartments she'd decorated, the work she'd done at a women's shelter two years ago. He told her about some of his favorite constructions, working on updating an old library on the Upper West Side, returning it to its former glory, a historic building in Harlem he'd helped repurpose for a community center.

They talked about nonsense, like the plethora of local gossip she picked up just going to the farmers markets and grocery stores, and which summer TV shows caught their interest, or which upcoming movies might be fun to see.

And they discussed more serious topics. Like his job with the Greenes and how he hadn't heard much from them since the wedding, even though the work was proceeding. He hadn't seen Anya since the wedding, which they both counted as probably good news. Secretly, Sabrina would have liked to know what had really been happening there, but she kept that to herself. They touched on her issue with Darren still calling, but those conversations made Nick so mad, she usually changed the subject.

They did not talk about what she intended to do at the end of the summer. They did not talk about the end of the summer at all.

But the rest of it was like…the sorts of things a couple talked about. The sorts of things a real couple did.

By the end of the third week—after they'd spent every single night together, mostly at her place but sometimes at his, and neither of them had left to return to their respective homes until morning when it was time for work—Sabrina was having a lot of trouble not thinking of this…whatever it was, as a relationship. The Not-A-Relationship label frayed at the edges and the writing got pretty blurry.

She was getting a little too comfortable with his weight in the bed next to her, and sleeping curled up against his side, and the way his scent was the first thing she noticed when she woke up in the morning —unless he was awake before her and woke her up with his hands and mouth. She noticed that first. Then she'd notice his yummy scent surrounding her. She got that tummy tightening shot of giddiness when she knew he was on his way over. And she savored the quiet conversations they had in the dark, either in bed or sitting on the deck late at night.

It all felt so… So right. So comfortable. That she kept forgetting it was only for the summer.

Which was a big problem because she'd promised him she wouldn't make that mistake. She'd promised Tabby she wouldn't confuse this with a relationship. She'd promised herself she wouldn't get herself hurt by getting emotionally involved in this summer fling.

And she was a little afraid she'd lied to all three of them.

But she refused to let that fear get in the way of her fun. Being with

Nick was *fun*. She could deal with the emotional fall out later, without either Nick or Tabby needing to know she'd gotten in too deep. She'd only have to acknowledge the lies she told to herself. And she didn't have to even face those lies until fall.

So she didn't deny herself time with Nick, as much time as he'd give her, but she also didn't push for more. She was a little surprised by how well this worked…for her as well as Nick. She didn't worry about him, about having to adjust herself to fit his schedule, about giving things up so she could give him all her time. It was freeing, knowing he didn't expect her around ever moment of every day. The fact that he preferred time alone gave her the freedom to go about her life, doing all the fun summer stuff she'd intended, and still having nights of amazing sex and conversation.

By the fourth week, she realized she very much liked this…Not-A-Relationship way of doing things. She didn't feel stifled even a little bit. It wasn't the picture she'd always had of a relationship, of what a relationship was supposed to be. Not at all like what her father had now with his wife. She'd always assumed that was the perfect way to be as a couple, what was *required* of being a couple. But… Well, she enjoyed the freedom of what she had with Nick a lot more than she had any of the relationships she'd tried to make fit into that perfect-couple mold. If she ever found an actual relationship that worked this way, she might just feel like she'd hit a jackpot of some kind.

The fact that she only wanted that "relationship" with Nick wasn't lost on her. She just chose not to think about it too closely.

The beginning of that fourth week, they were out at a local restaurant Tabby had recommended, reluctantly, to Sabrina, and they ran into Geraldine and Harold Roland. This time, Sabrina didn't choke on her own words or worry about the older couple finding out she and Nick weren't actually an item. They were out together. On something that looked like a date. They were sleeping together, spending almost every night together. Outside of the fact that they weren't, in fact, in a relationship, they could do a very realistic job of pretending they were since they were doing most of the things couples did.

And that wasn't lost on her either.

Geraldine brought up the design work for her charity again. It was a bit shocking to realize how much time had passed without her giving her future career much consideration. She'd pushed thoughts of that future to the backburner as deliberately as she'd pushed thoughts of a future without Nick to the backburner. Things to worry about later.

But the summer was half over. They were coming into August soon. Tabby got back from Europe at the end of August. Sabrina was going to have to face her future, one way or the other, soon.

Since she didn't want to think about the Nick part of all that, she agreed to call Geraldine the next day and discuss the project. It wasn't her specialty, she'd have to do a lot of research, but the more she thought about it over dinner, the more she thought she might enjoy the challenge. Something very different to the work she'd done before. The differences might make doing the work less painful, less of a reminder of what she'd lost.

She noticed she didn't feel the sting quite so badly when Geraldine brought it up. The hurt and anger weren't as breath-stealingly sharp. Progress. She'd take it.

"So you'll do the job?" Nick asked when they were in his car driving back home from the restaurant. "I wasn't sure you wanted to keep doing interior design."

She shrugged, leaning her head back against the headrest. "I wasn't sure I wanted to either. But it'll be a challenge. Geraldine seems like she'd be fun to work with." That earned her a snort from Nick. "And the work is so different... I don't know. Maybe it'll feel different. Maybe it'll lead me into a whole new field." She sighed. "Or maybe it'll confirm I can't... I don't want to do this work anymore."

"What happens if you discover it's that last thing?"

"I'll have to figure out what else I want to do, then, won't I?"

"Any thoughts?"

"Not a one," she said, sounding more despondent than she'd meant to. She had loved her work so so much. Always. She couldn't quite imagine giving it up altogether.

"You could always buy up old houses and flip them," he said, attempting to make his tone light. "You've been doing a great job with Tabby's house."

She chuckled because he was trying to help and because having him to talk to about this stuff did help. "I'd need capital and more interest in ripping out the guts of a house and building from the ground up. I'm less interested in that angle."

"You could do what Tabby wants to do, go for a reality TV show on interior design for one of the cable networks."

Now her laugh was genuine and loud. "Right. Because that sort of thing lands in my lap every day? Besides, I'm not already a superstar like Tabby. She has a chance at that cooking show. I'm a no one who doesn't have the kind of connections needed for that."

"I'd lay out real cash money Geraldine does, though," Nick said, glancing at her before focusing on the road again. "If it's something you want, I'd be willing to bet that woman would know someone who knows someone who could help. Probably another of her godchildren." He huffed out a little laugh. "The Greenes weren't the only ones at that wedding with influence and connections."

Huh. He was probably right about that. "I'm not really the TV show type," she said. "That's Tabby's thing. I don't have the temperament."

But it was an interesting point that Geraldine would have connections to make things happen. Maybe… Maybe if Sabrina did enjoy the work on the charity building, if she did a good job, Geraldine would be able to point her toward other charities that needed similar sorts of work done.

The *if* she did a good job part of that hung heavy on her shoulders. Her confidence had taken a hit at her last job. It wobbled when she considered putting pressure on her design skills again.

She went right back to wanting to hide in the sand and not think about it. She was out with a gorgeous man, looking forward to getting home and getting him naked. Not the time to think about her future.

Except she was running out of time. She really couldn't keep hiding from these decisions forever.

* * *

THE NEXT DAY, WHILE NICK WAS BACK AT HIS HOME WORKING, SHE took a break from hiding in the work on Tabby's second floor to do a little research. She went down a rabbit hole of design options for people with sensitivity issues and how to accommodate a range of elements into the interior of the center that would suit people across the spectrum of neurodiversity.

And she had fun with the research. She enjoyed the challenge, the new things she learned, the questions raised. She hadn't seen the layout for Geraldine's center so she didn't know what she'd have to work with, but she had *ideas*. Things she'd like to try. She had more questions. She felt the challenge of it rolling through her blood.

By the time the dogs reminded her it was lunch time—because they were very good at not letting her forget about food times, especially Justin; he might be skinny, but he ate like a small horse—she had a legal pad full of ideas, sketches, options, resources, more things she needed to check, sites with pictures of possibilities, a starter list of experts who were neurodivergent who she could potentially consult, and she was starting on to a second legal pad.

She hadn't felt this good about work in…probably a couple of years, she realized. Two, maybe three years since she felt so challenged and excited. She wasn't even officially working on the project with Geraldine. There was a board of directors she'd have to get through to be officially hired. But that didn't stop her excitement and enthusiasm.

Even if she didn't get this work, she realized she'd *enjoy* doing similar things. She just needed someone to give her a start.

She called Geraldine after lunch and asked if they could talk more about the project, let her know she'd been doing research and had some ideas she thought could really work. Geraldine's enthusiasm left Sabrina feeling a little overwhelmed, but in a good way. The way that made her feel valued for her skills—even if Geraldine hadn't seen those skills in action yet.

That feeling of having others appreciate what she could do… She'd missed that. More than she realized.

She was still flying on that high when Nick came over that evening with a pizza and a six pack of beer.

"I'm going to do it," she said, letting him in and kissing him soundly on the cheek because his hands were full and she didn't want to upend the delicious smelling pizza by throwing herself into his arms. She took the beer as she led him to the kitchen. "I'm going to try for the job for Geraldine."

"Sabrina that's great!"

He set the pizza down and drew her into a huge hug that made her smile and sigh, and that dangerous feeling in her chest made itself known, but she ignored it. She was too happy to worry about that right now.

He pulled back to look into her face. "Are you excited? Happy? When do you meet with the board? What's next? Do you know how long the project should take? Do you need help putting the proposal together?"

She laughed. "Stop! I don't know the answer to most of those questions yet. I'm meeting with Geraldine tomorrow to talk more. I am excited and very happy. I'll have to work the rest out as we go. Yes, I may need help with putting the proposal together since I've never done one as a freelancer."

She'd put proposals together for jobs before, of course, but always with the backing of an entire firm and with a lot of help and support. The fact that Nick realized this and offered to help without her even having to ask filled her with a giddy sort of delight. And it further softened that suspiciously soft feeling in the center of her, that emotion she wasn't going to look at. Sometime before the end of the summer, she'd have to acknowledge that feeling, if only to herself. But not yet. And definitely not tonight.

"This is now officially a celebration," she said. "And you even brought the pizza and beer!"

He kissed her, a kiss with so much delightful enthusiasm and heat she melted against him. It was on the tip of her tongue to suggest the pizza and beer could wait, when her cellphone rang.

She was so excited about this new adventure, so buzzed on Nick's kiss, she didn't check the screen before she answered.

She should have checked the screen.

Chapter Twenty-Five

"We lost the job," Darren said without preamble. "And it's all your fault."

Sabrina's mood took a decidedly less delighted turn from just moments before. She wished she hadn't answered the phone and could go back to the kissing Nick part of her evening.

"Can't talk. Don't care. Not my fault." She hung up before Darren could say more. Hearing his voice for even those two sentences had been more than enough. But the damage to her mood was done. She sighed and set the phone onto the kitchen counter next to the pizza box.

"What? Who was that?" Nick said, his scowl dark and ominous. Before she could do more than sigh again, he said, "That Darren creep? What did he say?"

"That they lost the multi-million-dollar project he couldn't manage after I left, and apparently, it's my fault."

Nick growled. A sound that went very well with his snarl. And for reasons that made no sense at all, but also a lot of sense, his fierce expression made her want to hug and kiss him again. And that soft feeling in her chest got a little bit bigger.

"That guy has some nerve," Nick said, his voice deep.

"Yes. He always did. Maybe my boss will see I was the one carrying Darren for the last few years, finally. My ex-boss."

His scowl turned more contemplative, less like he wanted to punch a wall, but he still looked snarly when he asked, "If your boss fired Darren and offered you your job back, would you take it?"

She hadn't even considered that as a possibility. Not once since this started. It seemed…very unlikely. Knowing Darren, she'd just assumed he'd find a way to talk himself out of any hole he dug for himself—blame someone else, like he was doing with her, spin the whole thing into some kind of positive, somehow worm his way out of the shit until he ended up smelling like a rose. He was good at that. Did that all the time. So it had never crossed her mind he wouldn't find a way out of this that left him still fully employed and still seen as an essential part of the company.

"It never occurred to me to consider that an option," she said out loud.

"Consider it now. He might get fired for all this."

She chuckled without much humor and took out some plates for the pizza. "I doubt it. He might not be as good at design and managing big projects as I am, but he's a genius at wiggling out of trouble and making himself seem like the only one who can fix things."

Another growl from Nick. This one did make her smile.

"I've worked with that kind of guy before," Nick said after a moment. "Pain in the ass to deal with."

"An understatement." She set the plates next to the pizza box, then opened the lid. Yummy melty cheese, pepperoni, and mushrooms. The good kind of mushrooms too, done so the edges were a little crispy. "This is amazingly good pizza. I didn't expect the pizza to be as good out here as it is at my neighborhood place."

"We're still New Yorkers. We take our pizza seriously."

"Because Tabby lives out here, I assume everything is fancy and gourmet, I guess. I keep expecting…I don't know. Goat cheese and some weird fruit Tabby would have to explain to me."

He snorted. "Who would do that to a pizza?"

She raised her nose in the air and affected a snooty expression. "Chefs, darling. Chefs!"

Her tone broke his scowl, and he gave her a reluctant smile as they took their plates and bottles of beer out to the deck. She purposefully left her phone back on the kitchen counter so she wouldn't have to hear it ring again and wouldn't have to see Darren's name pop up on the screen. She'd been tempted a few times to change his name to something rude, just so she'd be able to laugh when he tried to call her. But in the end, that felt like too much effort for someone she didn't want to deal with ever again. She only kept him in her contacts now, and didn't block a number for him which she could easily identify, so she'd know it was him calling and could avoid his calls.

The dogs followed them out onto the deck, but settled a few feet away, laying down to watch and wait. They'd both learned early on that with pizza they'd have to be patient for their sneaky bite of pepperoni. And for Justin mushrooms because he was a dog who apparently liked his vegetables.

Nick's expression returned to a scowl as they settled at the glass top deck table. "You distracted me with pizza talk."

"I was distracting myself."

"You don't want to talk about this? I'll let it go."

"No. I'm just still in avoidance mode. And I'd rather talk about the potential project for Geraldine's charity." She shrugged, took a bite of pizza and savored for a moment before continuing. "But to answer your question, no, I don't think I'd go back. I quit because my boss refused to support me, to have my back. I doubt that would change, even without Darren in the mix."

"You quit?" His brows raised. "I thought you were fired."

"Didn't give them the chance." She looked out over the rolling Atlantic, wishing she could recapture her earlier good mood. "Final straw. A meeting where Darren, once again, took credit for my ideas, my design work, work the client adored. The whole reason we got that particular job. I gave them something both gorgeous and practical."

She glanced at him. "This was for a series of restaurants—

expensive, fancy ones strung through Manhattan. Each one had to be unique, to make it a destination spot. There was a lot of money involved, a few celebrity chefs. I talked a lot with Tabby about the job, what she'd want, how to make a unique design that would also be practical for both staff and guests. You'd be surprised how few designers think about the practical side, how the waitstaff will navigate the table arrangement, or how the décor around the kitchen door can cause trouble. Especially with these trendy places. They want the flash. The ability to say there's no other restaurant like ours anywhere in the city—which is a tough ask, given it's Manhattan. And sometimes the designers get carried away and forget unique still has to be functional. I can do both."

She raised her chin a little, as if she'd have to defend that assertion. She'd had to before. Knowing her own worth, her own value and skill set, had taken her years. Getting past the idea that each success was just luck had taken time. But she knew her worth now. She knew she was damned good at her job.

"Anyway," she said after a sip of beer, "I came up with five unique designs, not just one, but five, that were also practical. And Darren took credit for them. And my ex-boss let him. When I tried to stand up for myself at the meeting where this was happening, I got the usual, and infuriating, 'there's no I in team' speech. I quit on the spot. Told them they could try to make my ideas work without me." She let out a snort that was maybe a little too petty, but her ex-boss and Darren both deserved it. "And they had no idea how to pull it off. Darren didn't anyway. He didn't even understand what I'd done, only that it was impressive and he wanted credit for it."

"I hate this guy more and more with every passing sentence."

"He got what he deserved. In over his head and out the big client." She huffed out a sigh. "Unfortunately, I doubt it'll cost him his career. Probably not even his job. He'll find a way out of it." She scowled now. "He'll probably say my designs were flawed. The ass." She looked Nick in the eyes and said, "My designs were perfect. Every detail. They're the reason the client hired us."

"I believe you. I'd prefer not to believe Darren will keep his job, but…" He snarled. "Those kind of guys always dodge consequences, don't they?"

"They do. And it sucks. But I'm going to move on to better things and let him try to wiggle out of this problem on his own."

"Good for you." Nick raised his beer to her. "And good for you for being strong enough to quit. I'm not sure I would have in the same circumstances."

"You would have. You wouldn't have let assholes treat you that way." She was certain of that. Nick wasn't the kind to tolerate assholes lightly.

He shrugged. "Early in my career? I might have. I was hungry and the assholes were plenty. To reach my level, I had to deal with a lot of crap."

"Then you went freelance and left it all behind."

"I needed…a different surrounding. Freelance was more of a necessity to get me out of the city. To give me time alone. I can be more flexible, and deal only with clients I want to deal with, if I work for myself."

She thought about Anya, and the Greenes, and his efforts to ensure he didn't lose them as clients. "Are you really free to pick who you want? Or does the money win out over the choice?"

He held her gaze and she wanted to fidget, to take back the comment. A lot of people didn't like to talk about money. But if she was seriously going to consider this path, this option of…being her own boss, she needed to talk it through with someone doing the work. He was doing the work.

Still, she opened her mouth to take back the question. Yes, they were fucking. And they spent almost every night together. And he understood some of her issue. But they weren't a couple, and this might be a step too far.

"Depends on the client," he said before she could speak. "It'll always depend on the client and the money and what you need most at any given moment for your job. Sometimes, you'll work for clients you like less because the money is good."

She realized Tabby did that, too. Catered for people she didn't like much because they paid her a lot and it was a step toward a bigger goal.

"But you'll also take on clients you *want* to work with even though the money isn't great," he continued. "The two things will balance out. And you'll have a choice in that balance." He shrugged. "I found, working in a bigger organization, that they always defaulted to the money jobs. And the more personal stuff, the stuff I might have wanted to do for other reasons, was dismissed as not 'worth company time.'" He huffed out a breath. "I hated that phrase." He met her gaze. "I haven't even told Diego this, but it was that phrase that was the last straw for me. Company time. Bothered me a lot."

"You're not a company, you're a human being," she said with little shrug. "And your time is more important than any company's time. Makes perfect sense to me."

And she recognized the sort of culture he was talking about. She'd had some of that at her last job, though they had let her take on smaller projects for the prestige element. They'd even encouraged her to do that. One of the reasons she had, until Darren, enjoyed working for that company. But having her leaders choose Darren over her... Yes, she'd been the one to quit and leave, but they'd driven her to it by letting her know where she stood in their opinion—and it wasn't high.

Sounded like Nick had gone through something similar.

"I told Diego, told everyone, my reason for moving out here was to get away from other people." He smiled a little. "That's true on some level. I really do prefer...need less time around people."

She wanted to ask if he thought she was crowding him but kept her mouth shut. This wasn't about them, and she didn't want to derail the conversation to make it about them.

"It's not that I don't like people. They're just...overwhelming sometimes. I like quiet. Need it, I guess." He stared down at his pizza, not looking at her. "Not sure I'll ever like being constantly surrounded by people again. At least not for long periods of time. Not every day."

"That's fair enough," she said because it seemed like he was waiting for her to say something.

"But…that wasn't the only thing that drove me freelance. I just didn't want to discuss the rest."

"You don't have to now." She leaned forward, resting her elbows on the table on either side of her pizza plate—which was mostly empty now except the few pieces of pepperoni she'd saved for the dogs. "We can move on to talking about something silly and unimportant."

He smiled and her heartbeat thudded a little harder. "In a minute, but I want you to know you're not alone. And that it's good, you leaving a bad situation. For a long time after I quit, I thought… I felt a little guilty. Like I'd given up a good thing for no real reason. My reasons were real. They were important. To me. But at first, I didn't fully believe that."

She felt every word in her gut, like he'd cracked open her brain and seen the things she was trying not to look at. Exposing her inner most fears even as she'd been trying to hide from them herself.

She felt guilty that the firm had lost the multi-million-dollar contract, even though they deserved to have. She felt guilty she hadn't helped Darren, even though he didn't deserve her help. Sometimes— not always, but sometimes when she was up in the middle of the night thinking too much—she felt like *she'd* been in the wrong to leave. That she was being vain, looking for praise and head pats. That she was being unrealistic, expecting people to see her value.

That last was the hardest fear to face and the one she shoved aside the most. It felt like she was being disloyal to herself on some level. She *was* really. She wasn't in the wrong to expect her colleagues to see and acknowledge her efforts and her value to the work. She *earned* their respect. And if they couldn't give that to her, she shouldn't be to blame for leaving a bad situation.

But in those moments in the middle of the night with her inner most thoughts, she didn't always see that logic.

And here Nick was, speaking directly to those fears. The fear of jumping off a cliff and taking on a task she wasn't sure she'd be able to succeed at. Doing something for herself that was hard. The easy way out was to try and get another job, with another company, and hope her ex-boss didn't spread negative things about her to the companies she applied to. But easy wasn't necessarily the *right* answer.

"Becoming my own boss scares me," she murmured. "All the responsibility. The risk of failure…" She picked at the label on her beer bottle. "What if I'm not good enough?"

"What if you are?"

Those quiet words hit. Hard. What if she was good enough? What if she could do this?

What if she succeeded?

"Lot to think about," she said.

"You've got time. The summer isn't over yet."

But it would be sooner rather than later. And that hung over them, too. She held his gaze for a long, quiet moment. Was he thinking the same thing? That they'd be over when the summer ended? Did that…bother him?

No. Stop, Sabrina. She'd promised herself not to get too involved. This was a summer fling. She could do a summer fling. She'd promised Tabby she wouldn't let herself get hurt. That she could be with Nick this way and not end up devastated when she left at the end of the summer.

She wasn't entirely certain she could keep that promise. But the least she could do was pretend to, for Nick's sake as much as for Tabby's. He'd said it himself, he was out here to be away from people. She didn't want to force him into something he didn't want. And she wouldn't. They had another month. That would be good enough.

It had to be.

CHAPTER TWENTY-SIX

Nick paced his house, glancing at the clock on his cable box every few minutes on his circuit through the living room. He had promised himself he wouldn't go to Sabrina until at least five every day. That he would spend the day working, and doing his usual thing, and not running over there the instant the idea occurred to him.

Which happened at least four hundred and thirty-seven times a day from the moment he left her in the morning until his required five o'clock deadline. Maybe more. He'd stopped counting after the first tortuous day.

The clock insisted it was four forty. Since it had been four thirty-eight like ten minutes ago, he was sure there was something wrong with that clock. He returned to pacing.

This had been his every day for the last month. And somehow, he didn't hate it. Well, he hated the waiting when he finished work early or when he got too distracted thinking about her and had to put the work away. That last should probably bother him more. And probably would if not for the clock in his head ticking down to the end of summer. That beating pulse that kept reminding him they were in August now. Sabrina left at the end of August.

He'd told himself that was likely why he couldn't seem to get enough time with her. That it was all down to the fact that they only had the summer, and he hated to waste any of that time. This couldn't continue into the fall. He knew that. Sabrina knew that.

In fact, she seemed content with it.

And no, that wasn't driving him a little crazy. Not at all. Not even a little bit.

She was giving him exactly what he'd wanted. What he *always* wanted with a woman. Space to be on his own and do his own thing, and then occasional company that ended with sex. Mind blowing sex. Best sex of his life. Okay, that last was purely a Sabrina thing. But the point was, she wasn't asking questions about their future. Wasn't insisting he tell her "where all this was going." She wasn't texting him forty-seven times a day. She didn't "drop by" with surprise lunches, or spontaneous "vacations," or any other sort of surprise that would just piss him off.

At least, those surprises had always pissed him off in the past. The disruption to his day. The assumption that he didn't have things to do. Or that he could just drop everything because someone else wanted him to. He hated surprises. He didn't have time for unplanned lunches and certainly not for that spontaneous trip to the Keyes one of his exs had tried to demand. Sabrina never forced her way into his day like that—at least physically—and didn't try to usurp his plans without consulting him. Not even once. She stayed away all day long, and never even texted him, and let him do his own thing until he was ready for them to spend time together.

He loved that. Of course he did. Loved it. It was perfect. Who needed texts all day long just to check in? See what someone else was doing. Find out if the new grout was working or how the tiling was going or if she'd talked to Geraldine or…

He glanced at the clock again. Four forty-eight. He went back to pacing.

Okay, maybe he wouldn't have *minded* a spontaneous lunch or two. He had to eat, right. So did she. That wouldn't throw his day off too much, just having lunch with her once in a while. And if that lunch led to sex… Well, he could always work a little later in the afternoon, make up for the time. Except then he would miss his self-imposed five o'clock time to go over to her. Wouldn't want to do that. He'd be able to make up anything the next day, then.

He paused in his pacing. What the hell was he talking about? She wasn't going to come over with lunch and an afternoon of sex because she knew *he* wouldn't want that. And he didn't. Of course he didn't. Would throw his whole week off. That would just irritate him.

Well, not the sex part. That part never irritated him. Left him exhausted. Spent. Delighted. Not irritated. The irritating part always happened when he had to get up and leave. Or when she left. He didn't like that part at all.

His cellphone rang and he pounced on it, jerking it from his back pocket to check the caller.

He scowled a little at the bite of disappointment when he saw Diego's name on the screen. He ignored it and answered the phone. "What's up?"

"How's things going with Sabrina?"

"Why the hell are you calling and asking me that at…" He checked the clock. "Four fifty on a Thursday? Don't you have work?"

"Took the week off. Staycation with the family. And Jessy wanted me to call and ask how things were going. I told her you'd be working and hated being disturbed. She insisted."

Nick grunted. He did hate being disturbed while he was working. Diego was absolutely right. He didn't point out he had, in fact, not been working because he'd been pacing the house waiting to go over to Sabrina's.

"Your wife is nosey," he said.

"Yup. So how are things going?"

"Great. Fine. No problems."

"Then why do you sound so tense? She start asking all the 'where is this going' questions you hate? Is she trying to plan how you'll keep seeing each other after the summer?" A little pause, and then, "She hasn't committed you to a spontaneous trip to a tropical island without asking first, has she?"

"No. None of that. Not even once."

"Is she bringing up the end of the summer? What you'll do after?"

"No. Hasn't even mentioned it."

"Not once."

"Not once."

"That should make you happy."

"Delighted."

"Then why do you sound so pissed off?"

"I'm not." He heard the snap and bite in his voice. Cursed in his head. "It's work. It's nothing."

"Uh huh." There was a long pause. "What are you up to tonight?"

"Heading over to have dinner with Sabrina soon." In exactly seven minutes. But who was counting?

"Cool. Cool. She insist on that?"

"No, of course not." In fact, she never mentioned it. She'd ask if he wanted to have dinner maybe twice in the last month. Most of the time, he just showed up with food or an invitation to dinner. And if she was in the middle of working, he went out and brought dinner back so she could finish what she was doing.

He stopped pacing when he realized what he'd been doing. Then shook off the slight twinge of…something and went back to pacing. Five more minutes.

"So… Everything is good then," Diego said slowly.

"Perfect," he snapped. Why was he snapping? He looked at the clock again. Four minutes. "I have to go."

"Okay. Before you go, a buddy's got a couple spare tickets to the Mets on Sunday. You free?"

Nick glanced at the clock again. "No. Sorry."

"Busy, huh. With work."

Nick opened his mouth and nothing came out. He was turning down Mets tickets for…no real reason. He didn't have plans on Sunday. He didn't work Sundays if he could avoid it, and there was no reason he couldn't avoid work this Sunday. He didn't have any immediate deadlines. In fact, he was in between deadlines. The Greene construction was on schedule. He'd turned in another proposal for more work just that morning. His next build wasn't starting for a few weeks, and the clients had already signed off on the final plans. There was nothing keeping him from going to the Mets with Diego on Sunday.

Except, if he went, he'd miss an entire day with Sabrina. And they only had a month left.

He didn't lie to Diego without good reason, though—tried never to about important things. Yet he was reluctant to tell him he'd rather stay out here with Sabrina because they had so little time. Why? He wasn't sure. He just didn't want to talk about it.

"Got plans already," he hedged. It wasn't a lie, exactly.

"With Sabrina?"

"Yes." Sort of. They hadn't technically made plans yet. But they would, right? Probably tonight. When he went over there in…two more minutes.

"Fair enough. I guess with only a month left…"

Nick scowled at the phone but didn't respond to that baited sentence.

Diego waited him out for another moment that felt longer than it was—because Nick still had a full minute before he could leave for Sabrina's and that didn't go any faster—then said, "Okay, then. Well, glad everything is going well. I'll let Jessy know. She'll be relieved for you."

"Great. Tell her I said hi."

"Will do."

He said his goodbyes and hung up before Diego started asking more questions Nick didn't want to answer.

He snatched up his keys and headed for the door.

Questions could wait.

CHAPTER TWENTY-SEVEN

When Sabrina opened the door for him, her gaze was turned inward, her expression distant. She leaned in and kiss his cheek, but the gesture was distracted.

It was a weird sensation, that moment. The fact that she was comfortable enough with him she still kissed him even in her distraction felt good. But also his first instinct was to ask what was wrong and what she needed him to do to fix whatever was bothering her.

That last part was…probably a problem all its own.

"You okay?" he asked, because that, at least, was something anyone would do.

"Fine," she said, waving a hand vaguely. "I just got off the phone with Geraldine. We've got a meeting on Sunday, did I tell you that?"

Shit. She had. Yesterday. Which meant he could have taken Diego up on the Mets tickets. Maybe he'd call back later and do that. Or maybe not. He didn't examine why he'd rather stay out here and be at home for when her meeting ended, so they could talk about it as soon as she was back. Didn't examine that instinct even a little bit.

"You did. Still think it's an odd day for that."

She smiled a little. "Only day we could get everyone together."

"Did something go wrong?"

"No. Not at all. Just worried about the meeting, I guess. Feeling excited but in over my head." She was still frowning.

"Something else wrong?"

"Well… Geraldine called my old boss for a reference."

"Shit. How did that go?"

"He gave her a glowing one. Which… I'm still not sure how to take that."

"Why shouldn't he have given you a good recommendation? You earned one."

"Yeah, but I also left in a huff over not getting credit for my work." He scowled at her use of the word "huff" and she raised a hand. "I know, it was a justified huff, and I'm making light of it on purpose because it still hurts that they were so willing to let me go and believe Darren more valuable to the firm than I was."

He closed his mouth.

"Anyway, that's why Geraldine called. To tell me what a glowing reference my former boss had given me and how impressed the others on the board of directors for the charity were. They're surprised I'd even consider their project. I'm… I guess stunned is the best word. I'm not entirely sure how to feel right now."

"Good?" he suggested as he followed her back to the living room. Justin and Princess followed along at his heels, Justin nudging against his leg until he scratched the giant poodle's head. Princess demanded attention the instant he sat down on the couch next to Sabrina. He gave the Pekinese her own scratch as he kept most of his attention on Sabrina's face and the myriad of emotions moving over her expression.

"A little," she admitted. "Good. Flattered. Relieved. I sort of thought he'd tell Geraldine I wasn't a 'team player' and give me a bad rec."

He wanted to growl at that for some reason so he shifted his attention more to Princess as a way to soothe his irritation with Sabrina's former boss. Though he did say, "A good recommendation was the least he could do."

"He called after I got off the phone with Geraldine." She blurted this out, like she hadn't intended to say it out loud. She blinked a few times before meeting his gaze. "He called and asked me to come back to work. I… I didn't actually think he would. Ever. But he did. He offered me my old job back."

"Did he fire Darren?" He was growling. He shouldn't do that. He cleared his throat.

"I didn't ask. I was in shock that he'd called and still reeling from Geraldine telling me he'd given me a good recommendation. I'm not sure I said a whole lot on the call, to be honest."

"Did he offer a raise?" There, that sounded less snarly and pissed off. Good. So long as they weren't talking about the asshole Darren, he could have this conversation without growling. Though he didn't have many kind feelings for her ex-boss either.

"He didn't mention money. Just said I should come into the office next week so we could discuss it."

"Are you going to?"

"I… I don't know." She gave him a little helpless shrug. "I don't honestly know. I like the idea of being in control of my time and clients, being freelance like you are, but it also scares the shit out of me, and a nice corporate job with benefits sounds…safer."

"Do you want safer?" he asked, now quite seriously. "Or do you want freedom and flexibility?" His turn to raise a hand and stop her before she answered too quickly. "I'm not asking that last question to make light of safety, by the way. Some people aren't cut out to be freelance—the financial ups and downs and the uncertainty aren't for everyone. Diego couldn't have done it. So I'm not being flippant. I'm asking quite seriously, which is more important to you right now? The consistency of a regular paycheck and the structure of a company someone else runs? Or the freedom and flexibility to choose your own clients and working colleagues but with the inconsistency and uncertainty that comes with that freedom?"

She frowned a little as her gaze turned inward, contemplating his question. While she did, he studied her face. A lot of emotion went through her expression.

"I'm honestly not sure," she said after a few moments. "I never considered freelance before, so I've never thought much about it." She winced and gave him a look from the corner of her eye. "Honestly, I wasn't sure I could work for myself. So I've never considered trying. But…"

"But now you are considering it."

"Geraldine's project has really sparked my creativity, that same excitement and fear I felt when I started working. So many ideas, so many ways I could make this work, and so uncertain I'm up for the job. And, while this surprises me a lot, I like this feeling. I'm not just making a rich person's Manhattan apartment look trendy enough for a magazine spread. I'm designing something that could have real impact on people's experience of their surroundings." She shook her head. "I'm not sure I'm saying this right, but it just feels more…important than the other work I've done."

She met his gaze. "And I'm not sure I'd be able to do this kind of work at my previous firm. Not sure I'd be allowed. The charity is well-funded, and this aspect of what they're doing is really really important, vital even, to the success of a center like this. But even then, the money isn't the sort of thing that would have tempted my previous boss. It's good for me, on my own. But…"

She ran a hand over her hair, the gesture loosening her bun so it lilted to one side. "I guess what I'm saying is I'd love to do more of the work I'm doing right now, for Geraldine, but if I go back to work at my old company, I probably won't get that chance. At least not very often. Not unless there's significant prestige involved, which there isn't in this case. And I want the chance to do this kind of work."

"Then take it. Either negotiate the freedom to take on these clients with your previous boss, find a company that will let you do this kind of work, or go it alone and choose the clients you want to work with." He leaned back a little. "Actually, you have a lot of options now."

"What if I fuck up the work for Geraldine?"

His knee-jerk response was to say "You won't," but that wasn't what she needed him to say. Instead, he said, "You might and that might limit what you do next. It's always a possibility in any work, but especially in work you're passionate about. But you either take the chance, work your ass off, and do the best you can. Or you play it safe. And maybe regret that more."

"All good talk in theory," she said, but with a slight smile.

"Have you talked to Tabby about all this?"

"Haven't had a chance to."

"You don't have to make a decision right away, right?"

"No. I have time."

"Then take the time. Do the work with the charity, see how that goes first. Give yourself space to think about the rest."

"If the job offer goes away because I take too long thinking?"

"It wasn't a sincere offer, and you'd have just had to quit again."

"Why are you making so much sense?"

"Because I'm not the one having to make the decision. Easier to see things when you're on the outside."

She leaned in and gave him a kiss, soft and gently. Enough to distract him from everything they'd just been talking about. He followed her a little when she pulled back before catching himself and straightening.

"Thanks for listening," she said, her smile as soft as the kiss had been. "I came out here for the summer to think about all this stuff." Her look turned wry. "I've been a little distracted, though."

"I'm not going to apologize for that even a little bit, you know."

She chuckled. "I'm not sorry about it either. And wouldn't change anything. But I suppose I really do need to think about all this more, instead of making excuses not to think about it."

For some reason, that comment filled him with foreboding, but he ignored it. "I don't know about you, but I'm starving. Why don't we eat now, and you can contemplate the entirety of your future after? You'll be able to think better on a full stomach."

"That's not what we usually do after dinner," she said, her smile deepening as she leaned into him.

"Then you can contemplate your future tomorrow." His voice dropped. And he was suddenly a lot less hungry for food.

"Tomorrow," she agreed, and kissed him again.

He pulled her close, sinking into the kiss this time. Food could wait.

So could tomorrow.

CHAPTER TWENTY-EIGHT

They spent Saturday together, mostly in bed, and then Sabrina made Nick leave early Sunday morning. Her nerves were a tangled mess over the coming meeting and she had to focus. And with Nick around, she didn't focus. Or, well, she focused, just not on anything but him.

She had to focus on the meeting.

And that focus paid off. It went so well she could hardly believe it. The board loved her ideas. Loved the thought she'd put into her plan for the interior design of the center. They had two autistic board members who provided her with some suggestions and possible changes or things to consider, all ideas that easily integrated into what she'd already come up with. They gave her some experts to consult, so she got information directly from people who were neurodiverse. By the end of the meeting, after the back and forth about ideas and options, everyone left excited about getting started. They had the budget they needed to make it work. Sabrina knew, using some of the contacts she'd made at her last job, she could get everything done within that budget. There were, at this point, no problems.

She could hardly believe how well it had gone.

The very first thing she wanted to do, besides collapse in joy, was talk to Nick and tell him everything. She glanced at the clock on her phone. It was late afternoon. She had a half hour drive back to the house. She could call him from the car, before getting on the road, or she could just get home and go over and see him.

She really wanted to see him when she told him the news. He'd been so damned encouraging and supportive, she was certain he'd be as happy for her as she was happy for herself. Something she was really going to miss after the summer.

A worry for later, she told herself as that little ping of sadness poked through her excitement. Right now, she would savor this moment of success and happiness. No telling how long it would last—she'd never done an interior without *something* going wrong and needing fixing or changing. Life, and work, were never that straightforward and easy. But in this moment, everything was on track. Nick was still right next door for her to talk to. And the rest...could wait.

She went home first, to ensure the dogs got out for a quick break and to give them the good news. They'd had to listen to her talk all about the project and rehearse her presentation. They deserved to know it had gone well, too. Once they'd been settled with a treat, she opened her phone to send Nick a text to find out if he was free for her to come over. She didn't want to just drop in on him because, even though they were spending so much time together, she didn't like to assume he was free for her at every moment. She knew how much he valued his alone time.

A return text didn't come right away, though. Usually, he got right back to her, within a minute or two. Twenty minutes passed this time, and nothing. Part of her grew worried—was he okay? Was he hurt? Had something bad happened?—but another part acknowledged that maybe he was just busy and didn't have time to check his phone or texts yet. Maybe he was too busy to see her today and just didn't want to say it out loud.

That latter thought put the brakes on some of her headlong joy. A stark reminder that they were a temporary fling. A mutually agreed upon temporary fling at that. He didn't want a relationship. He didn't want more than what they were already doing. And she'd *promised* herself she'd accept that. No asking for more. No pushing him into corners. She was a grownup, and she'd gone in with her eyes wide open to what this was and what he could give. She refused to demand more from him than he was willing to offer.

Including his time.

As far as she knew, he might have made plans with friends or just gone out and left his phone behind to disconnect. There was no reason for him to be waiting around for news from her meeting. Especially when she hadn't known when it would be over. He was supportive and encouraging. And that had been enough—so she told herself.

When a half hour went by and she still hadn't heard from him, she called Tabby, who'd also been encouraging and supportive and *was* waiting on news. They celebrated together on video chat, Tabby insisted Sabrina pop open something with alcohol in it—she picked a beer, Tabby poured herself a glass of wine—and they toasted to her successful pitch. Then they discussed Tabby's tour, which had moved on to Vienna, a place Tabby loved so much she wanted Sabrina to start saving so they could take a trip there together. Which sounded like so much fun, Sabrina did start mentally figuring out where she could come up with and set aside the money. They talked about how Tabby's book was doing and the execs from various food-focused television stations she'd met and talked to during the Paris food festival. They talked about what Sabrina would do about her career—she'd already told Tabby about the new job offer from her ex-boss, which she hadn't responded to yet. Like Nick, Tabby had asked about pay raises and the status of Darren at the company. All things Sabrina promised to ask about before making any decisions.

After the success of her meeting with the board of directors that day, though, she was more seriously considering going it on her own. She *liked* the work she was doing for them, and while she knew thing wouldn't always go this smoothly, that *this* job might not go smoothly —they hadn't gotten started with the work yet, and she hadn't been paid yet; a lot could still go wrong—but she had had fun getting ready for the meeting and felt charged up during and after. Feelings that had been missing from her previous work for a while. She thought she might enjoy specializing in these more challenging projects in the long run. There wasn't much her old job could offer that would make up for this renewed sense of purpose. Even if they fired Darren and gave her a big raise—though she might consider it if the raise was big enough. She wasn't that committed to going freelance yet.

All of this she debated and discussed with Tabby until Tabby had to go to make one of her events—her publisher had arranged a night at the opera for her, and Tabby loved nothing better than the drama of the opera, second only to food. After they disconnected, Sabrina checked her messages again. Still nothing from Nick. It had been a couple of hours now. Long enough, her worry was rising right alongside her insecurities. There was a weird mix of hurt, sadness that maybe he was finished with their fling early and she'd have to deal with all these emotions sooner rather than later, worry that something was wrong with him or someone he loved, and anger with herself for getting so attached to the man that she was fretting about the fact that he wasn't answering her text right away.

The smart thing to do would be to stop thinking about it. To get herself and the dogs some dinner. Or maybe take a walk on the beach first to burn off some of the residual nerves and excitement and fear from the day. Actually, as she thought about the walk, she decided that sounded like a great idea. And if she just happened to check in on Nick on the way, well, that wouldn't be a bad thing. Just the kind of thing a neighbor might do.

She was halfway out the front door with the dogs on their leashes when she paused to consider if what she was doing was a little desperate.

He was a grown man who needed time alone, and he hadn't responded to her text which meant he probably didn't want company yet. If she showed up and knocked on his door now, she'd be breaking the unspoken promise between them that this summer thing was casual, and they weren't supposed to be getting feelings. If this was the city, and Nick was her ninety-year-old neighbor, and they were having a heatwave, that would be a different neighbor situation. This wasn't the city, Nick was definitely not her ninety-year-old neighbor Mrs. Lee, and they were not having a heatwave.

Walk the dogs. Do not disturb the neighbor just because you've been sleeping with him.

She still walked past the front of his house on the way to a beach access path. She could have gone out the back door and through Tabby's backyard, but she wanted to check for Nick's car and she tried not to feel too weird doing that. His car was in the driveway. So he was probably home unless he'd shared a ride somewhere with a friend. She scowled at herself, feeling a little like a stalker, checking to see if he was home. What a ninny. She wasn't supposed to be getting this involved, damned it.

Hurrying past, letting Justin and Princess pull her toward the beach access road, she tried to ignore the guilt she felt—for allowing herself to get too emotional, too deeply involved. Tabby was right about her. She couldn't do casual. She'd fucked up. Big time. And she was going to get hurt. Damn it. She'd really tried not to let this happen. But she'd probably been doomed from the start.

Note to self: listen to Tabby over own hormones in all things going forward.

As she reached the edge of Nick's property and the small sandy path that led from the road to the beach, she passed a car she hadn't seen parked in the neighborhood before. A sleek, small, older Mercedes from a time when Mercedes had distinctive character. It was a nice car, deep metallic green with light leather upholstery. Sabrina wasn't a big car person, but her brother Sam was, and he bemoaned the homogenization of all modern cars enough, she could recognize an older, more unique car when she saw one. Sam would like this one.

Something about it struck her as weird, though. It was parked at a funny angel, just at the edge of the access path, taking up most of the walkway in front of Nick's house. Probably someone who'd come to the beach for the day and had used a free space in front of the residential houses to park rather than leaving the fancy Mercedes up on the main road where they should have parked.

Sabrina shrugged it off, even though something about it made her gut a little tight for reasons she couldn't decipher.

The dogs hurried her down the path and out to the beach before she could be nosey and look inside the car—which was good. She was having enough of a stalker evening checking on Nick's car in the driveway. She didn't need to add checking out the interior of a stranger's car.

The beach was crowded still, even this late on a Sunday afternoon. She walked the dogs close to the water in the harder packed sand, letting them roam out ahead of her, but she didn't take them off leash since there were still so many people.

The salty sea air blowing through her hair, the warm beach sand between her toes, the whooshing sounds of the waves rolling in, all helped soothe out her unease and restlessness. She'd had a good business meeting, and a great chat with her best friend, and the beach, though crowded, was the perfect way to end a day. She'd go home, have a nice dinner, maybe sit on the deck to watch the darkness roll in over the area, and then she'd get a good night's sleep—hadn't had one of those in a while since she'd been staying up too late with Nick. And tomorrow, she'd finished the work in Tabby's second bathroom. Then she'd start sourcing the things she needed for the center.

There. A plan. And none of it involved the sexy neighbor who was too busy to send her a text to say he was busy. Which was fine. He didn't owe her anything. They weren't a couple. Just a summer fling.

And she was better off dealing with these hurt feelings now anyway. Another month, who knows how deep she'd have let herself get. At least she wasn't in love with him yet. That would have been a disaster.

She was tempted to return via the backyard, to avoid walking past the front of his house and checking on his car again, which still felt too stalkery. She looked up at her temporary home from the edge of the backyard fence and decided going in that way was the wise thing to do, so she did. Hey, she could be smart about this kind of thing when she wanted to be. Brushing Princess off on the deck and getting the sand out of the dogs' paws in the back was easier anyway. No errant beach sand tracked across the entryway that she'd just have to sweep up.

For reasons she couldn't name, she wanted to check on that Mercedes parked in front of Nick's house. She didn't. But she really wanted to look out the front window and see if it was still there. She had no idea why, though she tried to convince herself it was because her brother would be interested in the car. The restlessness she'd managed to walk off on the beach returned, then. So she went to the kitchen and started getting dinner ready for herself and the dogs to keep herself occupied.

She debated for a full five minutes whether she should make enough for two or not, just in case Nick came over. She checked her phone. No text. Okay. Decision made. Dinner for one.

And no feeling sorry for herself allowed.

CHAPTER TWENTY-NINE

Later, she sat on the deck, in the dark, trying not to pay attention to the empty deck next door, or the fact that there were lights on in the house but she hadn't gotten any messages from Nick, carefully drinking a soda instead of the beer she wanted because... Well, drinking the beer right now felt like a sign she was deeply hurt, and she didn't want to admit to being deeply hurt because that would definitely prove she'd messed up.

Being with Nick wasn't the mistake. She'd messed up falling—

Nope. No. Not that. Not that far. Just...a little too far, a little too hard for a casual summer fling. She'd let herself get emotional. That was all. Only a little emotional, though. Not...that.

She sipped her drink and focused on the sounds of the waves hitting the beach, the cool breeze blowing across her cheeks, the little snuffling sounds from Princess where she lay a few feet away, and Justin's less delicate snort and whine as he chased something in his dream. All the good night sounds. Things that, if she focused on them, kept her from thinking and spinning pointless stories in her head.

And she did realize all the stories she was telling herself, all the excuses and scenarios she was making up, were all in her head.

Eventually, she'd bump into Nick or he'd text, they talked, she'd stop acting like a ninny. Eventually.

Her phone, where it lay on the round glass table next to her seat, dinged with a received text message. She debated a full forty seconds whether she should even look. It was late. She was…emotional. And pouncing on the phone felt desperate. It might not even be him. Other people texted her. Darren had stopped pestering her after the job fell through, so she was pretty sure it wasn't him. And it was too late at night/early in the morning for Tabby to text. If she was even up at this hour in Vienna, it was because she was partying or doing some sort of publicity schmooze and wouldn't have time for texting.

Unless of course she'd just met royalty. Tabby would definitely text her that the instant she was able to. They'd pinky sworn to that rule.

After another moment's debate, she picked up her phone.

Nick: *Sorry I didn't get back to you earlier. Something came up.*

Sabrina: *No problem. Hope everything is okay?*

Nick: *Fine.*

She waited for more, but the blinking text box remained quiet. So she said: *Okay, well, have a good night.*

What the hell else did she say? He wasn't telling her anything or asking her anything or saying anything. Just sorry about the late text, but then, nothing else.

No response for long enough, she sighed and put her phone back on the table. Whatever had happened today, he either didn't want to talk about it or didn't want to talk about it with her. Which was fine. He wasn't her boyfriend. She wasn't his girlfriend. They weren't in a relationship. He didn't owe her anything. And even if her gut was tight and her chest ached a little, well, that was her own problem.

Whatever had happened today felt like it changed everything, though. Her summer fling felt like it was over early. So she was just going to have to deal with that. And try to believe her logical self when that self said it was better this way. She'd been too close to…being even more emotional than she already was. Too close to tumbling over into something that would really get her hurt. This was better. Clean cut. Back to being friends or whatever they'd been before.

It's just texts and him not running over here, Sabrina, she snarled at herself. It's not the end of the world. It might not even be the end of the fling. Maybe he just had a bad night and needed some privacy.

Her scold didn't seem to help the ache in her chest, but she did feel silly for making up all the stories she was telling herself. Enough. Time to focus on something else. Her job. She had a lot to think about with that. She would finally finally think more deeply about her future.

She went to bed alone, after one too many sodas, still trying to convince herself everything was fine and she should be thinking more about her career future. She left her phone plugged in in a different room so she didn't spend the night checking for text messages.

Eventually, she slept, and eventually, the sun streaming in through the curtains woke her up. She forced herself to do her morning stuff, brush her teeth, take a shower, get dressed for the day, all while *not* running to check her phone. She wanted to get some renovation work done today, and then start on the center project, doing the preliminary sourcing.

When she finally allowed herself to look at her phone, there was a text message from Tabby—no, she hadn't met royalty yet, but she did have a great evening at the opera—but nothing from Nick.

Okay. Well. That was…fine. Just fine.

She walked the dogs, got breakfast, and got to work. She would not wallow. She had promised herself—and everyone else involved—she would deal with this exactly as it was. A summer fling, nothing more. And if it was over a little early or…whatever was going on, well that was fine. She had things to do, a life to reorganize, and a very exciting project to work on. If or when Nick felt like talking, that was fine, too. They could stay friends after this. In fact, that was part of the point, wasn't it? To acknowledge this was a summer fling and then *not* make it all weird for Tabby once she got back by being hurt and heartbroken. She didn't want Tabby to kill Nick. Or cut him out of her life because Sabrina did something stupid like fall in…too much like. So she would make an effort to remain friendly with Nick even if their fling was done.

She repeated this to herself through the rest of the tile work in the guest bathroom, all during lunch, and when she opened her laptop to start working on the new project.

Luckily, the research and sourcing, the challenge and excitement of doing work she loved, overwhelmed all other thoughts, and for several blissful hours, she only focused on the task she was doing. She was so involved that when her doorbell rang, she considered not answering it so she wouldn't have to break her concentration.

Princess took off toward the door, barking like a good guard dog. Justin sat up and stared at Sabrina, waiting for her to get up, too. She shook her head. Dog guilt. How could she ignore dog guilt? She pushed away from the kitchen bar counter where she'd been sitting working for the last three hours and stretched as she went to answer the front door.

Part of her brain was still on samples and costs of materials and how to get that extra quiet padding for the sensory room at a discount, so when she opened the door to see Darren standing there, she had to blink a few times to reconcile what she was seeing.

What the actual fuck?

"What the hell are you doing here?" she snarled. "How the hell did you find me here?" And that was some stalker shit she intended to tell her ex-boss about.

"That very nice woman Geraldine Roland, from the charity thing, told Gates where you were when she called for a reference. Not too hard to find you with that and a few phone calls to the charity's main offices. I have a winning personality. Didn't you know?"

She folded her arms over her chest, blocking the doorway, and scowled at him. He didn't look very good. Normally, he presented a sleek, fit, near-model level of put-togetheredness. He was close to six-foot, slim, with perfectly coiffed blond hair, clean shaven face, and handsome if you didn't know him. She was used to seeing him in hip, modern, slim cut suits that looked like they didn't quite fit but were designed to look that way. Her distinct lack of fashion skills left her in no position to judge his clothing. Still, she'd always thought his trendy suits looked a little weird on his taller frame. Today, he'd stuck to a t-shirt and cargo shorts, his short hair was messy, like he'd been running his hands through it, and there were deep circles under his blue eyes.

"Did Gates fire you?" she asked.

"Not yet. Might soon, though."

"You deserve it. If you'd done your own work and not tried to steal mine, you wouldn't be here."

"Can I come in and talk?"

"No."

He glanced past her to where Justin sat just behind her, watching the newcomer. Princess was jumping around at Sabrina's feet, barking at Darren, but so far hadn't lunged for him, so Sabrina let her make a fuss.

"Why not?" he asked without looking away from Justin.

"Because it's not my house. Because the dogs might get upset. But mostly, because I don't like you, and I don't want you inside. I'm considering calling everyone I know, and maybe even the police, since you tracked me down here without my permission, and it feels an awful lot like stalking."

"You know the police will take my side," he said, even though he didn't sound particularly smug about it. Just matter-of-fact.

The fact that she agreed with him irritated the hell out of her, but she'd deal with that societal failing later. "I have other people in my life who will object to this and make sure you know about it." She was thinking specifically of her brother. And probably Tabby—who could be a formidable enemy once made. "Why are you here?"

He glanced away, swallowing hard, and shifted from foot to foot. All nervous tics she'd never seen him make before.

"I… I came here to ask you not to come back to Tate Designs."

She blinked a few times. "You were calling earlier in the summer and begging me to help you." Not begging her to come back, though, she realized. Just to help him save the disaster he'd caused so he could look like the hero.

"If you take Gates up on the offer to return to work, I'll be fired. They'll choose you over me." He swallowed hard again and looked at her. "You're a better designer than I am. Always have been."

"And despite that, they chose you over me. What makes you think that would change?"

"Gates hasn't stopped talking about you since he heard from the Roland woman about this new work you'll be doing, about the work you've done for the company in the past. He keeps going on about how losing you was a big loss for the company."

"Gates let me go." And hadn't been singing her praises until he found out someone else wanted her skills—someone with money and influence at that! She'd walked because Gates didn't have her back and wouldn't acknowledge her contributions. Having him talk her up after he'd let her leave didn't change anything. He'd been happy to let her go so he could keep heaping praise on Darren. The fact that his chosen designer had failed while she'd gone out on her own and might just succeed on her own didn't change how he'd treated her in the two years.

"Well, he wants you back now," Darren said. "He wants these new clients you've landed."

She snorted. Of course he did. Tough luck for him.

"But I know you'll ask him to fire me before agreeing to come back," Darren finished.

"I considered it," she said.

"I won't be able to get another job in this business."

"That's not my problem."

"I know."

She blinked at that. She hadn't thought he'd acknowledge the fact that she wasn't responsible for his mistakes and his asshole behavior.

"I also know there's nothing I can say to make you believe I didn't want to see you quit."

"Of course you didn't want to see me quit. You were building a career off my ideas and work."

He shrugged. "Yes."

She blinked again. He was being remarkably honest about all this. She wasn't sure how to respond.

"But if you come back now, Gates will fire me. And I'll be out of the business. The whisper network is brutal in our field."

Yes, it was. Designers in the city got a lot of their new work through word-of-mouth recommendations, or were successful in their bid for that new work because of recommendations from past clients. If word-of-mouth turned against a designer, that could devastate any chance of getting new work. At least in New York. Which was why she wasn't sure she'd ever work in the field again after quitting. She'd been certain Gates would spread the word she wasn't a "team player" and no one would ever want to hire her. She was still worried about that, even if she went freelance.

"Still not my problem," she said. "You got yourself into this all on your own."

"I know. Which is why I know I have no right to ask for your help. But I'm here asking anyway."

"Why? Why go to all the trouble of tracking me down like this? It's making me less willing to do anything for you because I know you'll invade my privacy for your own selfish needs and ignore all my boundaries."

"You wouldn't take my calls."

"Boundaries, Darren. Does that word mean anything to you? I was setting boundaries and you kept ignoring them."

"You won't believe me if I apologize for that."

"Of course not. You're not sorry."

"You're right."

Well. Another acknowledgment that left her speechless.

"I'm selfish. I want what I want, and I'll do what it takes to get it." He shrugged. "I can own that."

"Okay." What was she supposed to say to that?

"So I'll make you a deal."

"Mm." Yeah, she wasn't going to like this at all.

"You agree not to come back to Tate Designs, and not only will I stop trying to contact you, I'll sing your praises to everyone I can. I'll talk you up all the time."

"While also making sure you look good in your stories?"

"Of course. No point in making myself look bad. But I'll ensure you look good, too."

"Not sure how that's supposed to motivate my choice."

"We wouldn't have to work together so you wouldn't have to worry about me stealing your ideas."

"Gates will fire you if I ask. That's why you're here. I don't have to work with you again no matter what decision I make."

"But if I get fired, I will use the whisper network. I'll spread rumors and lies and try to destroy your career like you destroyed mine."

"*You* destroyed your own career. Not me. I wasn't the one stealing another designer's ideas and work. And what you're doing here is blackmail. Not an honest request. That's not motivating me either. I can use the same back-alley tactics if you start down this road. It'll hurt both of our careers, but I'll go that route if you push me. I have other things I can do."

She wasn't sure what, yet, because she'd spent the summer fucking Nick instead of thinking about her future. But that wasn't something she intended on discussing with Darren.

He ran a hand through his hair, further messing the normally slick hairstyle. His blond hair was so fine, though, it mostly just fell back into place. That was just irritating. It made her very aware of her messy ponytail and her paint-stained t-shirt and shorts.

"I don't know what else to do," he said, raising his hands in a helpless sort of shrug she didn't really buy. "I need this job. I'll do what I need to to keep it."

"Fair enough. I know what I'm working with now." She wasn't about to give him the satisfaction of admitting she didn't necessarily want to go back to work at her former company. That she was considering either full freelance, or parlaying all this into work at a new firm. Let him worry for a few more weeks. He deserved it.

"What will you do?"

"You'll know when I do it. And now I know what to expect from you."

He nodded, looked down at his feet, then looked up and met her gaze. "I'm not…happy about doing this to you, you know."

She wasn't so sure about that. "You don't seem particularly sorry either."

"I can't afford to be." He shrugged and turned away from the door. "We understand each other."

"We do."

He nodded again and then left without looking back. She waited until she'd seen him get into his car—a sleek little electric blue Aston Martin that went a long way toward explaining why he couldn't afford to lose his job. She knew—or at least had a guess—what his salary was. He wasn't making Aston Martin money. Especially given what parking in the city cost. Even if he'd been making more than her. Which she suspected he had been because of *course* he had been.

Once he drove away, she closed and locked the door. Then stared at it for a long moment as she considered everything Darren had said. He'd definitely given her something to think about.

What she thought was that she didn't want to be in this situation, or work with any of these people, ever again.

And that she was…disappointed she couldn't talk about all this with Nick.

Yeah. That was the word.

Disappointed.

Chapter Thirty

A text came from Nick at dinner time, when she was sitting out on her deck trying to pretend she wasn't keenly aware of the fact that Nick hadn't been in touch at all for the last two days. Trying to pretend that she was okay with that and not really deeply hurt. She stared at the text for a long moment before responding.

Nick: *Are you free to talk now?*

Sabrina: *... I'm on the deck.*

Nick: *Should I bring dinner?*

Sabrina: *I already ate.*

She watched the three little dots come and go a few times, like he was typing something. But the only thing that came through was...

Nick: *I'll be there in a few minutes.*

She spent those few minutes screwing her face up into a smile, talking herself into a casual attitude. Hoping this wasn't some sort of breakup conversation because she'd have trouble holding on to her pretend upbeat mood if it was. She'd sworn to keep the fling casual, and she was determined to at least put in a good effort at making Nick believe she'd kept that promise.

Still, she found herself needlessly smoothing her t-shirt and running her hands along her shorts before she opened the door. She greeting him with a smile—was it too forced? It didn't feel too forced —and said, "Come on in. What's up?"

Too casual? Too chipper? Maybe. She was having trouble finding the balance here.

Nick didn't look very upbeat. In fact, he looked tired and sad. His thick dark hair was mussy and his t-shirt and shorts looked like they'd been slept in.

She pulled him in through the door, shooing the dogs away when they tried to crowd around to greet him. "Hey, are you okay? What's wrong? It's not Diego or his family?"

"Hi. No. Everyone is fine. Diego is fine." He frowned a little. "You have time to talk?"

"Sure, sure. Come on in. The deck or the living room?"

"Deck. Deck would be nice."

She led him out onto the deck and offered him the low-slung lounge seat next to the one she'd been sitting on. "Do you want a drink or…?"

He ran a hand through his hair, mussing it further. She found the mussed look adorable but didn't figure this was the moment for that observation.

"I'm good. Thanks." Then… "Actually, I could use a beer."

"Be right back."

He looked like he needed the drink. Whatever had happened in the last forty-eight hours, he was not "fine," and it was a big deal. And now she felt a little stupid for all the "summer fling must be over, and aren't I sad about it" thoughts. Well, maybe this was still something to do with that. But looking at how tired and worn he looked, even if it was, it wasn't the main thing.

She returned and handed him the cold bottle, trying not to frown down at him.

"How'd your meeting go on Sunday?" he asked, cradling the beer without taking a sip.

"Great. We can talk about it later. What's going on? No offense, but you look…" She searched for a word. He didn't look bad, because he never looked bad. She always found him delicious and gorgeous. But he did look worn out. "You look tired," she finished.

He snorted. "Yeah."

"Is it family?"

"No. Nothing like that. No one is dead or sick or anything. In fact, I'm not… I'm not even sure how to classify this."

She let out a long breath as she settled on the lounger next to him. At least it wasn't that level of serious. "So?"

"Anya came over on Sunday."

Well. That was a surprise. Not at all what she'd been expecting. And it did funny things to Sabrina's gut that she refused to acknowledge. Nick looked upset. He needed support. Not her pangs of weird jealousy that she shouldn't have.

"What happened?" she asked, keeping her voice level.

"I finally found out why she was acting so… Why the whole wedding thing was…the way it was."

"This doesn't sound good."

"It's pretty fucking awkward."

"Can you talk about it with me, or is it too private?"

He stared straight ahead for a long moment, still just cradling the beer. The dogs had settled on the deck too, Princess closer to Nick while Justin was in between the seats as if ensuring he had equal opportunities for random head scratches. Sabrina obliged the poodle because her nerves were humming and she needed the soothing gesture to stay calm for Nick's sake.

"I need to talk about it. She didn't say I couldn't. But…also, please don't say anything to anyone else?"

"Of course."

Wow. Whatever this was, it seemed serious. The same overactive imagination that had been concocting stories about how Nick was done with her now tried to insert all kinds of awful potential scenarios for what had happened to Anya. Which didn't help things any more than her brooding over Nick had. So she worked at ignoring her imagination's worried list of scenarios and just waited for Nick to talk.

"So…" He cleared his throat. "So the reason she was making a show of hitting on me and letting her father think she was interested in dating me and all that… There was more to it than just…personal interest."

She nodded. They'd suspected as much.

"Bianca's husband… He was someone Anya dated before."

That wasn't good.

"And he's continued his affair with her even after getting engaged to her sister."

"Oh shit."

"Yeah. Not good. She actually wanted out, but apparently, he's…persuasive."

Sabrina wanted to say "ew," but she didn't think this was the moment.

"Now, he's pitted them against each other, driven a wedge between them—though I get the feeling there was always too much sibling rivalry for them to be close."

"That's what I got from Geraldine, too," she said, keeping her voice low and quiet.

"Anya wasn't sure how to get out of the affair. She wanted to be done with him well before the wedding. But he wasn't letting her go easily, so she thought having another relationship with someone else would put an end to things. And that if she was with someone by his wedding, he'd stop cheating on her sister and be faithful."

Sabrina had a lot of opinions on that one, and the ability of cheaters to ever be faithful, but she kept those to herself, too.

"She picked me because, apparently, Brad's intimidated by me."

Sabrina couldn't help grinning at that. She knew it wasn't a grinning moment. But Bianca's husband being intimidated by Nick was amusing. "So she wasn't just enamored by your gorgeousness. She also wanted you as a shield between her and her ex, soon to be her brother-in-law."

His lip quirked at her description of him. "That was the thinking, yes."

"But then you showed up to the wedding with a 'girlfriend.'"

"And made things worse."

"Oh, Nick, that's not your fault, you know. You do know that, right?"

He ran a hand through his hair again. "I know. Logically. But I feel a little shitty about it now that I know what was behind everything."

And it wasn't lost on Sabrina that what she and Nick had done to dissuade Anya's interest was exactly what Anya had been trying to do to her ex. Except Sabrina and Nick had *talked* about what they were doing and communicated about the issue. Anya could have just talked to him and things might not have turned out the way they did.

"She could have talked to you earlier. Told you all this before the wedding."

He nodded, falling silent for a few minutes. Then he took a deep breath. "Anyway. The asshole is still trying to sleep with both women at once, and Anya doesn't know how to get out of it anymore since the guy is around all the time."

"He sounds like prince. What a jerk."

Nick snorted his agreement. "Anya's feeling trapped, because Bianca thinks it's Anya coming after her husband, the husband is still trying to get Anya into bed, and their parents are too delighted by Brad and his marriage to Bianca to see the tension or the truth. They like their son-in-law. And Mr. Greene is bringing him more and more into their main family business."

"Well none of that sounds good."

"Nope."

"Why did Anya come and talk with you? I mean, really, in the end, none of this has anything to do with you. It's not really your business."

"Nope. Which was why she came to me. I'm a neutral person. Someone with no skin in the game, so to speak. She needed someone to believe her side of things, I think."

"And do you?"

He nodded, his gaze on the ocean. "Yeah. Yeah, I do. Explains a lot. Especially the weirdly sudden way she started hitting on me. And the intensity of it all. But sounds like the rest of the family just think she's jealous and wants the guy for herself. Brad's encouraging that perspective."

"Of course he is." She made a face. "Did she ask you for help?"

"No. Actually, she just wanted to explain everything. And apologize."

"That was…"

"Unexpected?"

"I was thinking that was nice of her, but also unexpected." She stared at the side of his head. "This has upset you, though."

"I'm not sure I can keep working with the Greenes."

"Why? Specifically. Again, the interpersonal stuff doesn't have anything directly to do with you. You could finish the job and leave without getting further involved in the personal stuff."

"That's fine for this job. But they're asking me to do more work for them. And I was pretty fucking excited about that work until I had the conversation with Anya."

Ah. She was starting to see the problem here.

"But I don't want to be in the middle of their family shit. That's…" He spun the bottle of bear in his hands. "I went freelance so I could control who I took on as clients. It's not just about the money, it's about the freedom for me."

Exactly what he'd been asking her to think about and consider in her own career.

"I had 'family drama' enough growing up. My parents were… They aren't bad people. But they loved drama. They loved fighting and making up and getting into the middle of everyone else's business. There were always people coming and going from our house. And there was a lot of yelling, a lot of crying, and a lot of celebration all mixed up together. Which was fine for them because they loved all that. Called it *living*. I hated it. I just wanted quiet and to be left alone. To be alone for just a little bit."

He finally turned to look at her. "I got that finally when I moved out here and went freelance. The only drama I have now is work-related and most of that I can mitigate. It's not the same either. A contractor going bankrupt, and I have to scramble for a new one. A client changing some element last minute or wanting to add a new room or some bullshit. That's just the job. I don't mind doing the job. I just don't want…interpersonal drama in my life anymore."

"And working for the Greenes will ensure that family drama spills over onto you whether you like it or not."

He held her gaze, nodding slightly, though she thought unconsciously.

And suddenly a lot of things about Nick made more sense to her. She even understood. "I didn't grow up with a lot of drama around me, but…I've never been great with it either. I can sympathize. I never liked being in the middle of client personal issues."

"It happened to you?" He sat up a little.

"Sometimes. Sometimes I was just there during a fight, and they'd rope me into being a mediator. Sometimes they tried to get me involved. I hated it."

"But it never made you quit lucrative work," he said, sounding resigned.

"I didn't have that choice, remember. My firm wouldn't have let me quit."

"I have a choice. I'm just…not sure what to do with it."

"What did Anya say about that future work, after apologizing for getting you involved in all this?"

"Not much. Nothing about the work for her parents. She mentioned she might go travel, to get away from the new brother-in-law. I don't know what she'll do."

"You want to do the work, though? Ignoring the Greenes and their complicated soap opera lives, ignoring the money involved, do you want to do the work?"

"Yes. James wants to expand some property he has around a golf course, luxury houses he'll eventually sell, and he wants them designed to mesh well with the existing landscape and golf course. It'll be challenging. Some of the lots aren't very large or have weird formations I'd have to work around. I'd enjoy doing those designs."

"How often will you have to deal with anyone outside of Mr. Greene?"

He shrugged. "If Anya isn't helping him, then probably not much.

These are investment properties for him, not a family house, so it'll shift over to his corporation staff. But Brad is working for the firm."

"And Anya."

He nodded. "Although, I got the impression she was going to leave."

"Any idea what the son-in-law is in charge of?"

"He's a lawyer, so the legal stuff. Contracts and things."

"So you probably won't have to deal with him often?"

"Not in a work context, no."

"This is entirely up to you. I understand your dilemma. But it sounds like you might be able to swing this new work without getting roped into more drama. Less chance of it anyway, since you'll have so much less contact with the family. You could do the work, and just… leave the drama behind and come home. Especially now that Anya isn't dragging you into it all."

He nodded and glanced back at the ocean again. After a few quiet minutes, he finally took a sip of his beer. She focused on the ocean too, giving him time and quiet to think.

They sat there, watching the dark waves. The sea breeze ruffled her hair and brought the salty seaweed tang of the ocean to her stronger tonight. The night was warm, but not hot, and she was surprisingly comfortable, sitting in the quiet darkness with Nick.

She was nearly done with her beer when he finally spoke again. "Thanks for letting me talk about all this. I've been…thinking a lot since Anya left, but I felt like I was spinning my wheels. And Diego had some family stuff going on so couldn't talk."

The fact that he'd put her into the same category of confidant as his best friend made her stomach do a funny little tightening thing she tried to ignore. "Did it help? Talking it out?"

"It did."

"Decided what you'll do?"

"Not entirely. But… But I'm leaning toward taking the job and avoiding the family as much as possible."

"Best of both worlds," she said with a little smile.

They tapped their beer bottles together for that one.

Chapter Thirty-One

Nick continued to stare at the Atlantic, but most of his attention was on the woman sitting next to him on the deck. She was quiet too, just watching waves with him, absently scratching Justin's head with one hand, her mostly empty bottle of beer in the other.

He was acutely aware of her every movement, her small sighs and gestures. Acutely aware of the scent of her shampoo when the breeze shifted and brought it to him. The darkness beyond the deck added an air of quiet solitude, like it was just the two of them in the world. And if that had been the case, he'd have been perfectly content.

He'd debated longer than he should have whether to tell her everything he'd discussed with Anya. On the one hand, it wasn't his story to tell and Anya hadn't given him permission. But she hadn't explicitly said, "Don't tell that woman you're seeing." Which was good because he wasn't sure how he'd have reacted to that either. Especially since his supposed relationship with Sabrina wasn't just an act anymore. It was real. Or at least it was real for the summer.

But that was something else he'd been…debating.

He glanced at Sabrina again from the corner of his eye. She wasn't pushing him to talk more. She just sat with him while he stewed, giving him space to talk or not talk as he liked. That was new, at least in his relationships with women. He liked it. Most of his previous relationships had been with women who wanted to talk all the time. Talking all the time made his head hurt. His head already hurt from the Greene situation. But talking with Sabrina had actually helped.

That was also new. Wanting to talk about this kind of thing with someone he was seeing. Not just Diego. Not absolutely no one at all and he'd figure it out on his own. He'd *wanted* to discuss the predicament with her. Hell, he'd even told her something about his childhood he never talked about. Diego knew, of course, but like so much else, they didn't ever discuss it. It wasn't the kind of thing that really came up in conversation anyway. But it was the core of his reasons for not wanting anything to do with the Greene family's drama. He'd had more than enough of that as a kid. Still, in the past, it hadn't been the kind of thing he'd have shared with a woman he was seeing. The difference with Sabrina wasn't lost on him.

The city wasn't all that far away. Diego lived there, and they still managed to get together for visits and baseball and stuff. He went into the city for work a few times a year. It was just a drive.

The sounds of a set rolling in hard against the sandy beach drowned out the sound of his heartbeat, but only just. The rapid pounding realization that he wanted *more* with Sabrina... That he wanted this relationship to last past the summer... That he might be...

Well, that wasn't something he could consider yet. He just knew he didn't want what they had right now to end. Not yet. Not at the end of the summer. The realization that he wanted something different than he usually wanted with a woman was more than a little shocking.

He glanced at her from the corner of his eye again. At this point, in the past, women had started to pester him for a commitment. Sabrina liked commitment. She wanted a relationship. She'd agreed that wasn't what was between them. They'd both gone into this...whatever it was, with their eyes open.

And yet...

He set his beer aside, mostly untouched, and stood. She scrambled to her feet too, setting her empty bottle on the table before facing him. The way she blinked up at him, uncertain, like she wasn't sure what to do next, shifted something in his chest, very gently. Without a word, he pulled her close and kissed her. He wasn't sure of much in that moment, but what he knew for certain was that he needed Sabrina in his arms.

She held herself stiff for a moment, which surprised him, but then she relaxed and melted against him, wrapping her arms around his waist, and sighed into his mouth as she opened to him. The sensation of her in his arms wasn't something he'd gotten used to yet. He couldn't get enough of having her here, just like this, her body soft and warm and eager. He kissed her a little deeper and savored the way her scent wrapped around them both when he buried his fingers in her hair at the base of her neck, loosening her messy bun. She felt so damned right, but also new and delicate. Like he'd open his eyes and she'd be gone and this was all his imagination.

His fingers tightened in her hair. She groaned softly. And he was lost. She was here now. That mattered. This mattered. He urged her back toward the house, letting go of her only long enough to get the back door open. He left it open long enough to let the dogs slip inside, then closed the door and wrapped his arms around Sabrina again.

The living room lights felt bright after the dark deck, and he wanted that gentle dark intimacy again, but he was reluctant to stop kissing her. He let his lips travel from her mouth, down her throat, growled a little when she shivered, then took her hand and led her upstairs to her room. She pushed into the room ahead of him, though, as if she was in a hurry, and pulled him through the door, back into her arms.

He kicked the door closed because even though the dogs hadn't followed, neither he nor Sabrina wanted them wandering in. Then his full attention was on her, in the dark, the only illumination the ambient light coming in through her windows, the curtains still wide open. The overhead fan moved gently, swirling and cooling the air. The room smelled like Sabrina now. He wasn't sure he'd ever be able to be in here again without thinking of it as her room.

But that thought led him too close to other thoughts about the future. And for this moment, he really didn't want to think about any future beyond getting her naked and into bed.

The naked part happened delightfully fast as she pulled off her own t-shirt and bra on the way to the bed. The smooth heat of her skin never ceased to overwhelm him. He dipped is head, taking her nipple into his mouth, just to hear her gasp, to hear the little keening sounds she made when he sucked hard. Her fingers dug into his shoulders as she arched into him. He switched to her other breast, but he wanted her beneath him so he ignored her protest when he lifted his head and backed her toward the bed. Giving her a gentle push, she dropped onto the mattress with a little chuckle. That sound did things to him, sent tendrils of curling possessiveness through him that matched the heat already roaring in his blood.

He didn't bother to question the possessiveness. Right now, she was here, his, and she was all he wanted.

She wiggled out of her shorts and panties, shucking them to the side as he pulled off his t-shirt and shorts. He loved watching her get naked, and loved even more the way she stretched afterward, all lush and soft. All her beautiful curves and silky skin calling to him. He knelt at the edge of the bed and pulled her hips closer, her little gasp firing his blood. He kissed a sensitive spot on her inner thigh, near the top of her leg, because he wanted to hear that gasp again. Then he bit that same spot gently, because it made her squirm. The other thigh, his fingers firm on her hips, holding her when she jumped a little at the soft bite.

And then he licked into her heat, her pussy already wet and ready for him, tasting her as she moaned. She wove her fingers into his hair, holding him in place as he held her down. Not like he wanted to be anywhere else, but he loved having her hands on him, demanding and desperate. He licked into her, then circled her clit, sucking, feasting, as she panted and slowly, slowly lost control. Her skin flushed a delicious pink, her hips bucked against his mouth. He was happy to oblige, sucking harder, pushing harder, watching her face, her eyes closed, head back against the mattress. Her fingers dug hard into his hair, and when she came she cried out, the sound echoing in the dark room.

He loved watching her come. He wanted more. Wanted her desperate again. Wanted…

Wanted her.

He crawled up the bed to kiss her, caressing her as he went, finding all those sensitive areas that made her lose her mind just a little more. The side of her waist, her breasts, that little spot above her collarbone, the dip in her spine. She wrapped around him, the instant after he'd slipped on a condom, grinding and demanding. And now it was his turn to lose his mind. He slid into her wet heat, the sense of coming home and being exactly where he belonged a sensation he couldn't ignore but didn't think about. He wasn't able to think much by then anyway. Having her under him, and then on top of him, riding him, finding her own pleasure again as he flicked a finger over her clit… That glorious flush and her keening, panting. The way her eyes went unfocused as sensation took her fully. The way she shivered all over as she came again.

He launched up to take her nipple in his mouth as she trembled and clung to him. Then he rolled them both so she was under him again, and he buried himself in her heat again and again until all that wanting and desperation and need and…everything tightened and built and exploded in a rush, wringing him dry until he collapsed with her onto the bed.

Whatever common sense he had left was tossed out a window in that moment, with her panting beside him, them both limp and sweaty and spent. He didn't want to let her go at the end of the summer. He didn't want to let her go ever. But…

He had no idea how to keep her when he'd only ever driven women away. How did he hold on to this one?

How did he convince Sabrina to stay?

Chapter Thirty-Two

Sabrina tried to hide her surprise when Nick didn't leave quickly after breakfast the next morning. He usually had lots to do, and so did she, so they'd kiss goodbye at the door and he'd go back to his place, or she'd go back to hers, and they'd spend the day doing their own thing. After two nights of not seeing him, and building up a lot of unnecessary "end to their summer fling" scenarios in her head, she was just relieved he was here with her, and had trusted her enough to talk last night. But she'd also expected things to fall back into the normal rhythm they'd kept all summer.

He changed the routine by…snuggling next to her on the couch with his coffee, reading the morning news on his phone, not in any hurry to leave.

And while she liked the lazy pace and didn't want to hurrying him away, the change in weekday routine struck her as…odd.

Don't read too much into it, Sabrina. Maybe he just doesn't have work today.

She'd let her imagination run away with her already this week, and that had proved a useless exercise. She was not going to do that again. Whatever was between them, she was enjoying it, and him, and she would go with the flow of whatever happened, without twisting herself into knots trying to figure it out. He hated those "relationship" conversations. And they didn't have a future to talk about. So she wasn't going to bring that up. He wanted a lazy morning reading and sipping coffee with her, she'd take it. And then she'd let him go about his day while she went about her day, and not, absolutely *not*, get carried away convincing herself of things that weren't there. She'd done that before, and gotten her heart broken.

And yes, her heart would already end up broken at the end of the summer, but not because she'd convinced herself of something that wasn't real. She would see all this with clear, open eyes and take it for what it was.

Lovely, warm, sexy, fun. Some of the best sex of her life. A gentle, delightful routine. A good friendship alongside that excellent sex.

But *not* long term.

Her heart wanted to argue with her on that point. And her brain was definitely onboard with this argument. But her common sense had to prevail. There would be no pretending they were anything more than they were to each other, and that was that.

A buzz on her phone had her looking at the screen. She'd been expecting a text from Tabby, or maybe even Geraldine as they started work at the end of the week. But it was Darren of all people. "Checking" to see if she'd decided to take the job or not.

She rolled her eyes and flicked the screen to get rid of his message.

Nick looked up from his phone. "Everything okay?"

"Oh, yeah. No big deal. Just Darren."

His eyes narrowed. "What now?"

She realized in all the emotional kerfuffle she'd worked herself into, and then their conversation last night, she hadn't told him about her Sunday meeting with the board of directors or her Monday forced confrontation with Darren yet.

So she did. She started with the good stuff, the successful meeting, all the work she had to do now but how excited she was about it all. He set his coffee aside to give her a big hug and congratulate her. And when he asked why she hadn't told him sooner, and she raised her brows waiting for him to figure it out, he got the cutest patches of color in his cheeks when he scowled.

"Sorry," he said. "I should have been here so you could celebrate with someone."

"You had other things going on at the time. It was fine. We can celebrate tonight." And that celebration would be worth the wait.

"Where does Darren come in to all this?"

"That happened the next day." She told him about Darren showing up at her door, ran her fingers over his brows when his scowl turned so fierce at that news she thought he might explode, and then explained how Darren was a pathetic loser who didn't want her to take her old job back and get him fired.

"What an ass," Nick said, his voice very deep and rumbly. The scowl hadn't left his brow, but he no longer looked like he was going to chew up Darren's bones after he murdered him, so that was progress.

"An ass who's right that I don't want to work with him every again. It'll be either me or him at the firm."

"Have you decided to go back to your old job, then?"

"No. But..." She bit her lip and shrugged a little. "But I *like* what I'm doing now, with the charity. I... I know not every meeting will go that well, and that not every client will be this easy, or happy with my work. I've been through that already. And it's scary knowing I won't have a steady salary backing me up when things go wrong."

"You could go to work for a smaller company," he said. "Combine the best of both worlds."

"Yeah. And still be in a position to worry about other designers like Darren undermining me."

"That doesn't happen at every company," he said, pointing out the obvious.

She gave him a look. "That's not the point. The point is, I can either control the clients I accept and the work I do, or I can let someone else control which clients I work with. And...even with the lack of security, I'm leaning toward being able to make my own choices."

He nodded. "Big decision."

"Yeah. But not as hard as I thought it would be."

Something passed through his expression she couldn't read. His eyes narrowed just a little and his gaze unfocused as if he were thinking. She couldn't tell what had triggered that response, but she waited for him to tell her. Then he blinked back to his surroundings, and shook his head a little, and refocused on her. But he didn't say anything about what he'd been thinking.

She was curious enough she almost asked. Instead, she said, "So I still have a few weeks to make a final decision, but I'm leaning toward being my own boss. I'm just not interested in telling Darren that and letting him off the hook yet."

"He has earned every moment of agita the waiting gives him."

She chuckled and snuggled back against his side. "I'm glad I finally got to talk to you about all this. Talking helps put things into perspective."

"Yeah," he said quietly. "It does."

She enjoyed another half hour of just hanging out with him, and then her own work schedule poked her conscious. She had things to get done for the charity, and it was time she practiced working for herself. Which meant she had to be a better boss than her last boss had been. But it also meant she had to get to work. She patted his leg and stood up.

"This has been fun," she said, taking her coffee cup to the kitchen, "but I need to get to work now. And I suspect you do, too." She grinned as she walked back to him. "I'm enjoying being my own boss so far."

He chuckled as he stood and she took his coffee mug from him. "Just don't run yourself into the ground. That'll be an issue too."

Kissing his cheek, she shooed him toward the front door. "I'll need more than one client before I have that issue."

Princess and Justin followed them to the door so Nick leaned down to give them both scratches goodbye. Then he gave her a toe-curling kiss that left her blinking and a little dazed as he left. Wow. What was she supposed to be doing again?

Oh! Right. Work.

She was grinning when she closed the door, relieved as much as anything else that their summer fling wasn't over yet.

She was going to miss those delicious goodbye kisses. But it was lovely she still had them for a few weeks more.

* * *

WHEN NICK CALLED HER ON THURSDAY NIGHT, SABRINA ANSWERED A little breathless. "Hey," she said. "Listen, I need to work tonight. I'm afraid I won't be able to do our usual dinner thing. Do you mind?"

He scowled at the wall, but kept his voice neutral. "Sure. No problem. I was just calling because I wasn't going to make it over tonight. Need to work, too. Didn't want you to worry."

Actually, he'd been debating calling for an hour. He did have work to do. But he also didn't want to miss a night with Sabrina. And the fact that he wanted to drop everything to go over to her place made him…leery.

From the beginning, but even more so since the incident with Anya, he'd been reluctant to be away from Sabrina. Not for any good reason. The Darren thing seemed handled. Sabrina had solved—at least for now—her career crisis. He was doing good with work. Yes, they only had a few weeks left and that could be the reason he wanted to spend so much time with her, but he had a sneaking suspicion it was something else completely. And the idea scared the shit out of him.

He needed to keep some space between them. He needed some time alone. But even as he'd made the call, he'd been anticipating an argument. This kind of thing had always resulted in an argument, or a pout, or a tantrum in the past. He didn't want to fight with Sabrina. But he needed to be alone tonight—partly just to prove to himself he was still…okay.

The fact that she'd preempted him by saying she couldn't see him tonight was… Good. Yeah. It was good. No arguments. No drawn out discussions or anything. No guilt trips or complaints. They could do their own thing, and she wasn't going to bug him about it. That was good. Absolutely perfect.

"Great, then," he said aloud and his voice sounded a little rough. He cleared his throat. "Perfect timing."

"Yeah it was," she said. He could hear her grin. "You called instead of texting. How come?"

"Thought it was better to cancel plans with a call rather than a text." He scowled harder at the wall. He hadn't wanted to argue over text messages. And he owed her the courtesy of a call if he was going to break plans.

But mostly, he'd just wanted to hear her voice.

"That's very sweet," she said. Then, her voice full of bouncy happiness, she said, "I'm really glad you're the kind of person who understands needing to work and likes alone time and all that."

"Yeah," he said. "Me too." He was still scowling at the wall, though. What was wrong with his face? He made an attempt to relax.

"Okay, gotta go," she said. "See you soon!"

She hung up quickly after his goodbye, and he was left staring at the phone for a good three minutes before he shook his head and got back to work. But he spent entirely too much time dropping out of the concentration he needed to glance at his phone, sitting at the opposite side of his office, near the window. He wasn't sure why. This was what he wanted. He loved this. A woman who didn't argue with him when he had to call off plans? Didn't try to guilt him into dropping everything for her? That was…perfect. Absolutely, exactly what he wanted.

Completely perfect.

CHAPTER THIRTY-THREE

Sabrina immersed herself in the challenge of her new job and loved every second of it. She spent so much time working on the project, she'd had to call off plans with Nick a few times, but since he liked being alone, and they weren't in a relationship, and this was what *he* wanted, she never felt guilty. For the first time ever, she didn't feel guilty canceling plans with a man she was seeing. It was wonderful.

She missed Nick at night, of course, when she collapsed exhausted into bed, but those were the nights she'd have been too tired to do more than sleep anyway. And knowing Nick was good with all this let her sleep soundly.

She said as much on a call with Tabby the next week. "I used to worry a lot, when I was in actual relationships," she said as she scrolled through a website, looking for better sound dampening material, something she could also make look good. "Whenever I had to work late or got focused on a job. I'd feel guilty if I didn't stop and spend all my time with him. Like it was my responsibility to make sure we were together every moment we weren't working."

"I tried to tell you that wasn't necessary," Tabby said.

Sabrina laughed. "I know. I know. But it's what I thought a relationship was supposed to be, you know? Spend all your time together. That's the way Dad and Larissa are. And they have such a good marriage. Why be in a relationship if you weren't going to be together all the time?"

Constantly being around each other had been the base assumption underlying all her serious relationships. It hadn't really occurred to her that she might not want to be around the man she supposedly loved all the time every day.

But being attached at the hip to another human being was exhausting. And in the end, she'd always felt like she'd been doing all the work and sacrifice to make that closeness happen. She still liked two of her exes. They were nice men. But she was looking back on those relationships now, all her relationships, with fresh eyes, and seeing all the ways things had never been quite right. At least not for her.

"This has been illuminating," she told Tabby, who was on speaker phone, Sabrina's cell sitting next to her laptop on the living room coffee table. She sat on the floor to be on the right level with her computer and kept scrolling through sound dampening materials. "When I actually go into another relationship again, I want things more this way. I never realized how much better it was, being able to *not* be around each other constantly."

She tried not to sound melancholy when she talked about a future relationship. She only wanted Nick, and the thought of being with anyone else seemed…wrong. A lot wrong. But he didn't want anything beyond this summer, and she was determined to respect that.

"Glad to hear you're growing," Tabby said. "How's Nick with all this?"

"Good of course. This is what *he* wants."

And she finally understood the reasoning behind his preferences now. If she could have both, a relationship with him and still this freedom to lead her own life without constantly checking in and worrying she wasn't spending enough time in her boyfriend's company, that's what she'd want. That felt like the ideal relationship to her now.

Unfortunately, her ideal partner in that relationship was Nick. She couldn't imagine being this comfortable and happy with anyone else. She was in trouble, and she knew it. The emotions, the dangerous word… It was all right there. But she was also determined not to put that on Nick. Which meant no slipping up and telling him how she really felt. Respecting the limits they'd established for the summer.

And she couldn't even regret the upcoming heartbreak because thanks to Nick she'd learned something about what she wanted for her future. A lot actually. The kind of romantic relationship she wanted. The work she wanted to do. She owed him a lot for those realizations.

"Sounds like everything is working out great," Tabby said, sounding a little dubious. "I'm glad I won't have to kill him."

Sabrina chuckled. "Tell me about your stuff now. How's the food festival going?" Tabby was at another one in Italy this time, and Sabrina could live off her descriptions of just the pasta alone.

Just before they got off the phone, Tabby said, "You're sure you're good with the way things are going with Nick? I mean… At this stage, you're usually deep into your need for a commitment and wanting to spend all your time with the man you're seeing."

She was about to respond instantly with an "of course," but she wanted to give Tabby the right answer, not just the knee-jerk response. Was she okay?

Well, she didn't want this to end. She wanted more. She wanted… Her chest ached a little. She wanted always. But Nick didn't do that, and she was going to keep to the deal they'd made. But the other part, the space around their time together, the fact that they weren't living in each other's pockets… That she liked.

So she told Tabby as much. Not the part about wanting forever. That wasn't something anyone involved needed to know but her. Somehow it seemed like it would hurt more if Tabby knew how much Sabrina's emotions had gotten involved. Right now, that part, was hers to hold, gently and quietly, for her eyes only. Or well, in this case, her heart only.

"I've never known you to not want to live in the pocket of a man you're dating," Tabby said, and before Sabrina could respond, she finished, "but I like it. I like this more independent version of 'Sabrina in a relationship.' It's healthier."

Sabrina laughed. "I like this healthier attitude, too, to be honest. But don't let Nick hear you call this a relationship! We're not doing that. Fling. It's a summer fling."

"If you say so."

"It has to be. That's what we agreed. He doesn't do relationships." She was getting close to slipping and revealing the one thing she didn't want anyone else to know. So she said, "I need to get going. I have a call with the board of directors in a few minutes, and I need to get ready."

"Fair enough. I have a cooking demonstration in…" Tabby paused. "Oh shit. In like twenty minutes. I'd better go too. Wonder what the hell happened to my handler?" She said the word handler with a little snort.

They said their goodbyes and Sabrina determinedly put aside thoughts of Nick to focus on the work she was doing. She did have a call with the board this afternoon. And another call with one of the experts advising her. And tomorrow the work began in earnest. She was so excited she couldn't hardly wait. She loved getting into a space and filling it *just right* and making it look beautiful and functional. The thrill of getting back to the work she loved over the last few weeks did manage to offset the heartbreak she knew was on the horizon. Gave her something else to think about. And she had Nick to thank for that.

Even if he was also the source of her future heartbreak.

* * *

NICK TEXTED SABRINA, ABSENTLY LOOKING AT THE PLANS HE WAS working on. He needed to get this done and wouldn't have much time for the next couple of days. But for the first time in his life, he didn't want to cancel plans with a date. He missed her. Yes, he'd just seen her that morning. Still. For some reason, he missed her when they were apart.

He snorted to himself. "Some reason" was pretty fucking obvious.

But he wasn't going to look at that too closely. The approaching end of the summer, Tabby's return, Sabrina moving back to the city, those days were flying away, bringing the inevitable closer and closer. And frankly, he didn't want to waste a moment. But he also needed to get some things done or risk losing a brand new client he really wanted to work with.

She texted back almost immediately, and he ignored the tightening in his gut as he prepared for her irritation and anger. A knee-jerk reaction to other texts he'd gotten from other women. He expected a lot of recrimination and irritation. Or maybe a curt reply—those usually proceeded the "talks" that were the end of his relationships. He rubbed a hand over his face before he read the text.

What he got was…

Sabrina: *Of course! I have so much to do, this works out well for me too! Have a good time working. Text me when you're free.*

He was still trying to process her message when another one pinged through.

Sabrina: *Oh, wait, I'll be too busy to meet up this Thursday and Friday, just so you know ahead of time. Have fun!*

He blinked at his phone for a full minute before he realized he needed to text back.

Nick: *Okay. Great. Thanks for understanding.*

That was the only response he had because he was reeling from hers.

She replied with a smiley face emoji.

This all felt too easy. Too simple. Too right. She must be doing this on purpose. Some sort of trick to drive him nuts. To make him feel guilty. That's what the women in his past had done, spent a lot of time making him feel guilty for the time he needed alone. And some of them had used really sneaky, passive aggressive tactics to do that.

Except he knew that wasn't Sabrina's style. She was just following the parameters of their Not-A-Relationship. She wasn't the vindictive type—at least not meanly. She'd already told her former boss she wasn't taking the job to put Darren out of his misery. Nick would have dragged that shit out for weeks to make that asshole suffer. But not

Sabrina. She'd let the ass off the hook in only a few days. She wasn't vindictive or passive aggressive. She said what she meant. She was… fine with him having to cancel plans. She was really okay with giving him the space he needed. That was…great. Right?

Right. He was thrilled. Delighted. Relieved! He hated fights. Hated the accusations and recriminations and *drama* at the end of a relationship. Or in this case, most of the way through a relationship.

This was definitely better. Lots better. No clinging. No all caps text messages full of accusations of being too distant or breaking promises or whatever. This was exactly what he wanted.

Did she even miss him?

He scowled down at his phone. Why did he care? What did it matter? He wouldn't want her to anyway. Not really. Well, okay, maybe a little. Enough to actually want to see him again. But not in the chest aching, not-going-to-sleep-well-tonight kind of way. That way sucked. He wouldn't want her to go through that.

He rubbed a hand over his chest absently as he set his phone aside when there were no further messages from Sabrina. At least one of them should get a good night's sleep. That was good.

Everything was good.

* * *

When Nick arrived for dinner a few nights later, Sabrina opened the door absently, her face in her phone. She waved him in with a smile, but wasn't looking at him as she talked. He knelt down to greet the dogs, trying hard not to listen in to her side of the conversation. There wasn't much to hear from her end anyway. A lot of "uh huh" and "mm"s.

She finished with a, "Great. Yeah. We'll look at that tomorrow." And hung up.

Then she grinned at him, pulled him close, and kissed him.

Well. That part he liked a lot. He sank into the kiss. Wrapping his arms around her to keep her tight against him. Letting her now familiar scent sink into him, fill him up. He'd missed her, and he'd only been away from her a few days. He tried not to think too much about the implications of that. Right now, he didn't want to think at all.

She pulled back a little and smiled at him. "I'm starving. Thanks for bringing over dinner." She grabbed the bags of Chinese takeout he'd set onto the foyer side table before saying hi to the dogs. "That smells delicious."

"I got enough to feed an army, so we should be good."

They both glanced down at the dogs. Princess and Justin looked up at them with hopeful expressions.

"Tabby's going to kill me for giving them so many table scraps." Sabrina sighed. She patted his shoulders then took the bags and headed to the kitchen.

He followed, drinking her in, her relaxed shorts and t-shirt. Nothing fancy. She hadn't dressed up for him or anything. But for some reason, the easy summer outfit turned him on. To be fair, everything she did turned him on. He wondered if she'd be willing to wait to eat. They could always reheat the food.

"She called today," Sabrina was saying as she put the bags on the counter in the kitchen. "I can't believe she'll be home in just two weeks. This summer has flown by, hasn't it?"

Her back was to him as she took plates out of the cabinet, so she didn't see his expression. Which was good. Because the shock of what she'd just said stole his breath. He supposed he hadn't been paying much attention to the calendar on purpose. Hadn't really wanted to think about the end of the summer approaching. But two weeks? They only had two weeks left?

That couldn't be right.

She continued talking, and he had to blink to refocus on what she was saying. "I'll be mostly done with the center by then, I hope. We're a little behind. Do you think Tabby would mind if I bunked with her for a couple extra days? I'd better ask her. I'd hate to impose. She'll need quiet time in the house after all the travel and being 'on' for the entire summer."

He opened his mouth to say she could stay with him if Tabby wanted her house back to herself. Closed his mouth just as fast.

She kept talking, about Tabby, and the end of summer, and Tabby's return, and Nick just couldn't seem to focus because something was wrapped tight around his chest, making breathing hard. Was he having a heart attack? No. That'd probably hurt less.

He cleared his throat. "What will you do if Tabby needs the privacy, but you're not done with the center yet?"

She waved a hand, her focus on spooning rice onto their plates. "I'll figure it out. I can always just drive back and forth, although that'll be expensive for gas. Or maybe Geraldine will know someone with a spare room. Since it's the end of summer, I can probably find a room at that little B&B the other side of town." She poured sweet and sour pork onto her plate, gave him two pieces, then poured the chicken and cashew onto his plate before taking a couple of pieces for hers. "It'll only be a couple of days, I think. I should be fine."

She didn't even suggest staying with him. Didn't hint at it. Didn't glance at him and raise her brows, looking hopeful. Nothing. As if it wasn't even a possibility. As if he wasn't an option.

And that just pissed him off. He was standing right here. She could just ask.

She grinned and finally glanced up at him. "Deck or table?"

"Deck." They rarely sat at the table inside. Unless the wind was too rough or the weather stormy, they ate out on the deck. It was a clear, glorious night, the ocean roaring softly in the background. A good night to eat outside.

"You grab the drinks," she said as she carried the plates toward the door.

He gathered up the soda cans, then hurried to get the back door for her since her hands were more full than his.

"Thank you," she said, her smile wide as she went out onto the deck.

That smile went right through him, always made him feel ten feet tall. He had no idea how she did that to him. Made him feel so... He didn't know. Right. Good.

Happy.

"You could stay with me," he blurted before he thought better of it.

He scowled. He hadn't meant to say that. It wasn't the kind of offer he'd have made to anyone else.

She set the plates down on the table and sat, as if the world hadn't just shifted strangely. "That's sweet of you to offer, but I wouldn't want to impose. I'll get it figured out."

He grunted as he sat next to her. "I wouldn't have made the offer if it was an imposition." His voice sounded a little hoarse and deep. Like he was angry. He shouldn't be angry. Why the hell was he getting pissed off?

She leaned over her armrest and kissed his cheek. "I do appreciate the offer. Really. But we both know you'd be happier without an extended house guest." She grinned. "Have you ever had an extended house guest? Even Diego?"

"Diego has three kids and a wife. That's not a house guest. That's an invasion force."

She laughed. The sound light and happy, and she lit up with the humor. And that made a part of him light up too. But then there was this other part. The part that was extremely irritated by this conversation.

"Okay, maybe not Diego. But any other house guest?"

He opened his mouth to say of course, but then had to snap his mouth shut again. He went to family to visit, they didn't come to him. He didn't want his parents never-ending dramas in his quiet haven. He loved his family. He just didn't want them *here*. He also went to visit friends. And when a friend from out of town came into New York, they stayed in hotels in the city, and he went in to see them because who the hell would want to come all the way to New York City and stay all the way the hell out here?

The women he'd dated had stayed the night of course, but... Yeah, mostly he'd gone to their places. He hadn't wanted any of them to move in with him for even a short period of time. Hell, he'd had at least two breakups over the fact that he didn't want them to move in with him. But all those women had their own homes.

So does Sabrina, his inner bastard whispered, just to poke him.

But she didn't have a place out here where she was working. This wasn't like asking her to move in with him or anything. Just giving her a bed for a few days. Maybe a couple of weeks. And if he happened to share that bed with her, well, that was just…pragmatic. Like sharing a shower with her made sense because it saved water. Also resulted in some pretty hot sex, but that was a bonus.

"Well?" She raised her brows, a little grin tugging at her mouth as she waited.

"It hasn't come up before," he said.

"You've lived here for what? Four, five years? Not a single house guest?"

"Do you have a lot of house guests?"

"I live in a one-bedroom apartment in Brooklyn. And I have an air mattress stuffed into one of my few closets, taking up valuable closet space, because I occasionally have people stay with me." She turned to her food and popped an entire piece of pork into her mouth, like she'd just won the argument.

"That's Brooklyn," he said. "People *want* to stay in Brooklyn."

"You're literally *on* the beach. People want to stay on the beach, too."

"It's different. Anyone I know visiting New York wants to stay in the city, not out here."

"And no one in New York wants a convenient beach house to visit?" She dropped her chin and gave him a look.

He grunted and turned to his food.

Her quiet chuckle held too much triumph, and for some reason, that made him happy except still also very annoyed. What the hell had she done to him?

She was *right*. He hated having people stay in his home. It bothered the hell out of him, having other people's stuff in his place. Most of the time. Sabrina had left a few things there. The spare toothbrush he'd given her. But that had already been there. She had a pair of sleep shorts and a t-shirt in one of his drawers, which she hadn't needed to use because they always slept naked—who the hell wouldn't want that with her in bed with them? And she had left a full change of clothes in that same drawer. But again that was just pragmatic. They'd got a little carried away one evening and ripped one of her skirts. She'd had to go back to her place wearing a pair of his sweat pants, which did not fit her even a little. Although she did look pretty adorable in his sweats. After that, they'd decided her having something she could walk back home in stashed at his place was a good idea.

But that wasn't much. Not enough to bother him.

There'd be a lot more of her stuff in his house if she stayed with him while she finished her job. A lot more of her around. All the time. Even when she was working, she'd still be there every night. Every morning. Sometimes all day, when she wasn't on site. They'd be around each other a *lot*. There'd be another whole person in his home, maybe even there when he wasn't. The thought of that normally sent him running screaming into the night. The thought of Sabrina taking over his home…did not.

He shoveled in a mouthful of rice to hide his reaction to that. When he imagined Sabrina in his home every night, being there every morning, having whole drawers filled with her stuff in his bedroom, her laptop on his kitchen counter or at his table… None of that filled him with dread and claustrophobia. He liked the image.

"You've gone very quiet," she said. "Did I upset you? I really do appreciate your offer. But we both know you don't want anyone else staying in your house. It's fine! Really. I'll find something. It'll only be a couple of weeks at most anyway. Then back to Brooklyn."

She gazed out over the ocean, the sea breeze ruffling the little hairs on her forehead. She'd pulled her thick hair up into a messy bun. He loved when she did that because it gave him a chance to take her hair down.

"I'll miss it here, though," she said softly. "It's been a good summer."

It had been. The best summer. And he didn't want it to end.

He didn't want them to end. The thought of her leaving left him feeling hollow. The idea that he might not see her again was intolerable. Worse, that the next time he did see her, they'd have reverted to just being "Tabby's best friend" and "Tabby's neighbor" with no personal relationship between them. Maybe a sort of friendship, but nothing more. And the thought of seeing her and *not* being able to touch her made his head want to explode. He didn't *want* that distance between them.

He didn't *want* to let her go.

He blinked down at his food.

Fucking hell. He was in love with her.

Chapter Thirty-Four

"He did what?" Tabby asked, before her video feed froze because of bad internet at her side of the call.

Sabrina waited out the pause and then said, "He offered to let me stay with him if the job ran over."

"And you said?"

"No, of course. I know he just did it to be nice. And I know he'd hate having someone in his space like that. But it was so sweet and kind of him to offer."

"Uh huh. Why do you sound so chipper about all this?"

"I feel like I'm growing as a person. I didn't jump to take advantage of him, try to angle for a commitment I know he doesn't want. I didn't use his offer to insinuate myself into his life longer. And I didn't make the mistake of thinking the offer meant more than it did."

Another brief video freeze before Tabby said, "What else could the offer have meant?" Her eyes were narrowed, as if she wasn't sure what to say.

"You know, in the old days, I would have tried to use a casual offer like that to make a man commit for the long term. I would have tried to force a relationship. I would have thought the offer meant he wanted that commitment. But this time, I recognize it for what it is, and didn't let myself get carried away. I'm pretty proud of myself, to be honest."

She petted Princess where she was sitting on the couch next to her—and was careful not to let Tabby see Princess on the couch in the video. Justin sat on the floor at her feet, snoozing in a patch of sunshine streaming in through the back windows. The day was beautiful and bright outside, another glorious beach day, except the wind had kicked up so much it was blowing sand around hard enough to feel like scouring powder. So she'd spent most of the morning in the living room, trying to find a new source for a specific style of chair she needed because her last source had fallen through. She didn't even mind the hassle that was causing. Everything just seemed… She wasn't sure. Sunnier? That sounded weird. It was sunny out here a lot. She felt good. She felt good about her work, even with the usual issues that kept cropping up. She felt good about her summer. She felt good about the grownup way she was handling her summer fling.

And she really did feel proud of herself for how she was handling Nick's offer. She'd gone and fallen in love with him, and instead of pining away and attempting to coerce him into something he didn't want—which she'd have done in the past—she decided to put his feelings before her own. She would let him go, which would allow him to be happy, and that made her happy even as it broke her heart to leave him. The heartbreak felt more melancholy. Sad, but not as devastating as she'd have thought, because she knew he'd be happy.

It was a really strange state of mind. A strange feeling, to be so content knowing he'd be happy, even if that meant losing him. She wasn't sure she'd ever felt that way before.

She said as much to Tabby, trying to put to words the strange feeling.

Tabby stared at her so long, Sabrina thought the video had frozen up completely. She was about to offer to call back, when Tabby cleared her throat.

"You're in love with him."

"'Fraid so. I know you warned me this would happen. It did. My fault for not listening. But it's okay! I swear. You don't have to kill Nick. He can't help being loveable."

This brought another long pause from Tabby. "I've never met anyone who called Nick loveable before."

"That's surprising since he is."

"I agree. I just don't think many people realize it." Tabby shook her head. "And he offered to let you stay with him. He said those exact words?"

"He did. I'm not sure how he got them out. He looked a little stressed about the offer, to be honest. All adorably scowly. It was so sweet." And it was the moment she realized she wanted to put his feelings above her own by not accepting the offer. The moment when she realized not only that she loved him, she loved him enough to let him go.

"I'm…not understanding any of this, to be honest," Tabby said. "You love him?"

"I do."

"And you're *not* going to take advantage of his offer for a place to stay."

"No." She raised her hand to stop Tabby when she opened her mouth, but the gesture caused Princess to give her an irritated look, so she went back to scratching Princess's head as she said, "And I promise I won't impose on you either. I love you, too." She grinned.

"Sure. And thanks for that. But…"

"Thanks for not imposing on you, or thanks for the loving you part."

"The loving me part. Also, for not wanting to impose on me. You can stay with me that extra few weeks, by the way. It's not an imposition."

"You'll be just back from a long trip. You're going to need the time alone to come down from being 'on' so much."

"I will. But I can do that while you're around."

Sabrina was going to object again, but Tabby did her own hand raise to stop Sabrina mid-protest. "I'm still stuck on this Nick part," Tabby said. "Nick actually, in words, offered to let you stay *in* his house? Not, like, offered to find you a hotel or a B&B or something? Didn't tell you to ask me? He offered to let you move your *stuff* into his space?"

"Just for a week or two. He wasn't asking me to move in. Obviously. But yes, he did make the offer in those words. Well, not the stuff about moving my stuff into his space. But to stay with him, yes. And yes, I said no. Because I'm a grownup and shit." She grinned, hoping to make Tabby laugh.

Tabby did not laugh. She continued to stare at Sabrina in a way that made Sabrina think the video had frozen again.

After a full thirty seconds of Tabby staring, she blurted out, "Nick asked you to stay at his place?"

"Yes, yes. How many times do I have to say yes to that question? I know it's hard to believe and out of character for him. But he did do it."

For some reason, the fact that he'd been willing to make the offer, even though it would make him uncomfortable in his own home, had made her giddy. Delighted. Hard to deny the inner glow of pleasure, realizing he cared enough to make the offer.

"I can't get over it," Tabby said after an actual video freeze. "I suppose I just… Huh. Well." She blinked. "You…sure you don't want to, maybe, talk to him about the reason he asked you to stay? Maybe ask why he offered?"

"Why would I do that? I know the answer already. He was being sweet and nice. But he's hardly going to say that out loud. He'll just say something grumpy and wave it away." She grinned at the idea. That would be cute to watch. Still, she didn't want to embarrass him.

"I'm thinking maybe, *maybe*, there's a conversation there you two need to have."

"No. No 'conversations.' That's always been my problem. And that's exactly what we agreed wouldn't happen here."

"You love him, though. I think he needs to know."

"No, he doesn't. Oh my god, could you imagine! He'd be so upset."

"I… I'm not sure upset is the right word here."

"Listen, we promised each other this would just be a summer fling. I'm not breaking that promise to him." Bad enough she'd broken her promise to Tabby not to end up hurt. No more promise-breaking.

"Yeah, but things have changed."

"Not really." In fact, she was pretty sure she'd been in love with him since well before this summer even started. So nothing had really changed except that she recognized the feeling now. It didn't change the deal she'd made with him, though.

"I've never heard anyone sound so…happy about their own impending heartbreak, babe. I'm a little worried."

"You don't have to worry. I know it's weird. I find it weird, too. I've never *been* happy before a breakup. But… I don't know. I guess I like knowing I'm in love with him. Takes away the angst and questions."

"He should know."

"Tabby, no! Then every time I come out here to visit, he'll be uncomfortable and things will be awkward, and I don't want that. I'm keeping my mouth shut about this, and so are you." She pointed a finger at the screen just as the video froze again, so there was a still shot of her pointing a warning at Tabby while scowling. That was pretty appropriate.

When the video started again, she finished. "This isn't a problem that needs solving. It is what it is, and it's fine. I'm fine. Yes, I'll miss him a lot when the summer is over, and yes, I'm going to have a hard time getting over him." She wasn't sure she would, but Tabby was worried enough already. She didn't want to add that to the pile. "But none of that is *his* problem. And I'm not going to make things weird for us all by going and blurting out my feelings."

"Things are already weird," Tabby said.

"Can we change the subject?" Maybe Tabby would understand better after she got back.

To be fair, Sabrina was a little surprised by her own reactions, too. This wasn't a kind of love she'd felt before, and it took some getting used to. But it was worth it. Loving Nick was worth it. She just didn't want to keep justifying that to Tabby.

"Tell me about the last few stops on your book tour?" she said to force a new subject.

They finished the conversation a bit later after the video froze and didn't restart, although they could still hear each other, and Tabby promised to call later in the week. Sabrina sat on the couch for a long time, petting Princess and wondering if she'd done the right thing, telling Tabby. She'd had to get it out, though. The emotions were so big, so full, she was afraid if she hadn't said something to someone, she'd have spilled all this emotion onto Nick, and she really really didn't want to do that.

Mostly, because she was afraid he'd end their summer fling early if she did. She already knew what that felt like, even though it had been her imagination conjuring abrupt endings that hadn't been there. She didn't want the real thing. She wanted these last two weeks with Nick, loving him freely and without reservation. Admitting to him that she was in love with him would put an end to things too soon, and she selfishly wanted the extra time. So, no conversations about feelings.

The feelings themselves were enough.

CHAPTER THIRTY-FIVE

Nick picked up his cellphone, then set it down on his desk again for the hundredth time. He wanted to talk with Diego. But he didn't. He didn't want to hear the "I told you so"s, but he needed to talk to someone.

He'd fallen in love with Sabrina. He *loved* her. It was the strangest thing. Because he didn't actually feel all that different to how he'd felt before the epiphany. Which meant...

He'd probably *been* in love with her for a while now.

That wasn't good. First, it meant he didn't know his own damned mind and that sucked. But also, it meant he'd gotten himself into a hell of a mess.

She'd turned down his offer to stay with him. He still couldn't get over that he'd made the offer. But now that he had, the fact that she'd said no was really bugging him.

At least he knew why now, though. Because he didn't want the summer to end. He wanted her to stay out here, not go back to Brooklyn, and maybe... Well, moving in together felt too huge a step right after realizing he wanted to spend the rest of his life with one woman. But that was definitely on his list of things he wanted to happen in the future.

Never, not once in his entire life, had he wanted a woman to live with him. Not temporarily. Certainly not permanently. The mere idea of it used to send him bolting away so fast he left a hole in the wall. And he knew that's exactly what Diego would say. That this was something Nick had never wanted before and maybe he should go see a doctor.

He was giving a doctor visit serious consideration because this really wasn't like him.

Except, with Sabrina, it was. He liked the idea of waking up to her every day. Having her stuff overlapping his spaces. Liked the idea of her shampoo in a shower they shared, and her toothbrush next to his on the bathroom counter. Without meaning to, he'd been mentally considering an add on to the house so she could have her own office.

It was nuts. Diego would definitely call in a doctor if Nick told him all this.

Which was why he kept putting his phone back down. He kept picking it up because he was a little desperate to tell *someone* how he felt. Diego would tell him he should tell Sabrina. Which would just be horrible advice. Telling the woman he loved that he loved her when she was all set to move back to Brooklyn? No. Not gonna happen. She was better off not knowing anyway. That would just make her future visits with Tabby awkward. They'd made their no-strings-attached deal for this summer so things wouldn't get awkward during future visits. He'd stick with that.

No matter how miserable it made him.

The fact that it made him miserable at all was just astounding.

He picked up his phone again, checked the time. It was nearly five. Sabrina was expecting him. That settled it. No calls to Diego tonight and no "I told you so"s.

The fact that he flicked up the screen and hit Diego's number probably should have surprised him more than it actually did.

"What's up?" Deigo said, answering on the second ring. "Calling instead of texting again. Sabrina, right?"

"I asked her to stay with me a few extra weeks at the end of the summer and she said no."

A long silence at the other end of the line.

Nick felt the need to fill the silence with, "She won't be done with the job she's working on when Tabby comes home, so I said she could stay with me instead of getting a room somewhere."

More silence.

"Tabby will offer, but Sabrina didn't want to impose since Tabby will be tired."

More silence.

"If you don't speak soon, I'm going to assume we got disconnected."

"Still here. Processing."

"Stop processing. I just needed to say this out loud. It's fine."

"You sound fine."

"I am."

"You asked her to…move her stuff into your place, huh?"

"Only for two weeks. Or so."

"And she said no?"

"She said no."

"And that makes you feel?"

"Relieved, of course."

"You sound relieved."

"Fuck off."

"You called me, man."

Nick stared out his office window without really seeing the view of the Atlantic. "I might be in trouble."

"How so?"

"I'm in love with her."

"Yeah."

Nick switched his gaze to scowling at the phone before he put it back to his ear. "That's your response? That's all you have to say." The realization had hit him like a truck. Diego should have at least sounded as shocked as he did about Nick offering Sabrina a place to stay for a few weeks.

"Well," Diego said, "the you-being-in-love-with-Sabrina part is old news. I'm pretty fascinated that you'd want her to move her stuff into your space, even if it is temporary."

"What the hell do you mean 'old news'?"

"Well, yeah, Nick, you've been in love with this woman for, what, a couple years now." Another silence. Then, "Did you just… Did you just realize this?"

"Fuck off. I have to go."

"Tell Sabrina we said Hi."

"What am I going to do, Diego?"

"Probably ought to tell her you love her before the summer is over. Jessy tells me women like to hear that from the men they love."

"I knew you'd say that. It's terrible advice. Sabrina said no when I offered her a place to stay. What makes you think she…?" He trailed off. He couldn't quite bring himself to say the words. To hope.

And the fact that he was hoping Diego was right instead of panicking about it said a lot.

Diego sighed. "What you don't know about women is a lot."

"Don't quote *Moonstruck* at me." Jessy and her old rom-coms. Turned Diego into walking quote machine. "Answer my question."

"Go talk to Sabrina. Tell her you love her. Let the chips fall where they may."

"The last time you told me to talk to her, she didn't want to talk."

"As I recall, right after that you two got together. Finally. So, I stand by my original advice Talk to her."

"I thought the talk-to-her part was Jessy's advice."

"We share a similar view on these things."

Nick rolled his eyes.

As if he could see the reaction, Diego chuckled. "You wouldn't have called if you weren't looking for permission to talk to Sabrina, someone to tell you it was okay to be in love with her and to say that out loud."

"What if she's not interested?" he said, and ached with the words.

"Then you come into the city for a visit. I'll get you nice and drunk. We'll go yell at the Mets. And you'll eventually heal. It'll suck.

Heartbreaks do. But you'll survive. And it's better to try than to not to." Diego said the very last few words in a deep country twang, quoting a character from one of his youngest kid's favorite animated movies.

"Why am I taking advice from someone who just imitated the voice of a cartoon tow truck?"

"Because you know I'm right. And you love me, too."

"Fuck off. I'm going to Sabrina's now."

"Tell her you love her. It'll make you feel better."

Not if she didn't return his feelings.

"Text me. Or call again, if you need to talk," Diego said.

Nick hung up, wondering why he'd bothered to call Diego in the first place. Okay, it was nice having said all this out loud to another human. But the conversation hadn't really helped him. Sabrina had turned down his offer to stay with him. If she loved him, wouldn't she have said yes? Used any excuse to keep their relationship going? She didn't seem to care that the summer was coming to an end. That their relationship would be over soon.

Nick scowled at his computer screen. Why the hell wasn't she bothered by this? He sure was. Why was she just accepting the summer would end things between them?

He pushed back from his desk. That's what he wanted to ask her. That's the answer he needed. The rest…

Well, Diego might think heartbreak was acceptable. But Nick wasn't so sure. And if Sabrina was happy to let what was between them go so easily…

He couldn't finish the thought. He didn't know how to.

He slammed out the door, determined to get answers from Sabrina and settle this. One way or the other.

CHAPTER THIRTY-SIX

Nick waited an impatient four seconds for Sabrina to open the door, though it felt like four years, and when she did, she smiled wide and pulled him in for a kiss, and he forgot he'd come over to talk. Who needed to talk? What was there to talk about?

She tugged him inside, closed the door, then pushed him against the door and kissed him again.

He could get used to these kinds of greetings.

That thought reminded him why he was here. He started to lift his head, to pull back. They did need to talk, although he'd hate to prove Diego right. But then Sabrina dragged a hand down his stomach, reached down to cup his cock, and all thoughts of anything that didn't involve getting naked soon were obliterated.

He cupped her ass and pulled her tight against him, trapping her hand on his cock, letting her feel him getting hard fast, just for her. Then he reversed their positions so she was against the door and he could lean into her, feeling the full length of her. She giggled at the changed position and then groaned when he ground his hips against hers.

Desperate for more of that sound, he ran his mouth across her throat, kissing his way to one of her sensitive spots just beneath her ear.

She dropped her head to one side and he moved her thick braid out of the way to better access her warm skin. He could live on the taste of her. Silky and warm and a little salty. Her fingers tightened against his waist when he hit the delicate skin on her throat near her shoulder, and she ground her hips against his.

Which reminded him that they had too many clothes on still.

A cold nose against his calf pulled him abruptly out of his lust fog. He glanced down to see Justin and Princess sitting there, staring up at them. "Maybe we should go upstairs." He wasn't sure whether to be amazed or mildly appalled that those were the first words either one of them had said since she opened the door.

She glanced down at the dogs and laughed, the sound glorious and relaxed. Then she tugged his hand. He toed off his deck shoes in the entryway, and followed her as she led him up the stairs, shedding her own clothing as she went. Which gave him an excellent view of her ass when she finally wiggled out of her shorts and underwear—those got left on the newel post. Her bra and t-shirt were scattered on the steps.

The dogs followed them up to the second floor but were summarily left outside the bedroom when a very naked Sabrina closed the door on them. Nick pulled her into his arms the instant the door snicked shut. She was so warm, so soft, liquid heat as she flowed against him and set him on fire. He found her mouth, eager to taste her, taste all of her, delight in her. A voice very far at the back of his brain reminded him there were only days left before this was over, before he wouldn't be free to have her like this ever again, and that he needed to say something to change all that. Needed to *do* something to convince her to stay with him. To keep him.

But when she rubbed against him and whined that he wasn't naked yet and jerked his shirt off over his head with a delicious growl of impatience, that little voice at the back of his brain got buried under an avalanche of lust. He couldn't get naked fast enough. Though, he wasn't so impatient he couldn't take the time to make her scream.

He dropped to his knees and cupped her ass, pulling her close. She gasped and dug her fingers into his hair, holding her balance as he licked over the crease between her thigh and hip. She whimpered a little and her grip on his head tightened.

"I'm going to fall down," she muttered, pulling him closer instead of pushing him away.

He grinned against her lower stomach as he dropped delicate, teasing kisses over her skin, lower to the very top of her curls. "I'll hold you up."

"You're going to have to." She panted and then gasped when he licked into her pussy.

She was wet and sensitive and the instant he tongued her clit she started to quiver. He loved doing this to her, loved watching her skin flush and her muscles tremble as he licked and sucked and savored her. She came fast, her whole body tightening and then shaking with the release. And she screamed his name. He could live on that sound.

She folded over him, hugging his head, as her orgasm eased. He flicked his tongue against her one last time, but she jerked away. "Too sensitive. Need a minute."

"Happy to obliged." He stood and gathered her close, practically carrying her the last few feet to the bed. Then he laid down beside her and kissed her, his hand in her hair, loosening the braid. He was still half dressed, and that was a situation that needed to be taken care of very soon, but he didn't want to take his hands off her long enough to do it.

She solved that problem by gently unzipping his shorts and pushing the rest of his clothing down his hips. He had to help in the end, which required he move his hands, but he kept kissing her so he didn't have to release her completely. Once he had freed himself from the last of his clothes, he pulled her tight again, tangling his legs with hers as he sank deeper into the kiss. He only rolled away long enough to slip on a condom. Then he lost himself in her. Sank into her warmth. Sucking her nipples until she trembled. Gripping her tight as he buried his cock deep in her pussy, loving the way they both groaned, the way their voices mingled in the dim room. The rhythm felt both new and familiar. A lifetime and he was certain this would still feel new and familiar at the same time. A coming home and a surprise all at once.

He stroked into her at a steady pace, languid and hard. Letting the tension build, savoring each gasp, each panting plea. He fucked her harder when she demanded it, and watched her come apart for him before he finally had to let go.

The sounds of their heavy, raspy breathing as he collapsed beside her on the bed settled deep into him. He wrapped his arms around her and held her close. Just like this. He could live just like this. For the rest of his life.

But as his brain got access to his blood flow again, reality kicked back in. They had days before Tabby returned. They had to talk, to settle this. Now. Or he would lose her.

Before he could say anything, though, she gave him a big, happy kiss, then bounced out of bed. "Be back out in a minute." And she disappeared into the bathroom.

Okay, well, he supposed the serious conversation could wait until they'd cleaned up.

But after they'd both cleaned up, she threw on a skirt and tank top—without underwear or bra he noticed with no little pleasure —and dragged him back downstairs for dinner. "I'm starving after that," she said with a laugh.

She was so…happy. So light and full of enthusiasm and delight. And he loved it. But also…had she forgotten Tabby was back soon?

"Something good happen with the center today? You're in a very good mood." He tried not to sound annoyed by her happiness. He loved seeing her so happy. But he was having a hard time forgetting that they didn't have much time left together, and he wasn't happy about that at all. Did she even remember? Did she care?

"Nothing in particular," she said. "I am enjoying the work. The crew they have there, the volunteers, are really great. And so far, no huge disasters. We're almost finished. The board scheduled a big launch ceremony for the middle of September so we have to be done by then, but I think we'll make it. Everything is coming together."

She kissed him at the counter in the kitchen, then patted his shoulders and started taking things out of the refrigerator. "Hope you don't mind omelet for dinner. It's what I have on hand."

"Love omelets," he muttered, watching her bounce around. "Lot of protein."

"Anything you hate in them? I'm putting mushrooms, cheese, and spinach in mine."

"Everything but spinach."

She grinned. "You sure? My mom always told me it was good for my muscles."

He flexed his bicep, just to make her laugh, and said, "I think I'm good."

She did laugh and sidled up to him for another kiss. "Yeah you are," she murmured. Then danced away to start cooking.

He crossed his arms over his chest and leaned against the counter as he watched her. She hummed under her breath, and danced a little as she moved around. Her thin summer skirt tangled with her legs sometimes, reminding him she wasn't wearing anything under her clothes and that was a very convenient thing for later. But he kept coming back to...

Why was she in such a good mood when their time together was almost over? He was a little panicky about it all. Not least because he'd gone and fallen in love with her.

Which he was supposed to mention, wasn't he?

Yeah, he'd come over with the idea that they needed to talk. Diego had said he should tell her how he felt. Diego had been wrong before, though. And he talked out his ass most of the time. What the hell did he know anyway? Just because he'd been happily married for twelve years and had three kids and a loving wife and all that. He'd married his high school sweetheart. Nick shuddered at the thought of marrying any of the girls he'd known in high school.

Actually, he shuddered at the idea of marriage period. Or...well, he always had before.

He shook away that thought. He'd barely accepted he was in love with Sabrina. There was only so much change in perspective his brain could deal with.

"Are you going to the opening ceremony for the center?" he asked, to distract from the thing Diego said he should be talking about.

"I've been invited, of course." She didn't look up from gently folding her eggs when she said, "Geraldine said I should bring you, but don't worried, I made excuses for you."

"I could go. Not doing anything big in mid-September."

"Oh, but... Yes, well. That's after... After Tabby is back. I wouldn't want to impose on your time. It's fine."

She stumbled so much over those sentences, he frowned. But she didn't look up. And he was left wondering what she meant.

"Wouldn't be an imposition," he said, staring hard at the side of her face and wondering why she was in such a hurry to get rid of him.

Was that it? Was she happy because she'd be rid of him soon?

If that were the case, she wouldn't have dragged him up to bed the instant he walked through the door tonight, would she?

She waved his comment away as she pulled plates out of the overhead cabinets. "It's really no problem. Do you want toast?"

"No thanks." He frowned.

"You okay?" she asked as she slid his omelet onto a plate. "Problems with work today?"

"Nothing. I'm fine." He didn't sound find. He sounded grumpy and annoyed. He was grumpy and annoyed.

She narrowed her eyes as she handed him his plate. "Deck or table?"

"Deck," he grunted and carried both their plates outside, pausing long enough to let her open the back door.

He made an effort to set the dishes down on the glass-topped table gently, but he wasn't in a gentle mood. He was getting progressively more irritated. He just wasn't entirely sure what was irritating him so much. Seemed ridiculous that he should be mad that she was happy. He loved when she was happy. Made his own day better.

The timing, though... And the fact that she didn't want him at the center's opening party...

Was she really just ready to throw aside everything they had and go back to her life before...them?

She startled him out of his gloomy thoughts by reaching over and brushing her fingers across his temple. "You sure nothing's wrong? I didn't give you much of a chance to talk when you came in." She shrugged and smiled and even blushed a little which was pretty fucking delightful. "Is there something you need to talk about?"

"Why the fuck are you so excited to be done with me?" he snapped.

Chapter Thirty-Seven

Nick snarled and looked down at his plate. He hadn't meant to say that out loud, hadn't had any idea those words would just pop out of his stupid mouth like a stupid fucking admission.

Sabrina straightened away from him, blinking rapidly.

"Sorry," he said, without looking at her. "I didn't mean to…"

To what? Reveal he was upset because, even though the end-of-summer thing was his condition on their relationship, he now wanted to take it back and she didn't seem to care?

"I'm not… I'm not excited to be done with you," she murmured, so quietly he barely heard her over the sound of his own inner voice berating him for his outburst.

She sounded horrified, but maybe that was just because he was an asshole. "Forget I said anything. I shouldn't have." And he should never ever ever listen to Diego. Ever again. About anything.

"Nick… I don't understand why you're mad."

"I'm not. It's fine. Let's talk about something else."

"Obviously, it's not fine. You look like you could chew nails right now."

"Don't want to talk about it."

"Did Diego tell you you should?"

He made a face and rolled his eyes. Sabrina knew him too well. That was a big part of the problem. He loved that she knew him so well. Probably the only time in his life he *wanted* someone to know him this well. "Diego's an idiot."

"What is it?" she asked quietly. "What's wrong?"

"Nothing's wrong except that I don't want us to end because I'm in love with you, but you don't seem to care or mind that the summer is almost over, and that's fine since those are the parameters I set, but now I'm ticked off at Diego for telling me I should tell you anything since this just makes things awkward, and I'm not happy about that."

She sucked in her lips and stared at him through narrowed eyes. He kept most of his attention on his plate, pushing a few pieces of omelet to the side for Justin and Princess—who were both sitting a few feet away waiting for their signal that it was time for their part of dinner.

"I see," Sabrina said.

He was half holding his breath, waiting for her to kick him out, half hoping she'd just move on and pretend he hadn't said anything at all. He'd be happy with that last option. Thrilled even. If he was going to lose her anyway, no matter what he said, he'd prefer they went back to the moments before he'd blurted out his confession.

"This wasn't what I was expecting to happen," she said.

He sank a little further into his seat.

"To be honest, I've been a little surprised you weren't…ushering me out the door a few days early so you could get more time alone."

He scowled at that but didn't speak. He was afraid if he opened his mouth more shit would pop out, and he wasn't in the mood to make more of a fool of himself.

"If it helps the situation at all," she said, "you should know that I love you, too. And the only reason I'm happy is because I got one more precious night with you."

His scowl eased, and he finally looked at her, but he was having a hard time taking in what she was saying to him. "None of that makes sense."

She grinned. "Which part? The part where I love you, or the part where I consider time with you precious?"

"The part where you're in such a good mood, even though you say you love me and you're well aware the summer's almost over."

"Tabby told me to tell you all this." She laughed at that. "If we find out later she and Diego have been conspiring to get us talking, I'm going to have words for her."

"Already had words for Diego." His heart was hammering a little too hard. He clenched the arm rests on the chair.

"I wasn't going to say anything." Her voice was quiet again, though not so quiet he couldn't hear her over the gentle woosh of the waves. "I was going to let you go without…without burdening you with my feelings. I was going to honor what you wanted and not try to…to change your mind about us. Not talk about *feelings* and *relationships*." She gave him an exaggerated eye roll which surprised a rough chuckle from him. "I've always been the one to push that conversation, and even if I got what I wanted, it didn't seem to do me any good in the long run. So I thought I'd do this time different. Even though I fell in love with you, even though I've probably been in love with you for…oh, a while now, I thought I'd do the right thing and respect what you wanted. I thought it would make you happy. And, honestly, that's what made me happy."

"Are you telling me we almost fucked this all up with the very best of intentions?"

She made a face that was part wince part repressed grin. "Sounds like it."

He snorted. "Perfect. Fucking perfect."

The repressed grin broke through, turning into a full-blown grin. That smile… Every time. Just right to his heart.

"So now what?" she asked.

"Good question."

Now what? She loved him—and wasn't that the most spectacular thing to have happened to him in his whole damned life—so she wasn't in a hurry to dump him. That was good. But she still lived in Brooklyn, and he still lived out here. And that was…good? He frowned.

"What's wrong? Your scowl is back."

"You still live in the city. I don't want to live in the city."

"Of course not. You need your space and privacy." Her eyes narrowed a little. "And you need time alone."

He winced a little because, yeah, he still did. "I don't like the idea of being away from you for too long if that helps."

"It does actually."

She leaned against her armrest, leaning close to him. He let out a shaky breath as he scooted closer to her. Harder to keep his hands off her this close, but he was afraid if he touched her now, he'd derail one of the most important conversations of his life—Diego was never going to let him live this down—so he held himself still, close enough to feel the heat of her skin, to fill himself with the scent of her, but without actually touching.

"I'm not moving in with Tabby," she said, "because she'd hate that. And I'm not moving in with you for the same reason."

"I wouldn't hate it," he protested. He could adapt. It would mean having her with him all the time. He could adapt to sharing his space.

"Eventually," she said, with a smile. "Maybe eventually. But I think, for us, we need to do things…a little different."

Her gaze dropped a little, settling on his mouth, and it was distracting enough he almost missed the fact that she was still talking.

"…stay in Brooklyn. Turns out, I like not having to constantly adapt my life to fit the life of the man I'm seeing. I like the way we've been. Together but not in each other's pockets. Not attached at the hip as my mother would say."

"So, you're saying you want to still live in Brooklyn."

"My apartment is rent-controlled. I'm really not prepared to give that up yet."

Her mouth twitched with a grin, and he scowled a little just so she'd let out the grin.

"But," she said, "I think…it's not so far away. And maybe we could see how things worked like this. Our way. You living here and me there, but still together and getting together as often as possible? See if that works?"

She sounded so hesitant, but so open and vulnerable and willing.

He was a little awed by her. "If it doesn't? If you get tired of the distance between us?"

"We can just keep talking about it and what we want to do. We don't have to set anything in stone, right? That was always my big issue. Wanting things settled and settled in very specific ways. But maybe, maybe I don't need those specific ways. Maybe we need to find our own way."

He loved the idea of that. Almost as much as he loved her. "We could do that." He leaned in a little closer, close enough to feel her breath on his cheek. "So long as it means I don't have to let you go."

"And I don't have to let you go." She brushed her lips against his, so gentle and soft.

He buried his fingers in her hair and held her close as he kissed her, sinking into her. The chair armrests in the way were awkward, and there were dogs scooting under the table now, waiting for their bites of omelet, and the Atlantic roared louder as a set rolled in. But all he knew was Sabrina. And that perfect moment. Knowing she not only loved him, but she was willing to find a way for them to both be happy while being together. He never thought he'd find that in someone.

Now he had, he would never let her go. "I love you," he murmured against her mouth, because he wanted her to know. Wanted her to hear the words again.

"I love you," she said, sounding as relieved to say that as he felt hearing it.

He kissed her again, letting the relief and the love all out. Grateful for her.

Knowing he'd be grateful for her for the rest of his life.

EPILOGUE

Sabrina danced around her apartment, doing the last-minute tidying, knowing Nick was almost there, and so giddy she could hardly stay still. Every week was like this. For a year and a half. Every time she saw him, she got giddy and excited. She was sad to say goodbye at the end of their time together. But then she got to enjoy her week and work hard and not worry about what her partner was doing, or if she could or should do something that didn't include him. There was a lot of freedom in this relationship with Nick, in a way she'd never associated with relationships. It had taken her a little getting used to. But now, she couldn't imagine any other way.

This time, they had a full week together, too. There'd been debate, whether she would come out to him for Christmas, or he would come in to the city to her. On the one hand, the city was packed and a mess during the holiday season. No way around it. On the other, Tabby was having nightly parties for everyone and their uncle in the Hamptons, and Nick did not want to see all those people that often.

So they'd decided the city for most of the week, then a few quiet days in the Hamptons after the New Years parties were done and everyone was huddled in their homes for the winter.

The doorbell rang and Sabrina let out a quiet, excited little squeal before hurrying to let him in.

The sight of Nick on her doorstep never cease to take her breath away. So handsome and so…hers. Even after a year and a half, that still amazed her.

"You're here," she said, because she loved these moments, and jumped into his arms.

He wrapped her up with one large arm and nudged her inside so he could put his soft-sided travel bag down in the entryway. She closed the door, and then she was in his arms again, kissing him like she hadn't seen him in months when it had only really been five days. His eager growl made her stomach dance.

"Missed you," he muttered against her mouth.

"Missed you, too."

Early in their relationship, Sabrina had made the mistake of getting them dinner reservations occasionally for his first night there. They'd missed each and every reservation. Usually by hours. She didn't make that mistake anymore. Now, she laid out the delivery menus, and they ordered in food so this first night could be just them in their own little private reunion. Dinner reservations and anything that might require them to leave the apartment waited for night two. Or three. Or sometimes they just didn't leave the apartment.

"Good week?" he asked as he kissed down her throat.

"Great. You?" She pushed at his coat, letting it drop to the floor.

"Perfect." He pulled her shirt off over her head as she worked on his jeans buttons.

They didn't talk much more until quite a bit later. At least not about how their time apart had been.

Sitting on her couch, eating Chinese food, after mind-blowing sex, catching up on what had been going on for them during the week— though most of it they knew since they talked on the phone or video chatted every day—was one of her favorite rituals. And with her Christmas tree sparkling with multicolored lights in the corner of her living room the only illumination, the dark intimacy was even better.

"Tabby sends her regards," he said, and grinned. "And her reluctant understanding for why you're not coming out sooner."

She snorted. "I've been to enough of her parties. She's the entertainer. I'd rather spend the week up here fighting holiday crowds to see the Rockefeller Christmas tree with you."

"I'm not getting in the middle of that chaos without some sort of bribe, you know."

She grinned. "I have a bribe wrapped for you under the tree. Don't worry."

His eyes darkened a little as he glanced at the tree. "Do I get to open the present early or do I have to wait."

"You have to wait. But maybe the night before Christmas."

The speculative look he gave her got her tummy dancing and little tingles running along her spine. He was already half naked. Wouldn't take much to get him fully naked again. He'd slipped back into his jeans, but it was freezing outside and just starting to snow, which meant the super had the heat in the building cranked up to levels that would rival the sun. So Nick hadn't put on anything else besides the jeans. Much to her pleasure. She'd only put on a t-shirt and yoga pants herself because she'd had to answer the door for the food delivery. She liked her Chinese food delivery guy, but not enough to answer the door in nothing but a t-shirt.

She let her gaze move over Nick's chest, the dark hair emphasizing a lovely physique she just wanted to bury herself in again. He was as delicious as the food. More so. And she loved him so very very much it took her breath away. She leaned in and gave him a kiss.

A year and a half, and she still couldn't get enough of him.

She eased back, but reluctantly, so they could finish eating.

His knowing smile didn't help her concentration.

But he did return to the conversation. "Speaking of presents, Geraldine sent you one since you're not coming down until after New Year's Eve."

She grinned. Geraldine wasn't just a client anymore. They'd gotten to be friends even after the center had opened and Sabrina had moved on to different jobs—several of which she could directly attribute to Geraldine's recommendations.

The freelancer life had proved...challenging. And she'd considered going back to a job where someone else was the boss more than once. Nick had helped her get past the initial growing pains, talked to her when she needed to debate the pros and cons of having more consistent employment, never pushing her to go one way or the other. That had helped so much. In the end, it had been worth the effort, staying freelance. She loved her work so much more now, being able to choose the clients and causes she worked with, being able to challenge herself every day. And she had Nick to thank for helping her figure out how to do all this.

And Darren to thank for forcing her into it.

"Did I tell you I ran into Darren yesterday?" she told Nick. She was pretty sure she'd gotten distracted with his impending visit and forgot.

Nick frowned when he said, "Where?"

"Outside the old offices. I was heading to a meeting with a new client in the neighborhood."

"How's he doing?" Nick's scowl did not ease.

"Great. Still a trendy, user asshole who never did get fired." She shrugged. "He tried to be condescending, so I mentioned how Gates had called last week, wondering again if I'd consider coming back to work for him. That shut Darren up, and he was much more polite after that."

"You talked to your ex-boss last week? Why didn't you tell me?"

"Because I didn't. I was lying to Darren. I just wanted to see him sweat. He gets away with so much, it's kind of fun watching him squirm."

"Devious. I like it." Nick leaned in and surprised her with a quick kiss.

She preened a little, and considered going in for another kiss. "Well, he deserves it. The kind of asshole who always lands on his feet, no matter what." She shrugged.

"Are you mad he never got fired?"

She considered that. "Sort of. From a justice perspective. There was no real justice with him. He got to keep his job, despite being a deceptive, idea stealing jerk. And he still has all the trappings apparently, living so far outside his actual income it's ludicrous. But… I don't know. I love my current life so much, it's hard to be worried about him. I've moved on to much better things. Not having to deal with him has definitely improved my attitude toward him."

She did go in for another kiss. "Plus, I got the guy in the end. Perfect new career. Perfect relationship. I love my life right now. I'll take my happy ending over Darren's sneaky stress and trendy suits any day."

Nick smiled, but his gaze narrowed a little and he gave her a look she couldn't quite read.

"Give me a sec," he said, setting his Moo Shu pork on the coffee table.

He went to his soft-sided travel bag, still sitting where they'd left it by the door, squatted down and started digging through it, his back to her. She watched him, frowning a little bit.

When he turned back toward the living room, he held two wrapped boxes, one mid-sized square, and one small, long rectangular box. He held up the larger square, wrapped in a winter blue paper and circled by a gold ribbon. "This is Geraldine's present." He walked past the couch to set it under her tree. Then he returned to the couch and sat again, cradling the other present in his lap.

"I intended to give this to you on Christmas," he said, "but I'd like to…talk about it, so I think you should have it now."

Her frown deepened as she set her food aside and took the present from him. It was flat and narrow and long, wrapped in red paper decorated with little penguins. Almost too cute to open. She studied the box in her hands for a long moment.

She knew what it wasn't—what everyone else kept expecting from them. It wasn't a ring and there was no marriage proposal here. Because she and Nick had discussed that, and neither of them really wanted to get married. At least not yet.

Much to her surprise, she was the most adamant about that. She'd spent so many years thinking that was the only end result to a relationship, the only direction things could go. But she preferred what she and Nick had now. And she didn't want to screw it up with a whole wedding thing that might send her back into old relationship habits. She loved him so much, and she loved their relationship. She wanted things to stay this way. At least for now.

He'd agreed with her. Enthusiastically agreed. Took her to bed and gave her multiple orgasms agreed. So she knew this wasn't a ring. Box was wrong for it anyway.

But it was something he wanted to talk about…

"Are you going to open it or just stare at it?" he asked. "The paper is too cute, isn't it? You don't want to rip it."

She laughed. "A little reluctant to tear up the penguins, yes." She bit her bottom lip, then gave in to curiosity, despite the strange tingle of nerves in her belly. She did take the wrapping apart gently, at the seams where the tape held it shut, and grinned when Nick groaned at her slow process.

Inside the wrapping was a flat gold present box. And inside the box was…a key. A little silver key. She picked it up and frowned at him. "What's this?"

It wasn't his house key because they'd exchanged those already. He had one to her apartment, too. It wasn't a car key since it was too small. A storage locker maybe? But that would be a weird present.

"So…" He shifted a little on the couch, looking awkwardly nervous and deliciously adorable. "The key itself is mostly symbolic. I haven't done anything yet because I wanted to ask you first and have your input and…"

"Nick, what is the key to?"

"So, I've been thinking a lot about the future. And then this old house that needs a lot of work came onto the market, not far from my current place. It's huge. But they're selling it cheap because of all the work it needs." He shrugged. "Relatively cheap."

She snorted. Nothing in the Hamptons was "cheap." But she got the idea.

"Anyway, it's mostly the land that's valuable. And it's a nice chunk of land."

"You want to buy the house?"

"I do."

"Can you afford it?"

"I can."

"Why are you running this by me and giving me a key for Christmas?"

He pressed his lips together and let out a breath. "My idea was that I could buy the place and redo the whole thing so it could be a home for…us. Together. In one place. Eventually. Except with lots of room, so we'd essentially have our own parts of the house, and then could come together when we wanted to." He winced a little. "I'm not making this very romantic, and maybe I shouldn't have done this as a Christmas present. I did get you some other things." He said the last in a rush, like he thought she'd be disappointed if he hadn't.

She was not disappointed. In fact, she found herself blinking rapidly so she wouldn't let loose happy tears he might misunderstand. "You want to build us a house specially designed just for us? To suit us?"

He was half looking at her, half looking at his plate still on the coffee table. "Yes?"

The fact that he was asking rather than saying made her heart swell. She set the key aside carefully, next to their plates.

Then she threw herself into his arms so suddenly he "oofed" and fell back against the armrest. She laughed as she kissed all over his face. "I *love* this idea. Thank you thank you thank you! What a beautiful gift." She kissed his mouth before he could say anything, giddy with the idea that he wanted to build them a house.

When she finally came up for air, she was still grinning and even more happy to see the little sparkle in his dark eyes.

"It's going to take time," he warned. "And I still have to actually buy the property. Or, well, we do?"

"Yes. We. Can we go look at it while I'm there this time?"

"I…sort of already arranged a viewing and asked the seller to hold it for me until after that, and since the realtor is a friend, he's agreed."

"Nick! You're genius." And she kissed him again.

He was laughing this time when they came up for air. "I wasn't sure how you'd feel about a house designed to give us separate wings."

"I love it. It's perfect. It's perfect for *us*." And that was it really. They had their way of doing things, and their way worked for them, and this house idea worked for them, too.

"I want your input in the design. I won't do anything you don't like."

"I love you," she said with so much joy it just spilled out. "I love you, and I love this idea, and I can't wait!"

"You sure you're ready to give up a rent-controlled apartment?" he teased.

"I will be in a year. And, and…" She sat up a little, pulling him up with her so she could frame his face and make him understand something. "Even if we don't get this place, it's okay, because we'll find another place we can design just for us, and it'll be perfect. The *idea* is perfect, and we'll work out the details. Deal?"

"Deal." He cupped her face in one large hand, his soft smile doing more to her heart than all the silly love songs in the world. "I love you, Sabrina. And I'm really looking forward to designing a home for us."

"Me too, Nick." She grinned. "Both of those. Me too."

THANK YOU

Thank you for reading DESIGNED FOR YOU! I hope you enjoyed the story, and Sabrina and Nick's ever so slightly unconventional HEA.

I started writing this story in the middle of a Covid-19 surge, in the fall of 2021, while having to send my kids to school full time, and in a constant state of worry because my youngest still didn't have a vaccination available to him yet. I was also dealing with some side health issues myself, and there were a few other health issues happening in my family. All that compounded by the general state of the world, and I was so overwhelmed I could barely sleep.

Writing anything with too much conflict felt impossible. I just wanted to write something light, and sexy, and not too angsty, something that took place in a world prior to Covid. I wanted fun romance tropes, especially a Grumpy-Sunshine pairing (I'm not sure I accomplished that, but I did have it mind when I was writing—thus Nick *grin*), and I wanted something that would give my poor, overwhelmed brain a break.

Somewhat ironically, while I was writing this novel, I also took brief breaks to work on a couple of contemporary fantasy short stories, one of which has my most angry heroine to date. She is all anger. With few fucks to give and a lot of physical strength to back up her rage. And wow, was she cathartic to write! (That story will be in the upcoming collection *Haunts and Howls Where Demons Dwell*, releasing in October 2022.) So I obviously needed both light and angry in those same few months.

When I came back to this book to work on the edits, I wasn't entirely sure what I would see. My editor liked it, but when you're the writer, it's hard to judge your own work. Turns out I enjoyed it! That's always a relief. And I had so much fun working on the edits, I kept forgetting I was supposed to be editing. All of which is to say, this won't be my last contemporary romance. I have a short holiday contemporary romance story coming out late in 2022. And I have the first third of another contemporary romance in the wings, waiting for me to get back to it. I also think I might have to tell Tabitha's story because—aspiring TV chef? Yes, please.

If you've enjoyed this book and want updates on my new releases and upcoming books, the easiest place to do that is my newsletter (https://bit.ly/KatSimonsNewsletter). It's a monthly newsletter with updates, release information, news, occasional excerpts, cover reveals, and every so often a free story. I may talk about fiction I'm reading or things I'm baking, too. New subscribers get a free, exclusive short story in my Tiger Shifters paranormal romance series, a story which was originally written for an erotic romance anthology, so…yeah, pretty hot.

Outside of my newsletter, you can get updates on new releases at my website (https://www.katsimons.com), follow my author page at your favorite vendor, or follow my author page at BookBub (https://www.bookbub.com/authors/kat-simon).

You can also find me on Facebook (https://www.facebook.-com/KatSimonsAuthor), Twitter (www.twitter.com/IsaboKelly), or Instagram (www.instagram.com/IsaboKelly), though I forget to talk about my releases on Twitter and Instagram a lot, so less reliable place for new releases, but I do retweet a lot of animal and space pictures (though not many animals in space pictures *grin*). And I am also open to *receiving* animal and space pictures. As well as email from readers! I always love hearing from readers.

Thanks again for reading!

~Kat

Books By Kat Simons

Contemporary Romances

Designed for You

Poinsettias and Possibilities

Coming December 2022

Paranormal Romance

Tiger Shifters Series

Romancing the Leopard: A Tiger Shifters-Cary Redmond Crossover Novel

Urban Fantasy

The Cary Redmond Series

Cary Redmond Short Stories

Demon Witch Series

Contemporary Fantasy

Haunts and Howls Collections

Joan of Kerry Series

Tombstone Wizard

The Unshattered Sword

Destiny Through the Cats Eyes

Going Out of Business: Everything's for Sale

Coming August 2022

About the Author

Kat Simons earned her Ph.D. in animal behavior, working with animals as diverse as dolphins and deer. She brought her experience and knowledge of biology to her paranormal romance and urban fantasy fiction, where she delights in taking nature and turning it on its ear. Her Tiger Shifters series combines romance and the otherworldly with heart-pounding action adventure. Her latest urban fantasy romance series follows the adventures of Protector Cary Redmond as she tries to manage her personal life while saving the world. A lot.

Kat also publishes the occasional Contemporary Romance and has some Mystery stories due out soon.

For something a little different, Kat publishes fantasy, science fiction, and the occasional hockey romance under the name Isabo Kelly (http://www.isabokelly.com).

After traveling the world, Kat now lives in New York City with her family and a library's worth of books.

For more on Kat and her future books, you can find her at:

Website: https://www.katsimons.com
Newsletter: https://bit.ly/KatSimonsNewsletter
Facebook Page: https://www.facebook.com/KatSimonsAuthor
BookBub: https://www.bookbub.com/authors/kat-simons
Instagram: https://www.instagram.com/isabokelly/
Twitter: https://twitter.com/IsaboKelly

www.ingramcontent.com/pod-product-compliance
Lightning Source LLC
Chambersburg PA
CBHW030348200726

48286CB00013B/514